MY FAVORITE PLACE

BOOK THREE IN THE MINT CREEK RANCH SERIES

HILARY DARTT

ALSO BY HILARY DARTT

The Mint Creek Ranch Series

My Favorite Story

My Favorite View

Love Under the Arizona Sky

All the Stars

The Whole Sky

To the Moon

Arizona Heat

Pure Luck

Sweet Luck

Terrific Luck

Christmas Luck

The Seedling Homestead Series

A Summer of Wonder

A Dream of Home

A Promise of Forever

The Intervention Series

The Dating Intervention

The Marriage Intervention

The Motherhood Intervention

The Garden Club Series

Jasmine's Pact

Studying Sequoia

Just Holly

MY FAVORITE PLACE

BOOK THREE IN THE MINT CREEK RANCH SERIES

HILARY DARTT

For my parents.
There are no words to express my gratitude
for everything you've done for me.

PART 1

CHAPTER ONE

ABBY

ABBY FLORES REMEMBERED the exact moment she realized construction was a man's world. It was the same moment she made the decision to prove she could thrive in it.

She'd just turned fifteen, and even though her parents planned to throw her a massive quinceañera, she was even more excited about what was happening the day after the party. She was finally old enough to have a real job. To be on the payroll at her father's construction company, to pay taxes, and to open a bank account.

Even though she stayed up long past midnight dancing with her family and friends, she was awake well before her alarm went off at six.

Her dad walked into the kitchen as she was pouring him a mug of coffee. He accepted it, and his eyes twinkled at her through the steam. "Big day?"

"The biggest." She held up her own coffee mug for a toast. "To finally being a legal employee."

"Cheers," her dad said, lifting his mug to touch hers. "Although I have to admit, I'm sad to lose my free child labor."

They both laughed at the standing joke. Abby hadn't been on the payroll, but since she turned twelve and was able to work right along-side the crew, Ernesto had paid her in cash.

He reached out and curled a strand of her hair around his forefin-ger. "Your fancy hairdo held up."

"I know," Abby said. "I can't believe it. I'm going to have to braid it before we go."

Her dad made a dismissive sound. "Leave it. For the day."

It was still so dark outside that the kitchen window acted like a mirror. The hairdresser had worked magic on her long, thick hair, twisting the upper half into intricate swirls and letting the lower half hang long and curling down her back. Abby patted the top half. "It's not my normal work 'do," she told her dad. "But you're right. I should keep it as long as I can."

"You should do something about your face, though. All that makeup. All those young men."

He stood behind her, looking over her shoulder at her reflection. It was true: the mascara and eyeliner weren't normal for her. They made her look older.

She chuckled. "Daddy, you taught me early on how to handle the guys. I'll be fine."

Still, when they showed up at the jobsite — Ernesto's company was building a new hotel in their Utah hometown — he handed her his framing hammer. "Keep this in your toolbelt today. I have a feeling you're going to be fighting off the summer crew."

Abby had worked as something of a junior member of Ernesto's main crew since she was able to walk. Her role had evolved from a tagalong to gofer (the guys would often send her to retrieve certain tools or supplies), to apprentice, to, in more recent years, a full-fledged crew member.

Although construction was a nomadic business and workers came and went, Ernesto had a few loyal crew members who were like family to Abby. There was Joseph Scott, the foreman, who'd been with Ernesto since the early days of the company. And Christopher Hernandez, crew leader. The two of them oversaw everyone else. None of them had ever so much as looked at Abby sideways. They regarded her as another one of the guys.

But she had noticed that as she got older — and turned into a young woman — her father kept a closer watch.

Plus, school had gotten out the week before, which meant local teens and college students were looking for work. But Abby could handle herself.

When Ernesto handed her the hammer, she kissed him on the cheek before tucking it into her toolbelt. "I'll be fine, Dad."

And she was. More than fine. Her excitement over finally being on the payroll, officially, stoked the fire that fueled her productivity. All morning, she swung that hammer, helping frame in the walls for several rooms on the second floor. By noon, her arm was burning and her palm was blistered.

On a big project like that one, the construction manager usually set up an office — a portable building with enough space for a couple of desks, a filing cabinet, and a fridge. There was no official break room, so the crew members usually picnicked somewhere onsite. After retrieving her lunch from the fridge, Abby headed back up to the second floor. She sat down, her feet hanging over the edge, above what would eventually be the hotel's main entrance. And that's when it happened.

A kid about her own age, who she'd never seen before, came sauntering across the plywood that made up the unfinished floor. Abby figured he belonged to one of the subcontracted crews her father hired to help with such a large-scale project.

Come to think of it, judging by the stubble on his jaw, maybe he was a year or two older than she was. He wore construction boots and jeans, but he'd taken off his shirt and tucked it into his back pocket, the white cotton hanging down the back of one leg. And he had muscles. A deep tan, and really nice muscles. He was definitely older than her.

The onceover she gave him was unintentional, but the one he gave her seemed *very* intentional. He looked at her face for a full second — eyes and then lips — before his gaze traveled down to her breasts. She, too, sported a white T-shirt as part of her standard building uniform — and she was still wearing hers! But the way he looked at her, it was as if she were already naked.

He licked his lips, and she felt a shiver travel over her scalp. It was not an aroused shiver. She felt threatened, violated. So, she did what her dad had taught her. She stood up, gave him her biggest grin and offered him a hand to shake (he'd once told her she should spit a giant loogie or summon up a fart, but she couldn't bring herself to do it). "I'm Abby Flores. And you are?"

He blinked, stunned, which meant her confidence took him back a little. Abby was relieved. Maybe he was just a run-of-the-mill teenage boy gawking at a teenage girl who, if she did say so herself, looked drop-dead gorgeous with her fancy hairstyle and professional makeup job.

"Miles Taylor. Nice to meet you."

There was a beat of silence. Miles cleared his throat. Thankfully, he looked a little uneasy. "Mind if I join you?" He gestured at the spot where her lunch sat.

She didn't want him to join her, but her parents had taught her to be polite.

"I guess not."

There. That wasn't top-of-the-line politeness, but it would do. Only then did Abby notice that Miles was holding a paper bag, his palm curled around the top of it.

"Cool. Thanks."

She let him sit first, so she could leave some space between them.

Abby's acquiescence gave Miles some of his confidence back. He unrolled the top of his bag and peered inside, then looked at her and said, "You know, I think you might be too pretty to work here."

Abby's mouth would have dropped open, but, manners. She finished chewing her food, took her time swallowing, and then offered Miles the most withering look she could muster.

"Oh, do you, now? I'll bet you a hundred bucks I could frame more walls in an afternoon than you can, hands down."

"All I'm saying is, shouldn't you be, I don't know, in the office or something?"

That, right there, was the moment. It was the moment Abby made up her mind that she would become a successful builder. She was good, even at fifteen. She'd been taught by the best. Quality was everything. Mistakes happened, and they were fixed. All the elements of a project worked together like cogs in a motor: timing, precision, rhythm. The finished product was exquisite.

How many hours had she spent with her dad at construction sites, looking over blueprints and finding creative ways to give clients what they wanted, while staying within budget? This business was part of her blood. It was part of her family. And it would be her livelihood and her legacy. She would do it for herself ... and despite Miles Taylor and all the people like him, who thought women belonged in the office ... who thought women couldn't swing a hammer.

Abby never ate lunch with Miles again. In fact, she never spoke another word to him. If he said, "Hello," she responded with a curt nod. She would ignore him, but if her father ever saw that, she would hear about it.

Instead, she gave him a wide berth, and gratitude: he uttered the words that ignited her desire to prove that she, a young woman, belonged.

————

TRACE

AS AN ADULT, Trace Walker liked things just so. Every morning when he got up, he went straight to the kitchen, where his coffee sat, already brewed. He poured himself a cup before walking down the driveway to grab his copy of the *Daily Dispatch*. Then, he sat at his kitchen table, next to the window that overlooked Mint Creek itself, and read the paper front to back. After that, he ate and showered, then dressed and left the house. He fed and watered the horses, often along with his co-owners in the ranch, Cody Davis and Sawyer Nelson. They'd generally spend the morning tending the livestock, shooting the breeze, riding the fences, and making repairs around the property.

One hot, windy spring day, he went about his chores with his trademark work ethic and the enjoyment of checking off the boxes on his to-do list: *Repair the irrigation line. Check. Wash out the horse troughs. Check. Muck the stalls. Check.*

As he walked back toward his house, though, he saw a brand-new sports car coming up the driveway — *his* driveway.

For Trace, an unexpected visitor was almost always unwelcome. He felt his mouth settle into a grim line, and knew that his own mother would chastise him for greeting a stranger with such an unfriendly expression. Squaring his shoulders, he approached the driver's side as the car stopped. After a long couple of seconds, the window rolled down.

And Trace, despite the disruption to his normal routine, found himself grinning like a lunatic at the driver. She was stunning, to say the least. Eyelashes for days, an adorable dimple on each cheek, and a smile so bright, it almost blinded him.

As his eyes drank her in, his heart danced. It knocked against the inside of his ribs as if to say, *Are you seeing this?*

"Good morning," the woman said.

"Hi there," Trace said.

The eye contact made him freeze. It seemed to do the same to her. They remained there, staring at each other, grinning.

She recovered first. "I'm Abby. And I'm lost."

"Trace. And maybe I can help, Abby-and-I'm-lost. Where are you headed?"

He hoped she would say Mint Creek Ranch was her destination. Which was absurd, because nobody driving a car like that could possibly think they belonged in Prescott, Arizona.

She said, "I'm looking for an intersection, I guess. Williamson Valley Road and Saddle Horn?"

Why on Earth anyone would be looking for that intersection, Trace couldn't say. The two roads formed one half of the property line on an old piece of land that was overrun by weeds. But his mother would tell him it was rude to say so.

He couldn't stop himself from asking, "What are you doing out in these parts?"

Her smile disappeared. "Exploring."

Okay, Trace thought. *She's a closed book.*

He could understand that. A woman traveling alone probably didn't want to share too many details.

He relied again on the manners his mama taught him and said, "You're nearly there. It's been unmarked since three summers ago, when a microburst came through here and tore down the sign. Back out to the main road, hang a right, and go slightly less than three quarters of a mile. Saddle Horn Lane is a dirt road. Looks almost like a two-track these days. I would say you can't miss it, but really, you can."

She nodded. "I know exactly what you're talking about. I think I sped by it on my first pass. I was so caught up looking for a street sign, I figured that was someone's driveway. Anyway, thanks a lot. I really appreciate it."

As she rolled up her window, Trace tried to think of a way to ask for her number. His mind was so scrambled from the chemistry that he came up blank. She finished rolling up her window, then backed expertly out of the driveway. As she got back onto the main road, he waved, hoping she could see him in her mirror.

————

THE MINT CREEK Ranch changed Trace's life. He owed the place — and the city of Prescott — a debt of gratitude. Before Trace was one of the Mint Creek Ranch boys, he was a gangly, awkward eight-year-old. He wasn't one of those cliché loners, at least, not from the outside. Kids tolerated him. He never ate lunch alone or spent recess looking for someone to play with. But, he never really felt like he belonged, either. He felt *different*. Until he was eight, he could never put his finger on it.

Western-style decorations hung on the walls of the tiny two-bedroom house where he lived with his parents. Ceramic horse figurines and cowboy statues sat on the shelves. His dad, a car mechanic, and his mom, a teacher, dressed in leather boots, jeans, and button-up shirts. He did the same.

He had a bigger interest in Legos and library books than he did in fashion, and never even thought about how his wardrobe compared to those of his classmates. That is, until one hot spring day in the third grade. The air was stifling, and the school playground felt like an oven. When the teacher sent the kids outside, every part of Trace's body felt hot immediately: between his shoulder blades, the backs of his knees, especially his ankles in his leather cowboy boots. Sweat dripped from his hairline, and as he walked out to the playground, he wiped his forehead on his sleeve.

"Hot, huh?" Mindy Ray, his classmate, swung from the metal rings of the play structure, her long, dark hair swishing down to her waist. Trace took a moment to look over her outfit. The bright-yellow skirt and white striped t-shirt she wore looked about a hundred times cooler than his jeans and tucked-in plaid shirt. But, he didn't really have an answer for her — sure, it was hot, but wasn't that pretty obvious? He gave her a nod and climbed onto the platform to take his turn on the rings.

"Yeah, but Trace don't care if it's hot." The voice came from behind him. Trace turned around to see Jaden Billings giving him a once-over, like someone might examine an alien species. "He's some kind of cowboy, or something. Ain't that right, Trace?"

Trace recognized an unusual tone in the kid's voice. Him calling Trace a cowboy was definitely not a compliment.

Mindy, still swinging, giggled. "I know. It's like he thinks we live in Texas, or something. Giddyup." She landed neatly on the platform opposite Trace, and a couple of other kids laughed.

"Hey, y'all," one of them drawled.

Shocked, Trace felt his mouth drop open. If it were possible, his face felt even hotter, and he could feel his pulse in the tips of his ears, reminding him of the way he'd like to pummel Jaden's face, since he'd started the whole thing. Instead, he did what his mama taught him to do when someone was rude or disrespectful. He walked away. He jumped down off the platform before ever reaching for one of the metal rings. As he walked, his feet plowing through the wood chips, he heard the squeal of metal on metal. More laughter. More words spoken in fake Western accents. He made it to the edge of the grass before he felt the hot sting of tears in his eyes. And he kept moving.

A kid noticing the way he dressed was one thing. But *all* of those kids noticing the way he dressed, and acting like he was the only one who *didn't* notice? He felt blindsided.

When the bell rang and everyone went back to class, his classmates acted like everything was perfectly normal. But for Trace, everything had changed. That afternoon, as soon as he walked into his house after getting off the bus, he pried off his boots and threw them across the living room.

"What's the matter?" His mom came out of the kitchen just in time to see the second boot spinning through the air as it careened across the room.

"I need new shoes," Trace said. He could hear the pout in his own voice, and he was ashamed. He knew how hard it was to keep him in shoes. His feet always grew so fast.

"You didn't outgrow those already, did you?" his mom asked. "Darn it, Trace, those are brand new."

For the second time that day, Trace felt his face burning hot. "No, Mama. I didn't outgrow them."

He knew he shouldn't ask, but the words tumbled out of his mouth. "Do you think I could get some different shoes? Like tennis shoes or something?"

As he expected, the answer was a firm "no." Okay, not exactly, but a, "Well, I suppose we could go on down to the secondhand store and see if they've got a pair."

If anything was worse than cowboy boots, it was secondhand shoes you bought because kids teased you about your cowboy boots.

For the next week, Trace wore his cowboy boots to school every day. And every day, he avoided talking with the other kids. After all, who knew what else they were thinking when they saw him?

Exactly one week after he came home and flung those boots across the living room, Trace came home to his parents waiting for him in the kitchen, a plate of freshly baked chocolate chip cookies on the table alongside a full glass of cold milk.

Something strange was happening.

"Trace, honey," his mom said. "We have something to tell you."

His dad cleared his throat and drummed his fingers on the table. He must have come straight from work. Trace could see grease under his fingernails.

Trace couldn't imagine what they were going to tell him. Was something wrong? Had one of his grandparents died? Did his dad get laid off?

"Son," his dad said, "we're moving."

CHAPTER TWO

TWO WEEKS LATER, the Walker family packed their belongings into a single moving truck and headed north.

"You're going to love your Aunt Elaine and Uncle Tom, and your Aunt Lola and Uncle Wyatt," Trace's mom said, her voice different than he'd ever heard it, almost as if she might explode from excitement.

"If I'm going to love them so much, how come I've never met them before?"

His mom laughed, a high-pitched, birdlike sound. "It's so wonderful, honey. I grew up with Elaine and Lola. We were the best of friends. And as a life so often does, it took the three of us in different directions. We got busy and drifted apart, is all. But neither time apart nor distance have lessened my affection for them. They've asked your dad and me to be partners in the ranch up in Prescott."

"The ranch?" Trace wrinkled his nose.

"Yes! A real, working ranch. Trace, you're going to love it. And they each have a boy your age. I can sense this is going to be a great new beginning for you. For our whole family."

Eyes shining, she reached across the front of Trace to grab his dad's hand. They looked at each other over the top of Trace's head, and when Trace glanced from one to the other, he saw they were both smiling.

As they drove further and further north, the buildings seemed further and further apart. Dry, dusty cement and heat waves gave way to trees and shade and space. Lots of space. After about two hours, they came into a tiny, old-fashioned looking town, with a giant white building in its center.

"What's that?" Trace wanted to know.

"That's the county courthouse," his mom said. "And that, right there, is Two Scoops, the best ice cream place in town. And that —" she pointed at a bench sitting in the lush grass surrounding the big white building — "that's the best place to eat said ice cream."

"Can we get ice cream now?"

Trace's dad laughed. "Well, I don't think I can park this thing downtown. But we'll go this weekend and get a scoop."

"A double scoop?"

"Sure, a double scoop," his dad said.

Well, Trace thought, if his dad was agreeing to a double scoop, he must be really happy.

If Trace thought the little downtown looked nice, Mint Creek Ranch itself looked like heaven on earth. After turning off a long road flanked by wide green fields with plenty of trees, the moving truck made its way under a thick canopy of leaves and emerged onto the ranch property.

"This is it," Trace's mom breathed.

It wasn't as neat and tidy as Trace had imagined it. The grass and weeds were overgrown, and the buildings looked a little worse for wear. But he knew instantly: this was home. Everything seemed to sparkle in the early evening light.

"That's the main house, over there," Trace's dad said, pulling alongside a different building and putting the moving truck in park. Before they'd even finished climbing out of the cab, a stampede of people came through the front door. In the lead: two boys Trace's age. There was a jumble of adults, a bunch of laughing, and loud talking.

Suddenly, the two boys were right in front of Trace.

"Hey," said the taller one. He flashed a grin so wide, Trace immediately felt like they were friends. He stuck out his hand. "Cody."

"Trace."

Cody gave Trace's a good, hearty shake.

"Sawyer," said the other kid, whose shaggy blonde hair was a little too long. He, too, smiled and shook Trace's hand.

"Want us to show you around?" Sawyer asked. "Our parents said we had to."

Cody elbowed Sawyer, who laughed out loud. Trace found himself laughing, too.

"What? They did!"

"I know," Cody said. "But I don't think we're supposed to repeat that."

He looked at Trace and shrugged. "Well, you want to see the place?"

The two of them started to run — the precursor to the days and years that would follow — and as Trace jogged to keep up with them, he noticed something interesting: they were both wearing cowboy boots. And when he thought back to the moment before, when everyone had emerged from the house, he realized they were, too.

The three of them ran all over the ranch, from the first house to the second, third, and fourth, and then to the barn. They walked carefully through the yard of discarded farm stuff, tractor tires, fence panels, and giant wooden spools.

"Want to play hide-and-seek?" Trace asked, and within a few minutes, they were hiding and seeking and finding and laughing, and doing it all again. After a few rounds of that, Sawyer announced, "I'm hot. You guys want to go in the creek?"

Trace looked down at his clothes, and then said, "I've got no idea where my swim trunks are."

Cody made a dismissive gesture. "Go in your jeans."

The idea seemed impractical (what would the kids at his old school think about swimming in jeans?), but Trace was hot, and besides, he didn't want to disappoint his new friends. So he ran with them to the creek. Without even slowing down, the other two boys pulled off their boots and socks and shirts and splashed into the water. Trace followed suit, and gasped at the temperature of the water on his skin.

"Refreshing, right?" Sawyer hollered, pushing his arms over the creek's surface to splash Trace.

The sun sank lower in the sky and cast a golden light over the whole scene like magic. A while later, the sound of a bell ringing broke through the noise of splashing and shouting.

"Dinner bell!" Sawyer hollered.

"Good thing, too, because I'm starving!" Cody said.

"Me too!" Trace said.

They threw on their boots, grabbed their shirts, and ran back to the main house, where they ate a meal better than any Trace had ever tasted: smoked brisket, green beans, and biscuits with honey. After dinner, someone started a fire in the giant fire pit out front, and the boys roasted marshmallow after marshmallow. Their parents were so caught up in conversation, they lost count, and the boys polished off the whole package. Then, bellies full, almost sick on sugar, they flopped down on their backs on the grass.

"Boy, you can really see the stars up here," Trace said.

"Sure can," Sawyer said.

"Pretty incredible," Trace said.

"Sure is," Cody said.

After packing, loading the moving truck, driving, and the excitement of arriving, Trace was so tired he felt his eyelids getting heavy. Right before he drifted off to sleep, he thought, *This is perfect. This is exactly where we are supposed to be. This is home.*

THE NEXT DAY, Trace received his first up close and personal introduction to horses. The many long hours he'd spent admiring his parents' paintings did almost nothing to prepare him for that moment. Looking at two dimensional images was one thing. Sure, the oil-on-canvas horses hanging in his home looked athletic. Even in that format, a kid could tell horses were beautiful, powerful. But it wasn't until Cody led a massive chestnut horse out of the barn that Trace realized how big and imposing the creatures could be.

"This here is Shirley," Cody said, and Trace could swear his new friend was exaggerating his drawl. "Like Shirley Temple, the actress."

Even though the horse plodded toward him at a walk, and it seemed good-natured enough — she let a boy a fraction of her size lead her without ever once putting tension on the rope — Trace took a step back. His head came up to what he thought was the animal's shoulder. He had to tilt back to see her eyes. When he took the time to really look at her, he felt a bit calmer. Her eyes were a clear, warm brown, like the brandy his dad sometimes had before bed.

"She has really long eyelashes," Trace managed, and Cody and Sawyer chuckled.

"Well, that's not the first attribute a guy looks at on a horse," Cody said, "but maybe on a lady."

They were in stitches, clutching their sides as they cracked up. Trace couldn't be certain whether they were making fun of him, but he found the corners of his mouth tugging upward in a smile. As if Shirley understood that he'd relaxed, the tiniest bit, she lowered her head so her nose was directly in front of his face. Trace couldn't help himself. He reached out to touch her nose. He had to know if it felt as velvety soft as it looked. And it did.

"Careful," Cody said, his voice sharp. "You don't want her to mistake your fingers for carrots. Make sure to keep your palm flat like this." He held up his hand to illustrate. Trace flattened his hand.

"Want to ride her?" Cody asked.

A rattlesnake shook its rattler inside Trace's stomach. "I don't know."

"You ever ridden before?" Sawyer wanted to know.

Trace ran his palm over the massive cheek, which was sleek and smooth. The horse pressed her face against his hand. "Naw," he said, trying on the drawl. "My parents always told me we could get a horse one day, but that day hasn't come."

"The way I hear it, you'll be getting a horse of your own lickety-split." Cody spoke with such certainty, Trace didn't bother to question him.

"Which means," Sawyer said. "You might as well learn how to ride."

They didn't wait for him to answer. Sawyer took the lead rope from Cody, and Cody moved to Shirley's left side. "First thing is, you've got to learn how to mount."

He put his hands on the saddle horn.

In a move so effortless, Trace thought it resembled teleportation, Cody swung his right leg up and over Shirley's back. "That's it," he said. "Up and over."

As easily as he had mounted, he dismounted, and then he motioned for Trace to try. Trace copied Cody's motions: he put his left foot in the left stirrup, grasped the saddle horn, and hoisted himself up. It didn't feel nearly as easy as Cody made it look, but he did it, first try. Shirley seemed way taller, once he was on her back. He looked down at his friends. They both grinned up at him.

"You're a natural," Sawyer said.

Trace felt himself beaming with pride. "I am?"

"You are," Cody said. "But we're not going to let you loose quite yet. Let's do a few laps."

Cody picked up the lead rope again, and Trace was surprised to see no one had been holding it. The horse stood there, patiently, as if she were waiting for someone to tell her what to do next. This gave Trace a little comfort. He felt his shoulders relax.

"That's it," Sawyer said. "Keep your body relaxed."

"Ready?" Cody asked.

Trace nodded. Cody clicked his tongue and started to walk. Shirley started to move, and again, Trace marveled at how huge she was. After a few steps, he settled into the rhythm. It reminded him of a boat rolling over the choppy surface of a lake: up and down, up and down. Cody led Shirley into the corral and started a wide circle around the perimeter.

"So far, so good," Sawyer said. "If I didn't know better, I'd guess you grew up right here on this ranch."

"True," Cody said, his voice conveying surprise.

In that moment, basking in the glow of compliments from his new friends, Trace felt like he was on top of the world.

That feeling stuck with Trace throughout his childhood. Mint Creek Ranch was the first place where he really felt like he belonged. Not only with his parents, but with other kids, in his new hometown.

Eventually, Trace learned how to really ride. Not just sit astride a horse while someone else lead it around the property, but to trot, then gallop, then rope steers and horses. He was as comfortable in the saddle as he was on foot.

He, Cody, and Sawyer became like brothers, and when the Hart family moved onto the property, Montana Hart became like a little sister to him. The four of them played together, worked together, and squabbled now and then. But through it all, Trace knew his life was perfect. He wouldn't change it for anything.

———

TRACE'S first encounter with horses kicked off a lifelong love affair. He'd admired the horses in his parents' paintings, but no artist, no matter how skilled, could replicate what it felt like to stand right next to a horse, one hand on its warm neck, looking into its eyes.

Every chance he got, Trace ran to the barn. He became so efficient at his household chores that his parents joked they should've introduced him to horses long before moving to Mint Creek Ranch.

Soon enough, caring for the horses became one of his daily duties. His dad taught him how to feed and water them, how to clean their stalls, how to brush them, and eventually, how to rope and herd. Once he'd mastered those essential skills, he was allowed to take the horses out on the trails.

On his first solo ride, he did everything himself. He put the saddle blanket over the horse's back, and the saddle on top of that. He cinched it down and fastened it before adjusting the stirrups. He put on the bit and the bridle, laying the reins over the saddle. Then, with a growing sense of excitement, he mounted. And for the first time on his own, he led the horse out of the barn. As soon as he felt the afternoon sun on his shoulders and face, he smiled. He smiled so big that he was glad no one else was there.

At first, he let the horse walk. But he was a ten-year-old boy. And pretty much every boy he knew liked to go fast — even his dad. Sometimes when he and his dad went for a ride in the car and his mom wasn't there, his dad would look across the cab at Trace and say, "Pedal to the metal, right buddy?" And then he'd press the gas pedal practically down to the floor, making the car go so fast, Trace's stomach floated inside his body. Trace would give his dad a thumbs up and a grin — probably similar to the goofy expression he wore as he rode that horse out of the barn.

He didn't know how his parents would feel about him going too fast, so he kept the horse at a walk until they were around the corner. Then, he gave her a gentle nudge with his heels. She picked up speed, but barely. He couldn't blame her. The nudge had been somewhat … *tentative.* "Tentative" was one of his vocabulary words: *Done without confidence; hesitant.*

It seemed almost as if the horse could read Trace's mind or sense his feelings. Although he wanted to go faster, he wasn't quite sure if it was the best idea. But then something grabbed ahold of him. Something like courage. Or maybe stupidity. He leaned down over the horse's neck and gave her a nudge quite a bit more certain than the previous one.

They were off.

The acceleration was faster than Trace expected. He almost slid right off the horse's butt. He grabbed the saddle horn to keep himself in the seat. They were flying. He could hear the beat of the horse's hooves on the ground beneath them, but still, he felt like they were flying.

"Faster," he yelled, even though he knew that wasn't one of the commands the horse understood. Or maybe she did. She went even faster. She ran and ran. And she ran some more. She ran so fast, for so long, that Trace got tired of holding on. He'd heard from Cody, Sawyer, and all of their parents that he didn't really have to hold on tightly. But as new as the sensation was, he had a death grip on the reins. He brought the horse to a halt, marveling again at how she seemed to understand what he wanted.

When he turned her around, though, a realization knocked the wind out of him, as if he had fallen off the swings at school and landed flat on his back: when a horse runs really fast, for a really long time, she goes really far. Although it felt like they were running in a straight line, Trace had no idea where they were. The sun was a lot lower than he expected, too.

That excited feeling in his stomach did a one-eighty and turned to dread. What if he couldn't find his way back home? Boy, he would be in a world of trouble. More than once — more than one hundred times, maybe — one of the parents had mentioned that if a boy got lost on the property, he could die of starvation, dehydration, or hypothermia. In fact, Cody, Sawyer, and Trace had heard it so often that they usually rolled their eyes, figuring their parents were being dramatic.

But here he was, lost, with no idea how to get home. Just about sunset, too. How long had that darn horse run? Why hadn't she turned them around? Oh, but it had been so much fun! He couldn't decide whether to laugh or cry. At least no one was around to see the tears if he did. But still. Like his mom always said: crying didn't solve the problem.

"Put on your thinking cap, Trace," he said to himself.

Ah. Nature offered him one important clue: the sun was setting in the west. The creek ran north to south. And it ran along the western edge of the property. If he headed toward the sunset, he should come across the creek. And then, all he had to do was follow it south to the Mint Creek Ranch. Feeling better already, he turned the horse around. And because the sun seemed to be making a faster descent than ever, he nudged the horse, so she would go a little faster. She moved with confidence, and that's when yet another realization struck him: the horse would know how to get home. No one had taught him a command, like, "Go home." He said it anyway. Ears pricked, the horse picked up her pace even more. Not the full-out canter they'd done heading north, but fast enough. After what seemed like an eternity, the buildings of Mint Creek Ranch came into view. Trace couldn't believe the relief he felt. For a few minutes there, he really thought he might die out in the elements. He felt that grin spreading across his face again.

Something about the horse's run seemed a little jerkier, and he felt the saddle sliding around her midsection. As it slid, so did he. Within a few more steps, Trace felt himself unable to hold on to anything. His hands slipped off the horse's sweaty neck, and although his fingers could probably grasp her mane, he didn't want to hurt her. Grabbing the saddle horn didn't help. As he finished that final thought, he found himself flat on the ground, the wind knocked out of him again. For a split second, he had the thought that the horse might step on him, and he was terrified. Not for himself, but for her. His parents had told him that if a horse stepped on a human, it could break a leg. Most of the time, the damage was permanent, and the vet would have to put the horse down. Trace already felt guilty over it, and it hadn't even happened.

Fortunately, she was nimble. She stepped right over him. Her back legs didn't even touch him. He lay there, flat on his back, breathing heavily.

Less than a second later, the horse was back, the saddle hanging upside down below her belly. Suddenly, her giant, soft nose was inches from his face. She sniffed him, and he figured she was checking to see if he was all right.

"I'm all right, girl," he told her, and after a quick mental scan of his body, he realized he was. He might have a few bruises, and he defi-nitely felt a little breathless. But he was all right. A few seconds later, he heard another horse approaching. He couldn't make out the rider right away, but then he heard the voice. "Well, what do we have here?"

"Cody. Thank goodness it's you."

"You're lucky it's me. Any one of the parents would whoop you."

They both laughed then, because none of their parents had ever whooped any of them.

"Looks like you didn't cinch the saddle tight enough."

"Yeah, I figured that one out."

Cody sighed. "Rookie move."

Trace sighed as he sat up. "I know."

"What are you doing out here?"

"Thought I'd go for a ride. Solo."

"Didn't you tell anyone you were going?" Cody asked. He took off his hat and examined it, much the way Trace had seen Cody's dad do.

"No," Trace said. "But I should have. Right?"

"Right. What if you didn't come back?"

"Right. Then no one would know where I'd gone." Trace sighed again. "Maybe I should give up riding."

"Nah," Cody said. "Gotta get back in the saddle. I'd tighten it up first, though."

Trace did, and they rode home, side by side.

The more Trace rode, the more he wanted to ride. Over the next couple of years, he spent all his spare time in the barn or on the trails. He watched the more experienced riders take care of the horses and memorized as much as he could of what they told him. *Check the hooves daily. Feed grain, morning and evening. Always look for lumps and bumps or sores during grooming. Exercise a horse every day.*

One evening after a big winter storm blew through, Trace went to the barn to put blankets on all the horses. Sure, they had their own fur coats, but he'd overheard his parents talking about how temperatures would dip into the single digits that night. Even if the horses huddled together, he thought, they would be freezing, and he couldn't stand the thought of that. So, wearing his clunky snow boots, his puffy jacket, and his knit hat, he trudged to the barn. His gloves made his hands clumsy, but he managed. For their part, the horses seemed grateful. Some of them bobbed their heads in thanks, and some nuzzled his ear with their velvety noses. As he was tying a blanket around Cody's mare, Cinnamon, he heard someone come through the barn door, stamping their feet.

He turned around to see who had joined him. "Dad! What are you doing down here?"

His dad didn't answer right away. He unwound his scarf and brushed ice off it before pulling off his own hat. Trace could see kindness in his smile. "Your mom and I saw you heading out, and she asked me to come keep you company."

"That was nice of you," Trace said. "But the horses are keeping me company just fine. I didn't mean for you to come out into the cold."

His dad shrugged. "Can I give you a hand?"

Trace nodded and they walked together to the closet that held the blankets. "I've got almost all of them done. Just a couple more."

"It's nice," his dad said, "how you've been caring for the horses."

Trace shrugged. "I'm finding that I like them better than most people."

His dad laughed then, a great big belly laugh. "Me too, son. Me too."

Trace walked over to Sawyer's horse and laid a blanket across her back. As was her habit, she leaned into him. Sawyer said that's how she gave hugs, and it was the first hug Trace had received. He gave her neck a good rub.

He bent down to tie on the blanket, and as he stood up, he spoke without thinking. "It would be so nice to have a horse of my own."

His dad didn't respond right away, and Trace regretted his words instantly. Horses were expensive. He knew that as well as anyone. He had a good set of ears and a good memory. He could recall countless adult conversations at the dinner table.

He started to apologize, but his dad said, "I know you really love them, son. And you're great with them."

And that was it. Trace didn't say anything else, and neither did his dad. He figured he'd better stop while he was ahead, before he said something to upset his dad.

"I didn't tell you this before, because I didn't want you to worry," his dad said as they tied the last two blankets on the last two horses. "But your mom said they're expecting another storm. The real reason she sent me down here was so that you didn't get stuck in a blizzard between the barn and the house when you came back up. Now that you've got these guys all tucked in for the night, we'd better hustle."

Together, they closed up the barn. As they began the trek back up to the house, Trace's dad put an arm around his shoulder. Trace matched his dad's strides, his arm wrapped around his waist, and even though the first flakes of the new storm brushed his skin, he felt warm.

———

A WEEK LATER, the smell of bacon frying woke Trace up. Then he remembered — it was his thirteenth birthday. His mom was cooking his birthday breakfast, like she did every year: bacon, eggs, and chocolate chip pancakes.

His mouth watered as he sat up. Although he could hardly stand the thought of waiting, he shoved his feet into his winter boots and pulled on his winter coat. He had to feed the horses before breakfast. They always came first.

When he walked into the kitchen, his mom smiled at him and gave him a big hug. "Happy birthday to my favorite son."

"Smells good," he said. "Thank you for making breakfast."

"You know I'd never skip a birthday breakfast, even on a school day."

"I know. That's why you're my favorite mom."

She laughed at that, and then seemed to notice his jacket and boots. "Oh, your dad already went down to take care of the horses. Being as it's your birthday and all."

"I'll go help him finish up," Trace said. "We'll get it done faster that way. Then we can all enjoy breakfast together."

"No, no," his mom said. "The birthday boy can't eat a cold breakfast. I've already dished you up. Sit down and eat. Your dad shouldn't be much longer."

Trace pulled off his jacket and boots and set them by the door. By the time he sat down and picked up his fork, his dad came in, grinning. "Happy birthday, my boy!" He ruffled Trace's hair. "Eat up. It takes a lot of energy to be a teenager."

"Thanks for feeding the horses, Dad. I guess I'll go say goodbye to them before I leave for school."

His mom set his dad's plate in front of him and added another slice of bacon and another pancake to Trace's as she joined them at the table.

"So. What's your biggest wish this year?"

Of their own accord, Trace's eyes looked over at his dad for a beat, and then back at his mom. His dad could probably guess what his greatest wish was. But he wouldn't say it out loud. It was too big. He'd been expecting the question. Answering it was a birthday ritual. He'd prepared in advance.

"My biggest wish is to have the best year ever."

His parents looked at each other. Almost as if they knew. Almost.

"Can you be a bit more specific?" his dad asked. His eyes twinkled.

"I mean, I guess — I want to explore more, have more adventures, that kind of thing."

His parents nodded.

"What kind of adventures?" his mom asked.

Trace shook his head, stabbed a piece of scrambled egg with his fork. "You know. Camping. Rock jumping. Skydiving."

By the time Trace was finally dressed and ready for school, he didn't have time to stop by the barn.

"They'll be fine until you get home from school, sweetheart," his mom said, pushing a tray of cookies into his hands. "Be careful on the bus. I'd hate for you to spill the cookies."

With that, Trace was off. A minute later, Cody, Sawyer, and Montana joined him, and they walked down the long driveway to the bus stop together. None of his friends said so much as, "Good morning," and Trace was feeling a little miffed by the time the bus got there. They took their usual seats, the three boys squishing into the row directly behind the driver, and Montana across the aisle. They rode in silence, Trace getting madder by the minute. By the time they got to school, his face felt hot. Was it possible they'd forgotten his birthday? If it was, it was also pretty darn depressing. They'd remembered each other's birthdays. And Trace had been talking about it nonstop.

They got off the bus and walked to their respective classes. Trace, teeth clenched together in anger, didn't say, "Goodbye."

Idiots, he thought as he stomped off to his homeroom class. *You'd think the fact that I was carrying a plate of cookies would clue them in. But no. They can't be bothered to remember my birthday.* He fumed about it all morning, and then at lunchtime, he decided he didn't want to be mad anymore. He would give them a hard time, and then let bygones be bygones. Water under the bridge and all that. But when he got to their normal table, they weren't there. He scanned the hot lunch line, but they weren't there either. He couldn't remember whether he'd seen them carrying lunches that morning. They always sat together, and they always sat at the same table. So where were they? Maybe they'd made plans without him. He sat down and ate his lunch as quickly as he could, hoping no one would notice he was alone. Then, instead of heading out to the basketball court like he usually did, he went to the library.

"The library," he muttered to himself as he walked. "On your birthday. You're a loser, man."

Cody, Sawyer, and Montana weren't on the bus home, which puzzled Trace. Had they left school? And if so, why did they get to leave school on his birthday, and he had to stay? Again, he was fuming by the time the bus rolled up in the driveway. He half expected his friends to be there, waiting for him. Maybe even laughing at him for being the lone sucker who had to finish out the school day on his own birthday.

But they weren't. Sure he was being watched because his friends must be playing some practical joke on him, he hiked his backpack up on his shoulders, put his head down, and marched straight to his house. He put his backpack away, washed his hands, and went to the kitchen to get a snack. The house felt eerily quiet. Often, his mom was home to greet him. Even if she came home from her work on the property to chat with him for a few minutes before heading back out, there weren't many days when she wasn't in the kitchen to ask him how his day went.

And that day — his birthday — was one of those very infrequent days.

Trace wanted to cry. Instead, he grabbed an apple and a couple of cheese sticks and headed out to find the friends who never let him down: the horses. He stuffed the cheese in his pocket and took large, angry bites of the apple as he walked. He reached the core of the apple and the barn door at the same time. It was all part of his ritual. One lucky horse would get the core, and munch on it while Trace ate the cheese. He pushed open the door and then jumped. Cody, Sawyer, and Montana were sitting on the fence railing directly in front of him. Trace looked hard at Cody, then at Sawyer, then at Montana, and made a point of not saying anything.

"You think we forgot your birthday," Sawyer said, and Trace detected something in his voice. He couldn't quite put his finger on what it was, but it was something. And then Cody said, "Just so you know, we didn't."

"Yep," Montana said. "We didn't."

Nice of you to wish me happy birthday, Trace thought. He felt his eyebrows pressing down and inward. They were probably almost touching, he was so mad. He muttered, "Great," as he took a left to head toward the row of stalls.

"Hey, bud."

He jumped — again. "Mom."

She was smiling so big, Trace felt some of his own anger slipping away. "What are you doing out here?"

His dad was there, too, standing behind his mom. "There's something we wanted you to take a look at," he said.

Trace's heart raced. What could they possibly want him to look at? Had something happened to one of the horses? But no, they wouldn't all be standing around so calmly if one of the horses was sick. Maybe one of them had had a baby. Although surprise foals weren't common, they weren't unheard of, either. He took a few cautious steps toward the stall where his parents were standing. "What is it?"

"Come on over here and see," his mom said.

If anticipation could ever be an emotion, it was at that moment. Trace could feel his heart pumping the blood through his body. He could hear it whooshing in his ears. His feet moved in time to each pulse. He saw his parents glance at something behind him, but he was too focused on whatever was in front of him to look back. After what felt like about a hundred years, Trace was standing in front of his parents. His dad leaned casually on the half-door of one of the stalls, his elbow propped on top of it, his chin in his hand. His mom played casual, too, hands on her hips. But the energy in the air was anything but casual. Trace could feel it, zapping around between his parents, off of him, off the walls. That's when his dad tilted his head toward the open half-door. Trace crept forward, and looked in. He was eye to eye with a horse. One he had never seen before. When it saw him, its ears shot straight up and its nostrils flared. Its eye appraised him. Darn it if that horse didn't take a step forward and kiss him on the cheek. Trace's hand, with a mind of its own, reached up to touch the horse's cheek. They stood there for a moment, looking at each other. Then, Trace's mom said, "Well, what do you think?"

"What do you mean?" Trace said, afraid to believe it.

"Meet your new horse," his dad said.

Something exploded inside of Trace right then. He would call it pure joy, or straight-up happiness. It was like nothing he'd ever experienced. He wanted to shout, to scream. To run around the barn like a wild animal. But he didn't want his horse's first memory of him to be of a crazy kid. Still, it was as if she could sense his excitement. She pawed the floor with her right hoof. Even gave a little whinny.

"*My* horse?"

He almost couldn't believe it. He looked at his parents, whose eyes were shining.

"You've been so responsible," his mom said, and his dad said, "You've done such a great job with the horses. You're really turning out to be a great young man. We're so proud of you. Happy birthday."

Trace wrapped his arms around his mom's waist, and his dad encircled both of them in a big hug. After a couple of seconds, the events of the day made sense. Trace released his parents and turned around to face his friends. He pointed at them, accusing. "You *knew*!"

They were all grinning ear to ear. They said, "We knew."

Cody pointed at him. "You thought we forgot! We've been working on this surprise for weeks!"

"We agreed not to talk at all this morning. We didn't want to ruin the surprise," Sawyer said.

"You were so *mad*," Montana said.

"At lunch —"

"We begged our parents to let us come home," Montana said. "We knew they were bringing the horse this morning, and we wanted to help get everything set up."

"You *all* have been working on this for weeks?" Trace said. His voice was thick with emotion, but he was too happy to care.

"We got to help pick her out," Cody said, and Montana asked, "You really didn't know?"

Trace shook his head. "No clue."

Sawyer said, "We think you're going to love her. She's so smart. And she handles great."

"She's *fast*," Cody stage-whispered, and they all laughed.

"You want to take her for a spin?" his dad asked.

"Can I? She's brand new."

"Of course you can," said his mom. "We wouldn't get you a horse that we didn't think you could ride."

Trace turned to his friends. "You want to go?"

"We're ready," Cody said. "Our horses are saddled. We've been waiting for you."

Trace walked over to the saddles, but his dad put a hand on his shoulder. "We got you a new saddle, and gear, too. It's only fitting for a new horse."

Trace couldn't believe his ears.

"Everything's in her stall," Montana said.

Trace felt a little uncertain about going into a stall with a new horse. But when he opened the door, she stood calmly. Watchful, but serene.

"Why don't you talk to her for a few minutes?" his dad said. "Let her get to know the sound of your voice."

So he did. He put his forehead against hers and told her how excited he was to have her. Trace could've sworn she was listening, and that she actually understood his words.

After a few minutes, Trace rubbed her neck and ran a hand over her back. She remained still. He went ahead and put on the saddle blanket and the saddle, which didn't seem to faze her. Next, he gave her the bit and put on the bridle. Then he looked at his parents. His mom nodded. "Go ahead."

Trace took the reins and lead his horse (*his* horse!) out of the stall and through the barn.

Cody, Sawyer, and Montana were mounted up and waiting.

"Oh yeah," Cody said. "Happy birthday, man."

"Yeah," Sawyer said. "Sorry we didn't say so, earlier. We were afraid we'd ruin the surprise."

"But just know that we were *so* excited," Montana said. "We couldn't *wait*."

"It's okay," Trace said, and his friends burst out laughing.

"*Now* it is," Sawyer said, and Cody said, "But you should have seen your face on the bus this morning. Maddest I've ever seen you."

Smiling, Trace said, "Want to head down to the swimming hole?"

"You take the lead," Cody said.

Trace was grateful. If he was in front, they couldn't see him cry. As he brought his horse up to a trot, he felt the first tears running down his face.

He heard his dad call, "You're going to have to name her!"

And, as he brought her to a gallop, the tears really started to come down. He couldn't believe it. His very own horse.

CHAPTER THREE

ABBY NEVER THOUGHT of construction sites as dangerous places. No, a job was more like a giant jungle gym. As a little kid, fear wasn't even part of her vocabulary. She hopped from one floor joist to another, climbed unfinished walls, and swung from the ceiling.

Her dad's calls to, "Get down from there!" evolved to, "Be careful," and he shouted those two words more times than she could count. His crew members saw her coming and hollered, "Watch out! Here comes the tornado!"

The way everyone watched out for Abby, she never thought to watch out for anyone else. It never even occurred to her that a jobsite could be dangerous for the others.

Abby was twenty-two when it happened. She'd been a full-time crew member for seven years. They were building a commercial building — three stories. Her dad had come from another site to do an end-of-the-day walk-through. Abby was on the first floor, circular saw in hand, cutting two-by-fours for the guys framing in the interior walls. The sounds — the saw whining before it touched the wood, grinding while sawdust flew, and the end of the board clattering to the concrete foundation — were so loud, Abby didn't even hear her dad walk up. She jumped at the hand on her shoulder, but her sawing hand remained steady.

"You startled me!"

Her dad chuckled. "I'm glad to see you're such a focused worker. How's it going here?" Hands on hips, he surveyed the space. Abby felt at once proud and nervous. It had been a productive day. Also, he was a stickler. Every member of the crew knew that if something wasn't done right the first time, he would ask them to redo it. Although Abby was tempted to follow him as he began to walk around the first story, she instead picked up another two-by-four and set it across the sawhorses. Out of the corner of her eye, she could see her dad walking, examining. He ran a thumb over the head of a screw on one wall, then gave that board a gentle tap with his knuckles. He went all the way around the room this way. Abby was holding her breath by the time he made it back to her workstation.

"Looking good," he said. "If you aren't careful, you're going to become the foreman when Joseph retires." Abby stopped sawing and grinned at her dad. "That's fore*woman* to you."

"I suppose that's true." He gave her shoulder a squeeze. "I'm going to head upstairs, take a look."

Modern-day Abby didn't know why she hadn't said, "Be careful," like he'd said to her so many times. She winked at him and carried on with her work. He climbed the stairs, a hand against the unfinished wall for balance.

Once he was gone, Abby lost herself in the rhythm of the job. Choosing a board, measuring, sawing, setting it down. Lift, measure, cut, set down. And although the noise continued all around her as her crewmates hammered and drilled and sawed and shouted, the sound of the accident was unmistakable. A clatter, and then a shout. The sounds of a body thumping against wood, irregular. Grunting, more shouting. And then, the worst sight Abby had ever seen: the body of her father, limp, falling between the joists above her. He landed inches from where she stood. His hips hit first, and his back arched over the ends of the cut lumber. His head hit the concrete foundation with a sickening *crack*.

And then, complete silence.

Abby, the saw still in her hand, froze. She had the bizarre thought that she should scream, to somehow alert the rest of the crew that something was terribly wrong. But she couldn't find her voice. Or her feet. Fortunately, everyone else seemed to have found theirs. They came thundering down the stairs, emerging from the various corners, rushing to her father's side.

"Boss!" someone was yelling. "Boss!"

And then, "Someone call an ambulance."

"Don't move him," someone said. Someone else said, "Did someone call an ambulance?"

"I-I will," Abby said, her voice cracking. "I've got it."

She had a mobile phone in her car, and on numb legs she ran out to get it. She fumbled with the door handle, and with the phone. Her fingers shook so badly. It was everything she could do to press the right buttons. But once a dispatcher picked up, her voice sounded strong and clear as she gave the woman the address and asked for an ambulance.

She ran back inside, where most of the crew members had taken a step back from her dad. Only Joseph, the foreman, knelt next to him, a hand on his shoulder. Abby ran up and knelt on the other side.

It was bad, she knew that. She knew from watching her dad fall and seeing him land. But the expression on Joseph's face — and the fact that he avoided eye contact — made her think it was even worse than bad.

———

ABBY GLANCED in her rearview mirror and saw the rancher, Trace, give her a wave. She wished she had given him her business card, or something. Then he'd have her number. But her brain was fried from everything that had gone wrong that day, from the mix-up at the rental car company (she'd never drive a hot rod, if it were up to her) to the flat tire on the interstate, and she hadn't thought of it. She supposed she could go back there after checking out the property she hoped to buy.

If she did, though, she would have to come up with some kind of plausible excuse. The Mint Creek Ranch (there was a sign), a breathtaking property with rolling hills, old-growth trees, about a zillion head of cattle, and one very fine cowboy, wasn't a place where someone simply stopped by. If she hadn't been able to guess that from the geography alone (the place was practically in the middle of nowhere), the beyond-unfriendly expression on the rancher's face when she pulled up to his house would have been a dead giveaway.

But, that smile. When she rolled down her window and their eyes met, that smile had sent a buzzing energy straight to her lady parts. Which was very out of the ordinary. Most of the time, guys, even good-looking ones, didn't get Abby's libido going like that. Not at first sight, anyway.

She remembered Trace telling her to go less than three-quarters of a mile. In reminiscing over that one-minute encounter, she'd gone at least a full mile. She preferred her pick-up truck, but one benefit of a sports car was that she could do a quick one-eighty. This time, on her third pass, she saw the road. She took the left turn, enjoying how well the car handled compared to her truck. It didn't do quite as well on Saddle Horn Lane's washboard surface, but it wouldn't hurt to slow down and enjoy the scenery.

From what the real estate agent told her, this piece of property, a 100-acre parcel in Williamson Valley, had been a wedding present to a pair of city dwellers from the groom's parents.

The family came from a long line of northern Arizona ranchers, but the young couple chose to stay in Phoenix, where they both worked in electrical engineering. No matter how much the groom's parents pushed and prodded, the engineers couldn't be persuaded to move north, or even to put a weekend home on the property.

Real estate prices in Arizona had skyrocketed during the twenty years since, and the electrical engineers, no longer a young couple, wanted to sell the land to fund their retirement. So, Abby thought, it had served its purpose. They could use the land to live happily ever after.

And so could she.

She crested a little hill and got a view of the acreage below. She gasped — the landscape literally took her breath away as she stopped the car. She couldn't think of a more perfect place to build her dream development. All green grass and rolling fields, the land lay before her like an offering. Rock formations in tans and brown, evergreen trees in a deeper green, and smaller, flowery shrubs dotted the landscape.

Abby's hands came to her chest, and tears came to her eyes. Which was silly. It was a piece of land, that was all. But it was a beautiful piece of land. And her dad — her dad would be so proud. She parked the car, right there on the road, and got out. She would walk the place, step by step, yard by yard, acre by acre. She already knew in her heart that the land was *it*.

As reluctant to leave the pristine piece of property as she was an hour later, Abby had a flight to catch. And even if she wanted to (which she admitted to herself, she did), she didn't have time to revisit the Mint Creek Ranch.

As soon as she turned on the car, it made a loud beeping sound.

Abby groaned. "What now?"

The display on the dashboard read, "Low tire pressure."

Abby tightened her grip on the steering wheel and hit her forehead against it a few times, wailing, "Whyyyyy?"

She supposed she could take it as a sign. But she didn't know which way the sign was pointing. Was it saying, *You should stay here, in Prescott*? Or was it saying, *Everything about this trip has been doomed from the start. You absolutely should not build a life in this town*?

Leaving the car running, she got out and walked toward the rear. The driver's side tires looked fine, but the back one on the passenger side was completely flat. The only thing between the rim and the ground was about a centimeter of rubber. Abby groaned again. If the whole trip hadn't been going so terribly, she would probably cry. But the flat tire was the icing on the cake. So, she did what her father had taught her to do when everything was going wrong: she laughed. Perhaps the laugh sounded a little weepy, a little insane. But she didn't care. There was no one around to hear her.

Only, there was. "Hello," said a sexy, smooth voice behind her. "Flat tire, huh?"

Startled, Abby jumped as she whirled around. "You wouldn't believe it —" she started. Then she saw who the voice belonged to, and found herself speechless.

It was him. The guy from the ranch next door. He was still gorgeous, and his horse was even more so.

She chuckled, to herself. *The guy from the ranch next door*. That had a nice ring to it. Realizing that she might sound insane, Abby sucked in a breath and said, with as straight a face as she could muster, "Yep. About par for the course today."

She congratulated herself on the use of a golf metaphor. Golf was something all men could understand. Maybe that would impress this manly rancher. The guy from the ranch next door.

As she stifled another laugh, he said, "I fail to see the humor in this, being as you're a young lady out in the middle of nowhere." He pulled off his sunglasses, and his eyes smiled at her. "Ma'am, I've got to tell you, I've never seen someone laugh about a flat tire."

"You wouldn't believe it," Abby started again. "This is about the tenth thing today that's gone wrong. I'm only laughing because otherwise, I'd cry. If I don't hurry up and get this fixed, I'm going to miss my flight. Which ordinarily wouldn't be too big of a deal, but someone's waiting for me."

She was being purposefully cryptic, something she normally didn't do. But she normally didn't have a reaction like the one she was having to the guy from the ranch next door.

"That thing got a spare?"

Abby sighed. "I'm sure it does, but I haven't had a chance to look. I'd rather take your real horse back down to the airport than drive this thing."

As she spoke, she walked around to the driver's door. She hadn't even used the trunk yet, but the lever was easy enough to find. Sure enough, a panel in the bottom pulled up to reveal a spare tire.

"Yep, there's a spare," she said.

The rancher was already dismounting. In any other situation, Abby would feel a bit prickly about that. Did he assume she couldn't handle changing a tire? But in this case — only because she was in a hurry and *not at all* because he was five-star sexy, and cowboys were known for being chivalrous — she found the gesture sweet.

Still, she went ahead with assembling the tools and unscrewing the spare tire.

"You know your way around a tire change, I see," he said.

"I do," Abby said. She left it at that. She did know her way around a tire change, but still felt relieved when he said, "If you don't mind my help, the two of us can probably get you on the road a little faster. Give you some chance of catching that flight."

"Actually," she said. "I would appreciate it."

They worked together seamlessly, and within ten minutes, he was loading the flat tire into the trunk while she folded up the jack. He grabbed a rag out of the saddle bag and offered it to her just as she was wondering how she'd get her greasy hands clean.

"Thank you so much," she said, and he tipped his hat at her. To this, too, she had an unusual reaction: she wanted to kiss him.

"Any time. I hope you make your flight."

"Me too," she said. She glanced at her watch. "In fact, I think I will — thanks to you. As long as nothing else goes wrong."

"It'll be smooth sailing from here," he said. "I can feel it."

With that, he mounted that gorgeous horse and rode away.

Abby took a quick look at Mint Creek Ranch over her shoulder as she sped by a minute later. The drive back to the Phoenix airport was right about two hours, which meant Abby had plenty of time to take action. And to think. In that order.

As soon as she got on the highway, she called her real estate agent, who picked up right away. "What did you think?"

Lucy Marino was all business, straightforward, no-nonsense. Abby loved it about her.

"I want to put in an offer. Full asking price. Thirty-day escrow."

"That's it?"

"That's it," Abby said. Her voice held confidence. Sure, she felt a little nervous. But anytime a person made a big leap, nerves were part of the equation.

"Okay," said Lucy. "I'll write it up and send it in. I'll let you know the instant I hear back."

"I know you will."

Abby and Lucy had worked together on a few projects already: a commercial lot in Utah where Abby was building a retail building, a run-down ex-supermarket she'd remodeled into a strip mall, and a lot zoned for multi-family housing. While each project hit a snag or two, they were always able to get a deal through. So Abby was fairly certain Lucy could help her bring her vision for the property to reality, too.

"If you get this place, you going to move to Prescott? Wait — that's not how the locals pronounce it, right? 'Rhymes with biscuit.'"

"Right," Abby said. "I don't know if I'll ever pronounce it like the locals do." She sighed and looked briefly around at the mountains silhouetted against the pristine blue sky. "I *want* to move here. I really do. When I get this place, it's likely. Although, I'll have a hard time parting with my dad's house in Utah."

"You could always keep it," Lucy said. "The way you run your business, I think you'll have the cash flow."

"True. It's something to think about, anyway."

"Agreed. All right. I'll get this offer in and talk to you soon, okay?"

"Okay, thank you so much."

"Anytime, Abby. Drive careful."

The call ended, and music blared over the premium stereo system. Abby would love nothing more than to live in Prescott. Although that particular trip had been a bit of a whirlwind, especially with the travel delays, it had also been a nice break.

Instantly, Abby felt guilty for thinking that way. She'd spent the past several years being a caregiver for her dad, and while she *was* exhausted, she wouldn't have it any other way. She'd learned absolutely everything from him. It was only because of him that she was in the position to buy the property for her new development. And, if she could push it through, she'd have enough money to bring him out, too, and hire people to care for him.

———

THE SIGHT of her father in a wheelchair always gave Abby a little start. When she was a tiny girl, he seemed bigger than life, and she'd scramble up his back like she was climbing a mountain. She would stand on his shoulders, feeling like she was at the top of the world.

The way she thought of him — still — didn't jive with the reality: his body folded into the wheelchair. His shoulders were still broad, his long legs still sturdy looking, but he seemed smaller, somehow.

"My girl!" His voice reverberated throughout the room, strong despite the fact that he could no longer walk on his own. "I've been waiting for you."

Abby walked up to him and leaned down for a hug. His arms encircled her, and she was grateful that whatever else had changed, the comfort she experienced from his hugs remained the same.

"Well, how was it?" he asked at the same time she said, "Dad, it was perfect!"

"Tell me everything," he said. "I wish I'd been able to go with you in person."

It wasn't that Ernesto *couldn't* travel. But even though several years had passed since the accident, he didn't feel confident enough to navigate his way through a busy airport in his wheelchair, and he always said he didn't want to slow Abby down while she was working.

She insisted he wouldn't, but he insisted she go without him.

"Let me get us some drinks, and we'll go out onto the porch," she said.

"I'll get the drinks," he said. "You must be tired."

It was true. She rode the wave of exhilaration all the way down the mountain to the Phoenix airport. She was still flying high as she went through airport security and power walked to the gate. She felt alert with excitement as she sat in the chair, her thumbs flying over her phone screen, checking her emails and text messages for any news about whether the seller had accepted her offer on the property. There were no new messages by the time she boarded, and she shut off her phone as soon as she sat down. The next thing she knew, the plane was touching down in Utah. She jolted awake, but the adrenaline rush lasted only a couple of minutes before the bone-deep exhaustion set in as she drove to her dad's house. While some of the excitement was returning, thanks to sharing the news with him, she could definitely use a cold beer and a minute to sit.

"Meet you on the deck," she said.

Her dad nodded and powered his wheelchair toward the kitchen.

Immediately after his injury, she'd doted on him, trying to anticipate his every need before he mentioned it out loud. She felt like a butterfly. She would light on his shoulder, flutter away to get him something, and then return for only the briefest moment before going on another errand. At first, he needed it. Fighting through his own grief, he felt like his body failed him. Although his physical therapists marveled at how strong he was, how much he could do so quickly after his fall, Ernesto was beyond frustrated.

Over time, acceptance set in, and although he could do more for himself, Abby didn't let him. She wanted to take care of him in the same way he had always provided for her. She felt that somehow, if she cared for him, she could lessen his frustration, take away some of the sting.

She later realized that only Ernesto could do that for himself. Her realization came about the same time his did, and he sat her down and told her that she had to get on with it.

Remembering the conversation brought a smile to Abby's face as she pushed open the French doors that led to the deck.

Outdoor spaces had always been one of the best in Ernesto's designs. This one jutted out from the house in a way that made Abby feel like she was floating when she stepped onto it. A table and chairs sat at one end, and another row of chairs backed up to the house, positioned with a stunning view of the red rocks beyond.

A minute later, Ernesto joined Abby on the deck. He handed her a glass of seltzer water, with plenty of ice.

"Thanks," she said. "I needed this."

"I've got something stronger, if you want."

Abby smiled at him. "I could probably use that, too," she said. "The way my trip went. But I'm afraid I'd be snoring on the porch before you could get me home."

"I thought your trip went well. You said the place was perfect."

Abby took a long drink of the water, let the bubbles burst in her mouth before swallowing. "It is."

Evening sunlight poured over the landscape in front of them. The scene looked so soft. For a moment, Abby wondered how the sunset looked in Williamson Valley right then.

"The land *is* perfect. The trip — kind of a nightmare."

She told him all of it: the long security line at the airport, the flight delay, the rental car mix-up, the flat tire. When she got to the part about missing her turn and asking for directions at the Mint Creek Ranch, her dad's eyes started to sparkle.

"What?" she asked.

"What are you leaving out?"

Abby's body betrayed her. She felt herself blushing. "Nothing."

"Lies!" Ernesto pointed at her, as if to say, "Gotcha."

Abby laughed. "Well, if you must know, the rancher who gave me directions — let's just say he was easy on the eyes."

"Easy on the eyes, huh?"

"That's about the best description I can give, to my *father*!"

"Did you get his number?"

"Dad! No! I was there on business."

"I mean, did you get his number for business purposes? He could be a good ally, you know, in a neighborly way."

"Somehow, I didn't get the impression that he wants anything to do with an out-of-towner. He was pretty prickly when I drove up unannounced in my rented Mustang."

Ernesto shrugged. "Probably because he thought *you* were easy on the eyes, too."

"Da-ad," Abby said, breaking the word into two syllables, like she had as a teenager.

"What? You ought to be good-looking. You have my genes and

your mother's. God rest her soul. You know what they say about the acorn."

"It's the apple. Not the acorn."

"Whatever. I see some potential here."

"Let's talk about the property."

Eyes still twinkling, Ernesto chuckled. He took a drink of his water. "Okay. Let's talk about the property."

Abby pulled out her sketchpad and got to work, giving Ernesto the lay of the land, the hills and valleys, Granite Mountain. She held up her sketch for her dad to examine, and watched as his vision took shape. Instead of reaching for her pencil, though, he asked, "What are you thinking?"

She grinned. "I was hoping you'd ask."

CHAPTER FOUR

TRACE

AFTER THE STUNNING brunette in the Mustang drove away, Trace felt a little guilty for his reaction to her unexpectedly showing up at his place. Because he was an introspective guy (when he wanted to be), he spent some time thinking about the reasons behind his knee-jerk, prickly response.

Filling water troughs, Trace considered that as an adult, he still felt like his hometown was perfect. Sure, it had changed, grown. More traffic (and traffic signals), another movie theater, new restaurants. But it still had the same mountains, the same sky, many of the same people, who were still like family.

When Luis Hernandez had a heart attack, all the Williamson Valley neighbors created a meal schedule and delivered casseroles to Mama Hernandez. But they didn't stop there. Every day, someone showed up at the llama ranch to help with the chores. Trace was the first to sign up. They got quick lessons in llama shearing, stall mucking, and a llama's spitting distance. By the time Luis was out of the hospital and had recovered, the farm hadn't missed a beat. Everything was exactly as he'd left it.

One year, Hunter Inman, the youngest daughter of Hector and Jessica, owners of the Bright Moon Ranch, collied with another player during a soccer game and broke her arm. Her coach, the father of her longtime friend, comforted her while another parent, a doctor in town, splinted the bone. Within minutes, she was off to the hospital. And when she was cleared to play soccer again, the team held a little parade to welcome her back.

As for himself, Trace thought, getting in his truck to drive over to the hay barn, he enjoyed most of the perks of small-town living. When he went for breakfast at the Horse Shoe, the servers knew his order. When he went for drinks at the Watering Hole, whichever bartender was working that night would slide a cold one across the counter to him as he walked up. He knew what to expect — of the traffic, the weather, the people.

And Prescott knew what to expect of him, as well. He was a champion team roper, one of three legs that made up the Mint Creek Ranch boys, along with Cody and Sawyer. He'd never cross a friend, and nobody'd better cross him. Trace never forgot a favor, and he gave them out freely.

The rhythmic movement of swinging hay bales into the back calmed him as he continued thinking.

He was single. Happily. Trace loved life as it was. He didn't want anything to change. And hitching up with a woman was one surefire way to create change in a guy's life.

Sure, he dated. But, in a small town like Prescott, a guy couldn't date too much, or he'd be known as a player.

He was content being alone. His unexpected — and very tangible — reaction to the woman in the Mustang made him uneasy. *Was* he content?

Life was perfect. Until it wasn't.

A few months before, things had started shifting. Cody, who had taken some time off bull riding, went back on tour and promptly fell in love with the reporter covering his story.

Watching this romance unfold, Trace noticed the beginning of a change of heart. It wasn't that he wanted to get married. It wasn't that he was jealous. It was that, for the first time, he could see (to a tiny, minuscule extent) that falling in love might not be such a bad thing.

Not that he wanted change. Because he didn't.

But because he saw the way Cody and Tessa looked at each other. He saw, before his very eyes, that his friend would do anything for the love of his life — and she for him.

The sun felt hot on his skin now, as he loaded the last bale of hay and got back in the truck to take it over to the horse stalls. The physical labor, the burn of his muscles, the sweat dripping down his back, released the tension that such thoughts created in his body.

The thought had struck him recently — he braced himself for it again — that maybe once you had someone in your life, *that* became the constant. Maybe, if you found real love, then all the rest of life took on a new kind of stability. Even as he got out of the truck to put a bale in the first stall, he shuddered. Surely, this whole thought process would fade away. He was caught up in the romantic excitement.

After delivering another bale to another stall, he took a moment to reset. Like he did most days, he admired the view — Mint Creek Ranch nestled up against the base of Granite Mountain.

It was all rolling green fields, bisected into tidy squares by white fencing. Here and there, copses of old cottonwood trees, their leaves glittering in the sunlight, created shady oases for the horses and cattle. As kids, he, Cody, Sawyer, and Montana had spent lots of time in the shade of those trees, much of it in the creek that ran along the property's northern edge.

For the briefest moment, Trace considered driving right over to the creek and stripping down to his underwear to relive some of his favorite moments from childhood.

But, as it always did, his rational side took control. He had horses to feed and a City Council meeting to get to.

————

A WEEK HAD PASSED since Trace's unexpected visit from the sexy, Mustang-driving stranger, which meant it was Tuesday — the day the Prescott City Council held its weekly meeting.

Trace, who attended every meeting to keep an eye on how the city was developing, walked into the Council chambers and took his usual seat, in the first row, right behind the press table and off to the left, so he had a clear view of Ronnie Sunshine, the mayor. Maybe Trace should stop thinking of his last name as "Sunshine"; it was actually James. Good old Ronnie picked up the nickname in high school basketball, thanks to his bright-orange hair.

He greeted Trace with a cool nod, and Trace responded in kind. It wasn't that they didn't get along. It was that their relationship had been somewhat strained since high school.

And, okay, maybe Trace had a bit of a chip on his shoulder, but from his perspective, it seemed like the jocks looked down their perfect straight noses at the ranch kids. And Ronnie had only affirmed this belief when, junior year, Trace showed up to try out for the basketball team. While Trace laced up his basketball shoes — brand-new, sparkling white, purchased specifically for the tryout — Ronnie gave him a once over, snorted out a derisive laugh, and said, "You should've waited to buy those shoes until after the tryout, Walker. They're not going to see any time on the court."

Caught off guard and at a complete loss for what to say, Trace simply ignored Ronnie. He finished tying his brand-new shoes and went to line up.

What Ronnie Sunshine didn't know at the time was that Trace had some pretty decent skills. With four kids living on the property, the Mint Creek Ranch would not have been complete without a hoop and a half-court. Ronnie had no idea that Trace had a knack for hitting pretty much every shot he took. He had no idea that years of hauling hay, riding horses, roping, and doing whatever manual labor his parents came up with had made Trace much stronger than the average high school kid. So not only could he shoot, but he could pass, and he could run.

Ronnie didn't hide his disappointment when Trace not only made the team, but landed the first-string position.

Ronnie made the team too — second string.

Although the rest of the jocks accepted Trace with the requisite back slaps and good-natured teasing, Ronnie continued to give him the cold shoulder. Needless to say, they'd never become friends.

Years later, that held true. But, they did seem to share an interest in the buzzy "smart growth" of their hometown, and in that, they'd come to a sort of fragile understanding.

Ronnie Sunshine, Mayor of Prescott, sat facing the door. Trace could tell the moment Ronnie saw someone enter the room: his eyes focused, made a subtle-yet-noticeable appraisal, and then went straight down to the papers on the table in front of him.

That was interesting, Trace thought.

Trace waited until he could see the person in his peripheral vision. Gaze on the floor, the first thing he noticed was the heels. They were pointy and narrow, and made out of a material that closely resembled snakeskin. Only, it was pink. *Ridiculous.* Trace had never once seen a pink snake. The pants — contemporary slacks in a creamy gray — hugged shapely calf muscles. Maybe the heels weren't so ridiculous after all. And those thighs — they were just right for a man to hold onto when — *whoa.* Where was that coming from?

Trace forced his focus up to the woman's face, and he was even more stunned.

One thing about living in a small town was that a person could always spot a newcomer, Trace thought, and boy, howdy, was this a newcomer. It was Abby. The woman with the Mustang. The flat tire. The dimples. And she was beautiful. In a word, perfection. Like an artist had taken great care to carve her exquisite features: lush lips painted the same color as those ridiculous faux snakeskin high heels, almond-shaped eyes framed with long, thick eyelashes, and smooth, dark skin.

Their eyes met. Trace had a physical reaction. Electricity. It sparked through his body, leaving him vibrating.

Involuntarily, he gave her his sexiest grin. He had seen the tiniest hint of a smile on her lips, but when she saw his grin, hers disappeared altogether.

Shit.

She probably thought he was planning to hit on her. Not that he wasn't thinking about it. But he didn't want her to know he was thinking about it. Suddenly, her eyes focused straight ahead, and she strode past him and took a seat at the opposite end of the row. She smelled so, so good, like roses and vanilla. He realized he was inhaling, hard, through his nose, and hoped she didn't notice. He didn't dare turn his head to look at her, but out of the corner of his eye, he could see that she sat with her back straight, ankles crossed, and hands clasped atop a folder in her lap.

Trace would never ask Ronnie why the mysterious Abby-I'm-lost was at the meeting. But he would find out.

The seats in the chambers began to fill, and before too long, Trace could no longer see the gorgeous woman and her long black hair. Which was probably good. He had come to the meeting on business. An out-of-town developer was planning to re-zone a large piece of property adjacent to the Mint Creek Ranch. They wanted to put in several houses.

Trace couldn't stand the thought of that. Williamson Valley was known for its character, and that character was generous ranch properties, lots of open space, grass and air and sky. As soon as money-hungry developers started putting in subdivisions, that character would change.

He had come on behalf of himself and other Williamson Valley property owners, to speak against the rezoning of the property.

The night before, Cody and Sawyer had hinted that Trace might be overreacting.

"That parcel is what, a hundred acres?" Cody said to him. "I mean, even if they put twenty houses on it, that's five acres apiece. Those are decent-sized parcels."

Sawyer had nodded. "I heard through the grapevine that some of the parcels might actually be larger."

Trace, already so focused on what he planned to say at the City Council meeting, didn't think to ask Sawyer where he heard about the larger parcels. Instead, he said, "But this is how it's always been. We've never had a subdivision out here. Why start now? It's a slippery slope."

Neither of his friends seemed to think maintaining the area's character was as important as Trace did. When Cody changed the subject, Trace let it go. Which is how he showed up at the City Council meeting alone. Looking back on the night before, he couldn't help but wonder if what Cody and Sawyer said was true. Maybe it wouldn't be so bad to have a handful of houses sprinkled among the low, rolling hills of Williamson Valley.

But, there he was. He would at least say his piece. He checked his watch. It was three p.m., time for the meeting to begin.

With a whack of the gavel Trace considered grossly dramatic, Ronnie called the meeting to order. Trace tuned out most of the housekeeping, but when Ronnie announced the first presentation, Trace's ears perked up.

"I'd like to call to the podium Abby Flores of Premium Construction."

Trace could feel the interest building. Abby Flores. Apparently, the name didn't sound familiar to any of his fellow meeting attendees. And when Abby stood, the crowd gave a collective gasp. Trace watched as the woman in the pink snakeskin high heels walked to the podium, where she set down her folder before smiling at the Council members.

Well, I'll be.

The sexy temptress who'd made more than one appearance in his consciousness since she showed up in his driveway the week before worked for the developer who planned to ruin the place he'd always loved. It was only natural the developer would send out a beautiful woman to tackle this job. Well, Abby-I'm-lost didn't know who she was messing with.

As he listened to her speak, Trace realized he was in trouble. Not only did she sound intelligent and eloquent, but she had facts and numbers and drawings that *could* prove why rezoning the property might work. Trace knew the council wouldn't make a decision that day, but the longer Abby spoke, the more he feared the council members had everything they needed to go ahead with the rezoning.

She was so good that, for a moment, he thought he maybe shouldn't go to the microphone when she was done.

But Mint Creek Ranch came first, along with all the values he'd lived by since moving there. He wouldn't back down simply because the developer was pretty. Gorgeous. Smokin' hot. That's what the developer wanted. Abby was a pawn in his scheme to take over Williamson Valley.

Abby concluded with, "I expect I've answered all your questions, council members?" (which Trace thought was pretty cheeky).

After she returned to her seat, Ronnie opened the meeting for public comment. Trace cleared his throat and raised a hand.

"Trace Walker," Ronnie said, his tone bored and dismissive.

Trace could feel Abby's eyes on him as he approached the microphone. Silence descended. A little dizzy, Trace began to speak, careful not to look directly at Abby. He couldn't afford the distraction. She might hate him after he spoke, but she was an outsider. It shouldn't matter. His hometown was more important than any woman.

"I would like to urge the City Council to use caution when considering Ms. Flores's request. The character of Williamson Valley is a tradition, one that's important to everyone who lives there. Rezoning one piece of land will put us on a dangerous slippery slope."

Trace could hear the people behind him shifting in their seats. He was making them uncomfortable. *He* was uncomfortable. Earlier, he imagined making a long, impassioned speech. But in that moment, the clock ticking, the air conditioner whirring, someone yawning behind him, he felt uncharacteristically speechless.

"Mr. Walker," said Yancy Stringer, one of the City Council members. "To be clear, no one is talking about packing Williamson Valley full of apartment buildings or tract houses. This is one development on a rather large parcel."

Trace swallowed, nodded. "I know it's one development. But isn't that how any big change begins? With one small change? The second one is a little easier."

Yancy and Ronnie exchanged glances.

Ronnie said, "Thank you for your input, Mr. Walker. We appreciate it. We will be sure to take it into consideration when we have our discussion. Anyone else?"

Trace was dismissed — and embarrassed. The reporters at the press table were scribbling away on their notepads. There was no way his speech would escape being in the newspaper. Which meant people would be talking about it for a while.

ABBY

WHEN SHE'D FIRST LAID eyes on Trace Walker at the City Council meeting, Abby had to admit, she'd felt a jolt beyond the simple recognition of someone she'd met the week before.

It wasn't a little jolt. It was more of a zap. An attraction. He was good-looking. Not her type, with his cowboy hat and jeans and a five o'clock shadow — but handsome nonetheless.

She noticed him notice her, and she couldn't lie to herself: she liked the way he looked at her with intensity in his eyes. She wondered if she'd run into him in town, now that she'd be staying in Prescott. She hoped so.

She was already nervous about speaking to the City Council. After that lust-filled moment with the rancher, she was even more so. She hoped that if he could hear her voice shaking, he would attribute it to nerves, and not the fact that she knew he was watching her. Fortunately, he was behind her, and she finished her presentation with confidence. The council members looked interested and thoughtful, and she felt like she was paving the way toward their buy-in.

But then, *he* spoke. Trace told the City Council that her development was a bad idea. And damnit if she couldn't help but think he looked amazing doing it. The man looked great in jeans, for sure. But. He'd just made himself her enemy.

Unless she could convince him that her development was, in fact, a really good idea. She could be very convincing.

Still, she could already see that Prescott, a bona fide small town, was subject to all the small-town clichés: gossip, long-held grudges, tight-knit neighborhoods. The very last thing she needed was for people to think she was sleeping with Trace Walker in order to get her project through.

Sleeping with Trace Walker!

You made that leap pretty fast, woman.

The meeting was over, and she didn't think she'd made a complete fool of herself. The Council members didn't seem opposed to her development. They looked interested, and maybe even impressed with the care she put into her presentation. On still-shaky legs, she made her way out to the parking lot, breathing deeply to calm herself down.

As she reached her car, she heard someone saying her name. She recognized his voice — she had listened to him stumble through a speech opposing the project that was closest to her heart. Her first instinct was to jump in her truck and speed away. But even as an adult, she couldn't shake the good manners her parents had instilled in her. She stopped walking, sighed, and turned around.

"Yes?" She was going for icy, but Trace smiled back as if she'd offered him an ice cream cone.

Up close, he was even better looking, if that were possible. Intense blue eyes glittered at her, and that five o'clock shadow accented an angular, chiseled jawline. His teeth were straight and white, maybe a tiny bit too big. But that feature, along with his dimples, made for a pretty killer smile.

What was she thinking? Even a man with a killer smile could still be bad news. *Especially* a man with a killer smile. Hadn't she learned that more than once in her life? Quickly, she recalibrated.

"Is there something you wanted to discuss?" She arched one eyebrow, a practiced move designed to put a guy in the spotlight, make him feel like he was but a mere performer on a stage.

"As a matter of fact, I did," Trace said.

Abby raised both eyebrows then, as if to say, "Go ahead."

He rubbed his chin. "How serious is your company about this development?"

Abby let the smile fade from her face and said, "Dead serious."

"Y'all — your boss — couldn't be persuaded to change his mind about putting in a bunch of houses?"

Interesting. Like so many men before him, Trace assumed Abby was part of a team — not the owner of the company. Likely, he thought she was the face of the company, the one sent out to make deals, to charm people into what the boss wanted. Little did most people realize, Abby wasn't the face of her company. She was the brain, the heart, the very soul. But she wouldn't let Trace know that quite yet.

"I'm afraid not. We've done the research. Prescott — and specifically Williamson Valley — is perfect for our goals."

Anger flashed in those dark-blue eyes. "And what are your goals, exactly? To peddle the small-town dream to big-money city folks? To ruin the character of a place that's perfect as it is?"

A dozen years ago, Miles Taylor stood on the second story of an unfinished hotel building and, without even realizing it, showed Abby how men thought. And she took note. Instead of putting herself at odds with the men in the industry, she studied them. Starting when she was fifteen, she watched every move, listened to every conversation, learned all the nuances. Right now, Trace seemed angry, but for most people, Abby had learned, anger was a secondary emotion. He felt threatened. And *she* was the threat.

The best thing she could do was let him blow off steam.

At those three words, Abby felt a little shiver, a thrill. She could think of some ways they could blow off steam together. Not for the first time, she reminded herself that she couldn't think that way about that man. In the half-second it took Abby to go through that thought process, Trace must've gone through his own.

He sighed. "Look, I'm sorry. I'm sure you're just the messenger. And trust me, I don't want to shoot the messenger. Is there someone else I can talk to? The guy who makes the decisions?"

Hoping to defuse some of the tension, she offered him what she hoped was her most devilish grin. "Well, what do you know? You're talking to the guy who makes the decisions."

Surprise registered. He pointed at her, then looked around the parking lot. "You're —"

"It's just me."

"But — I thought —"

"You thought that only a man could run a construction company?" She knew she was baiting him, but she didn't care. No matter how much Trace loved Prescott, she loved her company more. She wouldn't let him stop her from building her dream project.

"No!" he rushed to say. "It's not that! With the size of the development you're planning on, I assumed it was a bigger company. That's all." He held up his hands, pleading innocence.

She laughed. "Well, whatever name you want to put on it, I know my situation is unusual. And I can tell how much you love this place. I could go on and on, explaining my rationale, giving you all the details of the project to put your mind at ease. I could tell you I have fallen in love with Williamson Valley and its open space. But at this point, I don't think you'd believe any of it. You seem pretty set on stopping me in my tracks. So for now, I guess we're going to have to agree to disagree. I plan to keep moving forward, no matter how hard you push back."

Some sassy, clever part of her wanted to turn around and add, "I might be persuaded, between the sheets."

But she didn't. Instead, she wished him a lovely rest of the day and walked back toward her truck. In her side-view mirror, she watched him walk away, and again, she admired the way he filled out those jeans.

She sighed. It *was* her dream project. And she *would* keep moving forward, whatever it took. But why in the world did she have to have an adversary? And why did that adversary have to be so darn good-looking?

———

THE NEXT MORNING, Abby sat at the kitchen table in her rented Prescott apartment (which she was calling her home office), hard at work on the designs for the different models in her new subdivision. Her phone rang, startling her. She noticed the time — an hour had passed since she sat down — before noticing the phone number: it was local. Although she was tempted to let it go to voicemail because she had so much to do, she knew she had to answer. It could be any number of people. The City Council secretary calling with a question or to set up a meeting, the real estate agent, Lucy, calling with details about the land, someone from the home goods store, calling about the curtains she'd ordered …

She took a sip of her coffee and then picked up. "This is Abby Flores."

"Hey, Abby, it's Montana. Montana Hart. Calling on official *Daily Dispatch* business. Have a minute?"

Abby's stomach dropped. Her teeth clenched. She held her breath, then released it. She detected nothing but friendly curiosity in Montana's voice, but still. A person had to be careful with the newspaper.

"Yeah, I have a minute." She kicked herself for saying, "Yeah," instead of, "Yes." Her dad would hate it.

"Great. I heard you were at the City Council meeting yesterday."

"Yeah, I — yes. I was."

"I missed it. I was out shooting a dog. Well, not *shooting* a dog. Taking pictures of a dog. We have this weekly feature, Dog of the Week, where we share pictures of a dog from the shelter, to help get it adopted. Anyway. Enough about that. I was wondering, since I wasn't there yesterday and didn't get a picture of you, if you might be available for a quick photo shoot."

"A photo shoot?"

"I know. It's awkward. Trust me, I'm so glad I'm the one *behind* the camera. My editor, Stanley, asked me to call you. Actually, he practically *begged* me to see if you'd be willing to let me take a couple pictures, so we have some to go with the story."

"The story?" Abby hadn't seen any reporters at the meeting. But she hadn't really been looking. She'd been so focused on Trace and her presentation … and Trace again.

"I mean, I guess —"

"Great!" Montana's enthusiasm made Abby smile. "What's your schedule like? I'm open all day."

Abby looked at the time up in the corner of her computer screen. Then she looked at the drawings she'd been adjusting when the phone rang. Then she glanced at her reflection in the mirror next to the table – hair in a messy bun, satin sleep shorts, a white tank top with no bra, and a silky turquoise robe. "I'm gonna need a couple of hours."

Montana suggested meeting at the property Abby was buying, and two hours later, Abby drove out.

When she turned off the narrow dirt road, she saw Montana's little hatchback already parked. A few yards beyond it, Montana stood, camera raised, the breeze blowing her long blonde hair to one side. As Abby approached, she turned around, and in her smile, Abby saw immediate warmth.

"Thank you so much for doing this," Montana said. "You're making my life so much easier. To tell you the truth, I hate photographing City Council meetings. I'd much rather meet someone out here where at least there's scenery."

Abby turned in a full circle, taking in the rolling grassy hills, the bright blue of the sky, the white fluffy clouds. "Yes, there's definitely scenery, isn't there?"

Montana rested the camera on her hip, like someone would do with a baby. "So what brings you to Williamson Valley property ownership?"

"Oh, I'm sure you've heard that it's, you know, a burning desire to completely ruin the atmosphere in Williamson Valley." She could hear the bitterness in her tone, and forced a laugh. "That came out wrong. Sorry. This is pretty much my dream project. This is my dream property. I'd like to live here, myself. The last thing I want to do is ruin it."

Montana took a deep breath and squeezed Abby's arm, as if they truly shared this burden. "Don't let Trace get to you. He's averse to change. It's not you."

"I take it you're a Prescott native, too? That's how you know Mr. Walker?"

Again, Montana laughed. "Yes, I'm a native. And I've never called Trace 'Mr. Walker' a day in my life. We literally grew up together, running every inch of the Mint Creek Ranch as kids. Along with Cody Davis and Sawyer Nelson. Trace is like a brother to me. I love the heck out of him, but I also know he can be a little … or a *lot* hardheaded."

Abby knew she should feel relief at the fact that Montana had acknowledged Trace's tendency toward stubbornness. But a fresh wave of nerves came crawling over her skin like a little army of insects. Montana grew up on the Mint Creek Ranch? With Trace! Great. Perfect. She, too, would probably hate the idea of the new development.

Before she could think of what to say, Montana jumped in yet again. "Oh, my gosh. I can read every thought you're thinking right now. Don't worry. I'm nothing like Trace. Okay, maybe we have a few things in common. But let's say I'm a little more open-minded than he is. I watched the online replay of your presentation at the meeting, and I can see the potential in what you're envisioning for your development. And, goodness knows, I could use another girlfriend. Seems like I'm always surrounded by men. Trace will come around."

At that last part, Abby made a face, and Montana laughed. "I know. Maybe he won't. But even if he doesn't, you and I can still be friends, right?"

Montana's optimism was contagious. Abby felt herself grinning. "In that case, I'd love to show you my sketches. Keep in mind, this is totally preliminary, since the City Council hasn't even approved the rezoning yet. But it'll give you an idea of what I'm thinking."

Back at her truck, Abby pulled the printed versions of the drawings out of the cab and spread them on the tailgate. Montana stood next to her.

"Oh, I see," she said. "You've got the house situated here for maximum privacy, right? The little hills will be between the houses, so neighbors won't be able to see into each others' windows. And this bank of windows is south-facing, right?"

One detail after another, Montana gushed over the drawings. Her approval brought Abby so much joy. Not that she needed approval, but it felt so good for someone to really see Abby's vision.

Once they'd looked at the last page, Montana beamed at Abby. "This is going to be amazing. I know it's going to happen."

And even though Abby wasn't as certain, she beamed back. "Thank you. You don't know how much that means to me."

"You know what?" Montana said, then. "This lighting is really nice. Why don't I get a couple pictures of you right here, with the property in the background? Maybe a few beside the truck, with the drawings, and a few without the truck?"

Abby had never played model before, but it was fun to pose for pictures. After about ten minutes, Montana said, "I think I've got what I need, here. Thanks again for meeting up. I'm sure you have a lot going on."

"No more than you do, I'm sure. Actually, it's good you got me out of the house. I've been obsessing over these drawings, and I need to stop by a couple of job sites this afternoon."

"Want to grab lunch?" Montana asked.

Abby looked at her watch, even though she knew it was close to noon, and her stomach told her it was lunchtime. "Yeah, I'd like that."

Twenty minutes later, they were seated in a comfy booth next to the window in the Burger Shack.

"Thanks for this," Abby said. "It's my first actual lunch invitation."

"Are you telling me none of the men in this town have asked you out on a date?"

"Ha. Yes. That's what I'm telling you. But I definitely give off a not-available vibe."

"Huh," Montana said, disbelieving.

"It's true. I have things to do."

"An entrepreneurial woman and all that," Montana said. "So, what projects do you have to check on?"

The server brought a basket of fries, and the women started munching on them. Inside, Abby cringed. It's not that she wasn't proud of her work — quite the opposite — but she knew that locals, especially those who had been around for a while, were predisposed to dislike what she was doing. She cleared her throat. "Well, there's that new retail building ... the one next to the dentist's office?"

Montana smacked the table. "That's *your* project? I had no idea. I love it! I'm so excited — like, *beyond* excited — they're putting a retail building in that space. Finally! It's always been such an eyesore. An empty field with lots of sticker bushes. Are you going to sell it? Lease it out? I can't wait to find out who's in there. You know what I'd really like to see? A store for women our age. With, you know, nice clothes. Not like those stores for teenagers. Maybe a shoe store. Yes! A shoe store! Wouldn't that be fun?"

Again, relief washed over Abby at Montana's reaction. The woman's enthusiasm was contagious. "A shoe store would be wonderful," Abby said. "To answer your question, at this point, I plan to hang onto the property. I'll lease out the spaces, but I'm not quite at the stage where I'm courting retailers. Not yet. You've seen it. We just got the walls up."

Montana clapped, her eyes alight with excitement. "Ooh! I can't wait. That's amazing! How have we not hung out? Where do you live? Why haven't I seen you around town?"

Laughing, Abby said, "I've got a little apartment downtown. But I still have my house in Utah. Since I actually moved here, I've been so busy. I'm up before the sun and head straight out to the sites. I work all day, can barely keep my eyes open through dinner, and then I crash. And get up and do it all again the next day. So that's probably why we haven't run into each other."

"Now that I've met you, you're not going to be able to get rid of me," Montana said. She lifted her soda cup. "Cheers!"

Abby lifted hers. "To friendship."

"To your new stalker. Speaking of that, I have a proposal."

"Well?" Abby said. "I can sure see your wheels turning. What are you thinking?"

———

MONTANA HART WANTED to buy one of Abby's houses. Abby couldn't believe it. It wasn't a traditional deal, but having the buy-in of a Prescott native meant more to her than any financial deal could. She spent the afternoon floating on clouds, in pure gratitude that she had her first buyer.

The fact that the rezoning wasn't yet approved was a tiny blip on her radar. What mattered was that she had the support of someone in her new hometown.

———

ABBY HADN'T SET up a *Daily Dispatch* subscription at her apartment yet, so she didn't see that day's edition until she walked into the convenience store to buy a sports drink. When she saw it on the stand inside the door, she froze. Then she smiled and blushed. Then, she walked out the door without buying anything because she didn't want anyone to recognize her.

Abby's dad kept a scrapbook of their company's projects, and she thought about it while she drove to the jobsite for the new retail building. Its pages contained blueprints, photos of jobsites, and newspaper clippings. Abby's name had been in the paper before, but never alongside a professional-quality picture that, even she had to admit, made her look like an actual model. Montana had worked some kind of magic. The picture in the paper looked like an ad for work boots, or maybe pickup trucks. Abby thought she'd be the first one to buy, if she was a stranger looking at it.

She made her rounds at the jobsites, pleased, as always, that she had such a good crew. Yet another lesson Ernesto taught her: great hires led to great work. A great hire wasn't always someone with the perfect resumé. It was someone willing to learn, ask questions, and do things correctly. Throughout the morning, as she checked measurements and window installations and prepped for electric, she thought about that picture in the paper. More specifically, she thought about the potential reactions to that picture in the paper. Although she momentarily felt like something of a supermodel, the people of Prescott would likely see her as a villain. She almost couldn't wait for lunch time to get home and on her computer, where she could look at the digital version of the newspaper and see reader comments.

In her apartment, she reheated leftovers from the previous night's dinner — old-fashioned spaghetti and meatballs — and poured herself a generous glass of merlot. She didn't have to go out again that day and figured a little liquid courage couldn't hurt. Seated at her kitchen table/desk, she opened her laptop and pulled up the *Daily Dispatch* website. And there it was. The picture made her smile all over again.

"Looking pretty good, Flores," she said to herself.

Her stomach fluttered with nerves as she scrolled down to the story. She took her time reading it, and found the reporter, Tessa Kincaid, offered an accurate and balanced representation of what happened during the City Council meeting. Although Abby knew a more in-depth story may follow, this one contained only the facts, including the breakdown of similar rezoning proposals and whether they passed or failed. Abby saw the pass-fail split was about fifty-fifty. She shrugged. She'd made her presentation, done what she could do, and the decision was out of her hands.

"And now, for the comments."

She braced herself and scrolled down. The fluttery feeling in her stomach transformed to a heavy sensation she recognized as dread. She wished she could say the comments were fifty-fifty, positive-negative. From what she could see in a quick glance, though, they were overwhelmingly negative about the idea of the Sunset Valley development.

I sincerely hope the Council will deny this request! This town can't handle any more traffic!

Why the Council would even hear this developer's presentation is beyond me! No more development in our small town!!!!!

"Five exclamation points," Abby said, letting her head fall into her hand for a moment. "Maybe I should stop reading these."

But she plowed on.

No. Just no. The last thing we need is a project of this size.

Don't let another developer try to ruin our small town. Say NO to big-city business.

Abby rolled her eyes. She wasn't even big-city business.

I hope all you fellows on the Council can see past the pretty face. This development is going to be ugly.

"Well, at least they think I'm pretty."

Abby closed her laptop. There was no use reading any more.

Maybe she should get out and go for a walk. But if she did, would she risk being accosted? Now that everyone had seen her picture on the front page of the newspaper, it was possible they would recognize her around town. All the fun of being an imaginary model faded away.

Her phone rang, and Montana's name came up on the screen. As soon as Abby answered, Montana said, "Whatever you do, don't look at the article online."

"Too late," Abby said, bolstered by Montana's effort.

"I'm sorry," Montana said. "I should have warned you."

"You couldn't have known," Abby said.

"Oh, yes. I could have. Happens every time. Knowing you're new to these parts, I should have told you when I took the photos that you should absolutely avoid the comment section. Take note of that for future reference, would you?"

Abby laughed. "Noted. That was nice of you to call."

Montana groaned. "If only I'd called a *little* earlier."

"Then I would've missed the one comment about me being pretty. Great photos, by the way."

"Thanks. Couldn't go wrong, really. What are you up to?"

Abby told her, and they talked for a few more minutes before making plans to go out that Friday. Abby felt a little guilty staying in town over the weekend. When she first started working in Prescott, she stayed in a hotel and went back to her dad's every Friday, returning to Prescott Sunday night or Monday morning. But after a month sticking to the hectic schedule, she simply couldn't any more. She practically had an IV drip of caffeine, and her hands shook constantly. Her stomach was always upset, and she had daily headaches. And, according to her dad, she looked a mess.

"Monkey," he said to her about a month before, "I say this in the most loving way possible. But you look terrible. The bags under your eyes are as big as the nail pouches on a toolbelt. Your skin's a weird color. And look at you." He pinched her arm. "You're wasting away. You're too skinny. I think you're coming to see me too often."

She opened her mouth to protest, but he held up a hand. "Besides, when you're here, you interrupt my binge-watching. During the week, I like to watch that home makeover show. But I reserve my weekends for that treehouse show, you know the one? And when you're here, I can't watch it."

"But couldn't we watch it —"

"No. I don't want to watch it with you. You talk too much. Always trying to guess the ending." She knew he was lying. His eyes held mischief, which gave way to concern. "Monkey, it's too much for you. You worry about me too much. I'll be fine. This is only temporary."

Ernesto knew Abby dreamed of moving to Prescott permanently. He had said he was willing to move there, too, if she got the development through. But, that was still a big *if*.

"So for now," he said, as if he'd gone through the same thought process she had, "you come every other weekend."

Thinking about her evening out with Montana — a night out on the town, for fun — Abby smiled. Her dad would be fine. He would be happy as could be watching his treehouse show. And after a late night on Friday, Abby could stay in bed all day Saturday and Sunday if she wanted.

She supposed she would never stop feeling like she wasn't doing enough for her dad, but she also knew a little time for herself would do her soul good.

CHAPTER FIVE

EXHAUSTED AFTER A LONG, hot day of riding the ranch to check the fields, Trace walked into the Watering Hole with a hankering for a cold beer. Maybe two. Grateful for the air conditioning, he pulled off his long-sleeved shirt and let the cool air hit his sweaty t-shirt.

He was set to meet Cody and Sawyer, who'd spent the day in Flagstaff scouting cattle to buy. Instead of the guys, he saw Montana. Her long blonde hair made her easy to pick out of a crowd. And, since she was like a sister to Trace, he always spotted her quickly.

And, because she was like a sister to him, irritation ran hot through his veins as soon as he realized who sat across the table from her.

It took a moment to register. First, he noticed Abby's profile, her long lashes, her full lips. What struck him as odd, though, was that she wore a white ribbed tank top, like an undershirt, which showed every curve, and a pair of carpenter jeans. Leather work boots completed the ensemble. Where were those snakeskin heels and curve-hugging pants?

What struck him as even more odd was that he felt totally aroused.

Get a grip. The woman humiliated you. Trace's face burned at the memory of Abby's smug expression when she revealed she was the developer who wanted to build that eyesore development.

Montana spotted Trace, raised a hand in greeting, and smiled. Trace started to smile back, but then he remembered that he was irritated with Montana. Why did the woman have to go and befriend everyone she met? She never knew a stranger. Which was fine in middle school, because she could open the door for Trace with his biggest crushes. But Abby? Why did she have to befriend his new, mortal enemy? His *sexy* mortal enemy? He let the scowl freeze on his face and offered the most minimalist wave he could muster. Fortunately, his friends chose that very moment to show up. Cody draped an arm over his shoulders, and Sawyer smacked him on the butt and headed for the bar.

ONE THING that never changed about living in a small town was that a guy couldn't go anywhere without running into someone he knew. Sometimes, it was one of Trace's mom's old friends, clucking at him for buying a dozen doughnuts on a Saturday morning ("All those for you, huh?"). Sometimes it was a woman he hadn't called for a second date (he rarely did), looking down her nose at him from her spot at the bar.

On one late spring day at the grocery store, it was Abby Flores, wearing skintight yoga pants that left nothing to the imagination and made Trace's jeans feel a little too snug. He hated his body for reacting to her. Waiting at the butcher's counter, Abby had one of those small hand baskets hanging from her elbow. She didn't see him, and he hoped to keep it that way.

He would have made a clean getaway, too, except he heard a voice he recognized right away, and it made him stop in his tracks.

"Hey! Aren't you the gal who's trying to develop the entire Williamson Valley?"

Trace unfroze, and keeping his back to the butcher's counter, faked a deep interest in the packages of on-sale pork chops.

The voice belonged to Hector Inman, the owner of the Bright Moon Ranch. Hector had taken a laissez-faire attitude when the Mint Creek Ranch boys stole his tractor as teens, and as they grew into adults, they always shared a good rapport. Still, Trace had seen Hector's mean side. He was a frequent audience member at City Council meetings, and a vocal one. At one point a few years back, he even ignited a protest when a different developer proposed building a thousand houses on open land next to the airport. Although his message was good — he had a legitimate concern for water supply, since they did, after all, live in the desert — his methods were a little ... incendiary. Red-faced and loud-mouthed, he'd been involved in several shouting matches that Trace could remember, and probably more he didn't even know about.

Once, at the Iron Brand Steakhouse, when a rancher from a neighboring town walked in and took a seat, Hector threw down his linen napkin, let his utensils clatter onto his plate, and pushed back his chair so hard, it fell over. With all the restaurant patrons looking on, he stormed out, muttering at the top of his lungs about how they let *anybody* in that place.

The fact that Trace could hear an edge to Hector's voice as he spoke to Abby at the butcher's counter should bring him a certain level of happiness. After all, their sentiments were probably similar, when it came to a new development in their neighborhood.

But for some reason, Trace felt instantly protective.

"That's me," Abby responded, her voice self-assured.

"If you're not careful, we'll run you right out of town," Hector said, quiet but menacing. "I don't know what you think you're playing at, trying to change the landscape of the area we've all worked so hard to preserve. But you're about as welcome here as a burger on a cowboy saddle."

Still facing away from them, Trace moved a little closer. Absentmindedly, he picked up a few packages of turkey, one at a time, and set them down — ground turkey, Italian turkey sausage, a turkey breast.

"Thank you for your opinion, Mr. ..."

"Inman," the man said. "Owner of the Bright Moon Ranch."

A beat of silence ensued, and Trace thought the two of them might be shaking hands. Why Abby would shake hands with the wizened old rancher, Trace didn't know.

"As sorry as I am to say this, I think you will be even sorrier to hear it," Abby said. "I have a feeling we'll be seeing a lot of each other. You might as well get used to me."

Grumbling, old Mr. Inman walked off. Trace couldn't put a finger on exactly why he was smiling as he walked away from the meat and toward the freezer section to grab the frozen dinner he'd eat that night, but he was. In fact, he smiled all night.

CHAPTER SIX

DURING THE NEXT couple of months, Abby settled into a nice routine. She spent her weekdays working: planning, building, assessing. Every other weekend, she visited her dad. They didn't watch a single episode of the treehouse show together. And on her weekends in Prescott, she hung out with her new friends, Montana and the *Daily Dispatch* reporter, Tessa, whose arrival from Phoenix sparked more of the small-town drama with which Abby was becoming familiar.

As short a time as she'd been in Prescott, she'd already gathered enough information to put together Tessa's story: A year before Tessa's arrival in town, Cody was preparing for the bull-riding championship when his sister, Annie, returned to Prescott, fleeing her abusive boyfriend in Texas. She spent a month in hiding. The Davis family was practically Arizona royalty, and if anyone knew Annie was back in town, word could get out … and her boyfriend could find her.

The night before Cody was set to leave for the championship, he and Annie went out dancing, to get out of the house, blow off steam for one evening.

But a big city reporter saw them and couldn't resist the scoop. Whether she knew about Annie's history or not didn't matter. She sent the photo to her editor — at the biggest newspaper in the state — and they published it. Annie's abusive boyfriend saw it online and came to Prescott in a rage, ready to kill her.

When he showed up at the front door, Cody called the police, who were able to arrest him before he hurt Annie.

Cody was so shaken, he couldn't compete. He withdrew from the tour (in which he was a heavy favorite to win) and headed out of town. Overcome with guilt, he stopped talking to Annie, who was also overcome with guilt as she blamed herself for Cody missing out on the championship.

Nine months later, Cody decided to take another crack at the bull-riding championship. Still wary of reporters, but also aware of how important the news coverage was to his hometown, he agreed to let the *Daily Dispatch* assign one person to cover his story ... as long as he and his friends could vet the person ahead of time.

That person was Tessa.

On Tessa's first night in town, Montana took her to the famous rodeo dance. Abby missed out on that — it was the same weekend as one of her visits to her dad — but she definitely heard about it when she got home.

Before Cody realized who Tessa was (the real-life Tessa looked nothing like the woman in the photo from the background check), they danced the night away. To hear Montana tell it, "It was hot. Like, romance-novel hot. They couldn't get enough of each other."

In fact, they'd been so unable to tear themselves apart that Montana couldn't warn Tessa that she was dancing with the subject of her upcoming assignment.

The next day, when both Cody and Tessa realized they'd be working together for three months, the world stopped turning. Or, as Montana said, Prescott's world stopped turning.

Tessa wasn't what Cody expected. She met the stringent requirements he, Trace, and Sawyer had come up with ... except one. She was a woman. A good-looking one.

At first, Cody and Tessa clashed. But their attraction remained, and they grew to trust — and love — each other.

The Mint Creek Ranch crew brought Tessa into the fold.

Abby, for the most part, enjoyed that same warm welcome from Cody, Sawyer, Tessa, and Montana. They invited her to be part of the Kincaid-Davis Wedding Planning Team, and included her in everything they did as a group.

Meanwhile, Trace held her at arm's length. He'd seemed so friendly that day when he helped her change the tire on that impractical Mustang. But after that, whenever he looked at her, his expression was cool, at best. Sometimes it was downright icy. And she wished she could change that.

———

TRACE

SOMEHOW, Abby Flores managed to integrate herself into the fabric of Prescott, and more specifically, Mint Creek Ranch, over the next couple of months.

Not for the first time, Trace thought about her while he did his morning chores. Actually, "somehow" wasn't accurate. Montana had made Abby part of the group. She had a knack for that. Much to Trace's chagrin.

Summer was in full bloom. The leaves on the big cottonwood trees were thick and full, and they fluttered in the breeze. It was hard to believe that in a few months, Trace would be breaking the ice on the horse troughs.

His horse, Heidi, walked over to where he stood outside her stall. She put her head over the gate and he placed his hand on her nose. Heidi was Shirley's great granddaughter, and she bore some of her predecessor's best features — the softest, chocolate-colored nose, a towering height, and a knack for bringing Trace into the perfect position for roping a steer.

"You're right, Heidi," Trace said to the horse. "I think a ride is exactly what I need to clear my head."

As if she understood, she stamped a foot.

"Give me ten minutes."

He fed and watered the other horses. The rest of the chores could wait. He brought Heidi into the barn and saddled her up. The way she trotted out into the sun, hooves high, chin up, ears pricked, made Trace think she needed the ride as much as he did. Once they were outside, he brought her up to a canter and let her choose the path. As he suspected she would, Heidi took off toward the creek. A well-worn trail ran along it, and she hooked a left when they got there.

Trace had been riding the ranch and the area surrounding it since he was a kid. Heidi couldn't take him anywhere that he couldn't find his way back from. He gave her the reins and let her keep running. The light down by the creek was crisp, the colors bright. As he relaxed into the rhythm of Heidi's stride, Trace found his mind wandering back to Abby. Again. He pictured her face, heard her laugh, and then found himself having the same thoughts he'd had several times since Cody met Tessa.

He always told himself that he didn't want things to change. But change was inevitable. It was happening around him. Cody and Sawyer were still his best friends — always would be. But marriage changed things, didn't it?

Trace, for his part, had always imagined the three Mint Creek Ranch boys as bachelors into their golden years, but seeing his friend so happy, so satisfied, made him question whether that scenario was even what he wanted anymore.

THE RIDE cleared Trace's head, and when Sawyer invited him to dinner for the Steakout's Friday fish fry, he figured a night out with a friend would do him good. They stopped at the hostess stand to chat with Lucy Garcia, a friend from high school. Before she could lead them to a table, Sawyer muttered, "What a coincidence."

That was about the same time Trace spotted Montana and Abby sitting at the bar. Montana didn't look one bit surprised.

"Fancy seeing them here," Trace said.

He glared at Sawyer, positive he and Montana had planned this. Sawyer held his hands up to profess his innocence. "I didn't know, man."

Trace shrugged it off, even when the four of them ended up seated together in the dining room. It was just one dinner. He could handle it.

Maybe it was his relaxed mental state after the long ride earlier in the day, or maybe it was because he was getting used to having Abby around, but Trace didn't mind. He even had to admit to himself that he enjoyed Abby's company.

Which was a good thing, because something weird was going on between Sawyer and Montana.

"Actually, I'm kind of glad we ran into you guys," Trace said at one point. "I've been wanting to install a new ceiling fan, but I wasn't sure about the wiring. I want to get one with one of those dimmable lights —"

"I'm sure all the ladies will truly appreciate that," Abby cut in.

Is that what she thinks of me? Trace played off his hurt and rolled his eyes.

"The only thing I know about wiring is that I shouldn't mess with it," Trace said.

"Well, at least you know that," Abby said. "I can help you. For a small price."

Trace was about to say, "Forget it, then," but she went on, "I could use some advice about fencing. For the new development."

Oh. "Sure. I can help you with that."

"Well, let's hope Abby has the sense to listen to you," Sawyer said, his tone harsh.

Montana rushed to say, "He didn't mean you, Abby. He meant me. Sawyer feels like I don't always listen to him, or take his advice."

"Correction," Sawyer said. "I feel like she *rarely* takes my advice. Maybe even never."

Montana looked as if someone had slapped her. She excused herself to go to the bathroom, and after a few minutes, Sawyer did the same. They came back a few minutes later, and if Trace wasn't mistaken, Sawyer looked steamed.

"I think we can all agree we're surprised at how well tonight is going," Montana said, lifting her wine glass. "Actually, I'm not that surprised. I really love the two of you." She pointed at Trace and then Abby. "And I knew it was only a matter of time until you learned to like each other. At the very least."

Trace and Abby looked at each other. Something strange was going on.

"I agree," Abby said, slowly. "This has been a very nice evening."

It looked like she might have more to say, but she pressed her lips together and took a drink. Trace nodded. Because it was obvious everyone was waiting for him to say something, he finally spoke. "I agree. This is the first time we've been in a social setting and Abby hasn't put up a forcefield between us."

"Me?!" Abby said, her cheeks immediately going rosy. "That was a forcefield of self-protection! From the fireballs you shoot at me every time we're in the same space!"

Sawyer held up his hands. "Okay, okay, kids. We were just talking about how well the evening was going. Can we keep things civil?"

Trace laughed, pleased with her reaction. "I was trying to get under her skin."

"And since the evening has gone so well," Montana said, shooting Trace a dark look, "I thought this would be the perfect time to share our big news."

Trace yelped when someone kicked his shin. It could only be Sawyer. "What did you do that for?"

"Sorry, man," Sawyer said, in a tone that implied he wasn't. "Restless leg syndrome."

Trace leaned down and rubbed his shin.

"What Montana's trying to say is —" Sawyer started. She cut him off.

"What I'm trying to say is that Sawyer and I are both buying property. We're both building houses."

What?

Trace forced a smile even as the panic set in. "That's great," he said, turning to Sawyer. "So you're moving out?" That would change *everything*. In every vision Trace had for his future, the three of them lived their entire lives on Mint Creek Ranch. Sawyer couldn't leave. Could he?

"Just next door."

The realization dawned. Not only was Sawyer moving off the ranch, but he was buying a property in Sunset Valley.

"You're buying one of Abby's properties."

"Two, actually," Montana said. "One each."

Wait a second …

If Sawyer and Montana were buying property from Abby, that meant Abby had held out on him, too.

"You knew about this?" he asked Abby, who simply said, "It wasn't my news to tell."

"How long?" Trace asked.

He felt like he might pass out.

"Well, it's going to be a bit," Montana said. "Since we're still waiting on all the permits."

"No," Trace said. "I mean, how long have the three of you been keeping this secret?"

"Few weeks," Sawyer said, his voice quiet.

Trace shook his head. He gave Montana and Sawyer one more glare before folding his napkin and setting it on his plate. He got up and walked out of the restaurant without another word.

He couldn't believe what he was hearing. Storming out of the restaurant was childish, sure, but he didn't care. A few weeks ago, two of his best friends buying property from Abby would have been the very worst scenario imaginable. That night, he discovered an even worse scenario: those two friends keeping a giant secret.

If he were being rational, Trace thought as he strode across the parking lot and away from the scene of the crime, he would tell himself that it was only natural they kept it a secret. One thing *he* hadn't hidden was his dislike of Abby and her development. Of course Sawyer and Montana were afraid of how he'd react when he found out they were working with her. A couple of cars zipped by. Trace wondered if he should try to hitchhike home. The last place he wanted to be was in Sawyer's truck with him.

If he were being rational, he would tell himself that the Sunset Valley development promised to be a pretty decent place to live. He couldn't really blame Sawyer and Montana for wanting to be part of it.

He wasn't being rational, though, and that was the rub. He was being emotional. The first emotion he experienced was anger. Underneath that, he felt betrayal. They had to know that he loved them. If they were happy, he was happy (eventually). Even if he was upset at first, he would get over it (eventually).

The fact that they'd walked around for weeks hiding something this big from him … that was way worse than any property deal they could make.

At that point, Trace had made it more than a block. He heard footsteps behind him. Fast footsteps, which meant they belonged to someone short. He knew only two people whose legs could match that rhythm. And only one of them wore high heels.

For a full minute, he debated turning around to wait for Abby. If he kept walking at the pace he'd set, she'd never catch up with his long strides. And if he turned around, he'd have to face her.

She'd been part of the deception. Guilty by association.

He groaned, hating himself for his train of thought. His rational side chimed in, reminding him that even though Abby had known, it wasn't her secret to tell. The two of them weren't even friends. They were acquaintances. And not even friendly acquaintances. Taking a deep breath, he slowed down. The footsteps behind him maintained their pace. He turned around and waited.

His breath caught. Even in her current state, rushing along to catch up to him, a cloth napkin clutched in one hand, long hair flowing out behind her, she looked beautiful. It was an observation, he thought, not a declaration of his attraction to her.

"Thank goodness you stopped," she said, breathless. "These are my power shoes, not my power-*walking* shoes."

Trace couldn't help it. He barked out a laugh. "Very funny."

"Can I talk to you?"

He shrugged. "I guess."

She stood directly in front of him, catching her breath. "I'm sorry."

He shook his head. "You have nothing to be sorry for. You're a property owner, not my friend."

Darn it if her shoulders didn't slump at that. "I know. I'm not sorry for not telling you. I'm sorry that Montana and Sawyer made such a mess of this, frankly. They've been so worried about how you would take it. Plus, with Tessa and Cody's wedding coming up, they didn't want to steal the spotlight. To be fair, Sawyer didn't even know I owned the property before he fell in love with it on the Internet listing."

Trace threw up his hands. "But he didn't even *mention* that he was thinking of buying land."

"He said he thought you might hate him moving off Mint Creek Ranch."

Oh.

Trace nodded. He couldn't believe Sawyer had shared all this with Abby. And Sawyer was spot on. Trace did hate the idea of Sawyer leaving. And that fear — of one of their trio leaving the ranch, leaving *him* — was another emotion overriding reason.

Abby seemed to be trying to decide what to say. She pursed her lips. He wanted to kiss her. He wished he could strike that thought from his mind.

After a minute, she spoke, deliberately. She was choosing her words carefully. "I'm going to be honest with you," she said. "The thing is, you've been pretty outspoken about Sunset Valley. Honestly, I can't blame them for being afraid to tell you — afraid it would turn into a big fiasco when we're all gearing up for this wedding. That was their biggest concern. Your reaction to them keeping a secret from you was second to that. A close second. They've both been anxious to tell you, but weren't sure of the right timing. I can't tell you how to feel about it. But I want you to know, it's been eating away at both of them. I hope you won't hold a grudge for too long."

If anyone told him two weeks ago that Abby Flores would bring him comfort during one of the toughest moments of his adult life, Trace would have laughed out loud. But, there they were. She soothed his emotional side and appealed to his rational side, calming him down as if they'd been friends, or lovers, for a long time.

"Thank you for sharing all this," he said. "I guess I owe you honesty, too. For me, the worst part is that they kept it a secret. But even when I walked out, angry about that, there was this voice in my head reminding me that I've been pretty difficult to deal with. I actually get why they didn't tell me. I wish they had, though."

"So … you're not angry at *me*?" Those dimples flashed, and Trace reached out and squeezed Abby's shoulder. "A little. But I think I can get past it."

"Thank goodness for that," Abby said. "I feel like you just finally stopped hating me."

"Hating you?" he repeated. "I've never hated you. I hated what I thought you stood for. But I think I'm coming around."

They stood there, smiling at each other, until Trace suddenly realized quite a bit of time had passed.

"Well, I guess that's everything," he said. "I would offer you a ride home, but I saw Sawyer leave a few minutes ago. Apparently, Montana's in the kitchen washing dishes, since I'm pretty sure we all left her with the bill."

"Should we share a taxi?"

Trace nodded. "Sure." Abby made the call. They talked for a few minutes, until the taxi came. Before Abby got out, she said, "Again, I'm sorry. I wish I could've stopped the train wreck that situation turned into. For what it's worth, both Sawyer and Montana are truly concerned about your feelings. They wanted to protect you. They want you to be happy for them."

Trace nodded. "I understand. Thanks for talking me through it."

When Abby got out, Trace realized he felt her absence like he'd removed a warm sweatshirt. Unexpected, he thought. About as unexpected as the fact that she managed to smooth his ruffled feathers.

Wonders never cease.

PART 2

CHAPTER SEVEN

ABBY COULDN'T BELIEVE she was standing at the edge of the dance floor at Tessa and Cody's wedding reception. As busy as she'd been the past few months, the wedding had come up fast. She allowed herself to reminisce as the wedding guests chattered.

Montana was buying one of her houses, and so was Sawyer. Thank goodness Trace knew … the secret had felt like a ticking time bomb. But, she reminded herself, Trace's reaction to Montana and Sawyer's property purchases wasn't *really* her business. Besides, they'd come to a fragile understanding during all the wedding planning. She glanced at him. No, they wouldn't call each other friends, exactly. But they weren't mortal enemies, either.

The DJ's voice came over the speakers, then, pulling Abby away from her thoughts. "Why don't we get the whole wedding party out on the floor for this next one?"

The guests cheered, a few whoops and hollers sprinkled in.

Oh, no, Abby thought. *I can't dance with Trace.*

Her traitorous mind started the movie reel of the day, delivering images of every moment Abby had felt attracted to him. That morning, when he handed her the box of flowers, and she felt his callused hands brush hers when she took it. She'd actually pictured his hands running up her bare torso and cupping her breasts and thought, *I wonder how that would feel.*

Later, when they ran outside to help Sawyer and Montana fix the tables after the storm, and he grinned at her as they set up the chairs, her body had a visceral reaction. After the wedding ceremony, when they walked back up the aisle, she experienced a strange sense of relief when they met in front of the altar. A tingling, vibrating energy ran through her body from the place where her palm touched his bicep.

Obviously, dancing with him was out of the question. The heat was already pooling between her legs at the thought of their bodies touching, swaying to the music. Having just watched Cody and Tessa's first dance, Abby was already at the edge of the dance floor. She made a quick decision, and backed up into the shadows before Trace could find her.

She tiptoed her way around to the front of the Davises' house and collapsed into one of the chairs on their front patio. From here, she could still hear the music. The song — something about never-ending love — was perfect for the newlyweds, even for Montana and Sawyer. But it wasn't perfect for Abby and Trace.

Sure, he had become friendlier throughout the weeks they'd spent preparing for the wedding. But, at his core, Trace still didn't like Abby or what she stood for. And he never would. Even if the man made her weak in the knees, even if his smile sent her heart all aflutter, they would never be anything more than two people with foundational differences who barely tolerated each other.

As Abby found herself wishing that she'd remembered to bring her champagne glass with her when she snuck away, she heard someone coming around the corner.

Probably someone else trying to escape.

Because her gaze was already fixed on the ground, she saw his boots first. Her body recognized and responded to Trace, leaning toward him before her mind consciously realized it was him.

He jumped when he saw her, and then he laughed. "You scared me!"

"Sorry," Abby said, her heart already picking up its pace. Would he know she was trying to avoid dancing with him? Would that bother him? Worse, would he be relieved? Had he come to that very spot to avoid dancing with *her*?

Without warning, a giggle escaped.

A muscle tensed in his jaw. He thought she was laughing at him.

"Don't be sorry," he said. "I'm actually supposed to be on the dance floor, but when I got out there, my dance partner was nowhere to be found."

Something in his voice shifted as he spoke. His tone went from friendly to curious, and Abby knew he was trying to make a point.

"I know. I'm sorry." She would have continued speaking, come up with some excuse for leaving. But he held up his hands. "No apology necessary. I probably wouldn't want to dance with me either, after the trouble I've given you."

Was it her imagination, or did Trace actually look chagrined?

"That's not why I —"

Quite suddenly, Trace was sitting in the chair next to Abby, and her hands were in his. "I want you to know that I'm sorry. I'm really, truly sorry for the way I've acted. Look, you look like you could use a drink. I know this isn't what you'd expect, Abby, but I'm going to go get us each a sparkling water. I've had enough to drink in the past two days that I could forego beer for a week, and that's not something I thought I'd ever say. Be right back."

And then, he was walking away, and she admired his backside until it disappeared around the corner. Trace returned a minute later, a sparkling water in each hand.

"Thank you," Abby said, careful to avoid touching his hand when she took the cold can from him. "I'm so thirsty."

Trace settled himself on the chair next to Abby's. She froze, momentarily, at the thought that he planned to hang around.

"Long day," he said. He surprised her again by tipping his head back and closing his eyes. It was perhaps the only time she'd ever seen Trace relaxed.

And oh my, is he handsome. His eyelashes were longer and thicker than she thought, and the line of his jaw … he looked like he belonged in an old-fashioned cigarette ad.

"I can feel you looking at me, Ms. Flores," he drawled.

"I've never seen you so relaxed, is all."

He sat upright and opened his eyes. "I reckon that's true. When people talk about the Mint Creek Ranch boys, you'll never hear them say I'm the easy-going one."

The introspection — at least, spoken out loud — seemed uncharacteristic. But, Abby reminded herself, she didn't know Trace very well at all.

"Why is that?"

He offered her a rueful smile and took a sip of his drink. "I could highlight a few of the defining moments in my life," he said. "But suffice it to say that I've always loved this place, and my life, as they are. And, as the three of us were growing up, I was the cautious one. The responsible one. The one who thought long-term about keeping this place exactly as it is. Now," he said, holding up a pointer finger, "that's not to say I didn't get involved with the shenanigans. But I was always the planner, the lookout guy. The one minimizing our chances of getting in trouble. I was the risk-assessment guy before that was even a thing."

Abby smiled. "So that's why they made you Cody's manager while he was on tour."

Trace shook his head. "*I* made me manager."

Disarmed, Abby laughed. Then she found herself saying, "I have to admit, Trace, I've never seen this side of you before. And, if I'm being honest, it's not so bad."

———

TRACE

EVEN AS ABBY said she'd never seen Trace relaxed, he was thinking the same: it was the first time he had ever seen Abby with her guard down.

He wanted the moment to last forever.

After he handed her the sparkling water, he felt the intense urge to grab her hand, pull her to standing, and lead her out onto the dance floor after all. Because he felt an even more intense urge to wrap his arms around her and feel her body against his. The last few bars of the song faded away, and something fast, with a heavy beat, came through the speakers.

As unaccustomed to the feeling as he was, Trace almost didn't recognize it: regret. He wished he hadn't tried to avoid dancing with her in the first place. He should have been a man about it and spent those precious moments close to her.

But, in this moment, they were talking like old friends, and there was something to be said for that. He'd even revealed something about himself to her, with an honesty he'd never imagined they would share.

"Tell me about you," he said.

Her expression took on a little more intensity. She went from unguarded to interested, and maybe even slightly cautious.

"I don't know if I want to," she blurted, the words loud and close together. Then she laughed, her dimples flashed, and again, Trace wanted to reach for her hand.

"Sorry," she said, massaging her temples. "Like you said, it's been a long day. Not to mention the fact that I feel like you already dislike me, so I don't know how much more you want to know about me. I'm thinking, the more you know, the less you like me. If that's even possible."

Trace had to admire her courage. At the same time, he felt guilty. "It's never been personal. It's not about me liking you. It's about the fact that I don't want a development next door."

Abby shrugged. "I get that."

She must have decided it was okay to proceed, because she said, "I grew up on construction sites. My dad owned the company, so I tagged along with him wherever he went. When I was really little, I was his gofer, finding the tools he needed, holding the end of the measuring tape, hammering a nail every once in a while. I loved watching the crew. There's a certain rhythm to building, you know. The sounds and the smells and the sights. Wood being cut, walls going up. It was only natural that as I got older, I did more. I'd been watching so long, it was just a matter of picking up the tools and getting to work."

Trace loved watching Abby as she spoke about her childhood. A faraway look had come into her eyes as she remembered. And although she seemed hesitant at first, the words flowed freely now. Trace surprised himself by picturing her as he'd seen her a few days ago, in work boots, jeans that hugged her curves, and a white tank top that showed off the beautiful color of her skin and her toned arms.

"So I guess you starting your own company was kind of a given?"

She shrugged, and if he wasn't mistaken, she looked sad. "Maybe, one day. It was definitely within the realm of possibility, but a few years ago, my dad had an accident." She took a drink of her water, and even after she'd rested the can on the arm of her chair again, it was a moment before she spoke. "I felt like I had to start to take over the company. Not that I didn't want to. And not that it wasn't a true gift. My dad, he's a great businessman. So, he handed me a nest egg, really."

Sensing the topic was more complicated than he'd originally thought, Trace wasn't sure whether to ask any more questions. But the more Abby talked, the more curious he became.

So he said, "But?"

She laughed, a breathy, shaky laugh that proved his suspicions that it was an emotional topic.

"I felt — and still feel — like I don't know if I'm up for the task. On one hand, I want to fulfill my father's dream, since he can't do it himself anymore. And on the other hand, I have dreams of my own, you know?"

"What are your dreams?"

He shouldn't care. He shouldn't feel so compelled to get to know her. But he did.

Her expression softened when she smiled at him. "When I was a little kid, all I wanted was to have my own place. And a horse. I don't know if you remember me saying, that night we had dinner at the Davises', that from the moment I saw that Appaloosa at the rodeo, I wanted one. It's been my lifelong dream."

"I can relate. I wanted a horse so bad when I was a kid. It was all I could think about. I pined after it."

Abby laughed. "That's how I've always felt. I know, now that I'm an adult, horse ownership doesn't seem like much of a lifelong dream. Obviously, my dream evolved a bit. As you probably know, I don't even have a horse yet. But anyway, that horse eventually began to represent more to me. My dream is to eventually create something of my own. To leave a legacy." She shrugged. "With the Sunset Valley subdivision, that legacy is to help other people have something of *their* own."

That was actually a beautiful sentiment, and when Trace opened his mouth to say so, Abby held up a finger. "Look, I know you hate the idea of Sunset Valley. I've wished so many times that I could somehow make you see what I envision. It's not a money-making scheme or a business venture. To me, it's a chance to create a community people can call home … one they can love, where they can create a beautiful life."

For a moment, it looked like she had more to say. But then, she leaned back in the chair, her eyes on his.

"I feel like a pretty big jerk," Trace said. "I didn't realize the development was so … personal to you. I admit, I thought it was all about the money."

She smiled at him, again, and in that moment, he felt like she knew him. And wrapped up inside her was every bit of feminine magic he'd ever heard about. If he didn't know better, he would think her smile revealed that she was some kind of sorceress. Because, quite suddenly, he had the startling realization that she was the most beautiful woman he'd ever seen, or would ever see again.

As suddenly as he had the realization, her smile widened.

"Why, thank you, Trace," she said. "That really means a lot, coming from you."

Not sure whether she was being sarcastic or not, he went for simple. "You're welcome."

They sat there, grinning at each other for a few beats before Trace realized he could hear the melody of a slow song coming from the dance floor at the reception. Again, he acted without thinking things through. He stood and offered Abby a hand. "I do believe we missed our last dance," he said. "Would you like to dance with me now?"

She hesitated, and in the split second he waited, panic overtook him. He shouldn't have asked. He should never have expected her to want to dance with him, after the way he'd treated her over the past couple of months. Was he crazy? But then, as he was about to say, "Forget it, never mind," her hand was in his.

He felt a rush, like the energy from a big gust of wind that came across the desert, rain on its heels. Their eyes met, and he felt something he'd never felt before: a surge, a connection. He literally felt it in his body, an electric sensation from his hand to his heart and then outward. He knew this moment was fragile, delicate, like the thin china plates and teacups Elaine Davis kept in the hutch of the buffet in the dining room. He knew he had to handle it with care.

And then she was in his arms, her body pressed against his. She smelled like roses and vanilla, and the skin on her lower back was as smooth and soft as buckskin hide. Dancing with her was different than he expected. He *had* thought about it; he knew they were supposed to dance together at least once during the reception.

Through the lens of anger he usually wore when thinking about Abby, he'd imagined she would feel rigid and immovable. But in reality, she felt soft and supple and liquid. Something strange was happening. As they swayed together on the Davises' front porch, in time to the slow and heady love song, he found himself thinking about sex with Abby Flores. As he inhaled the scent of her perfume, felt her skin under his hand, he was picturing her naked, strong, and confident. She would probably want to be on top, straddling him, riding him … he felt himself going hard and adjusted the arm around her waist to keep her from noticing.

———

ABBY

THE SONG ENDED. Another one, with a fast, heavy beat, replaced it. And while Abby could hear it, feel it, everything but Trace slipped away into the background.

Their bodies pressed together, the two of them stood on the Davises' front porch. They stopped swaying. Took a step back. Abby thought they must be having the same realization at the same time: *This is crazy.*

Instead of releasing her hands, though, Trace held onto them. For the briefest span of time, less than a second, his expression conveyed something Abby had never seen before. Not when he was looking at her, anyway. Warmth, affection, tenderness. And her own reaction: shock. Was she imagining these things? She blinked, once, hard. He grinned at her. Devilish.

"Why, Abby, I must say I'm surprised at what just transpired."

His pronounced drawl made Abby smile. She blushed. "I dare say, I'm a bit surprised, myself."

Her mind raced. What was going on here? What did it mean?

"Would you care for another dance?" he asked.

Would I?

"It probably isn't the best idea."

His big hands still enveloping hers, he said, "Well, my lady, I dare say, sometimes the worst idea is the best idea."

She found herself laughing again, and then being pulled into his arms.

"This song is a bit too fast for my taste," he said.

"Mine too," she said. Again, they started to sway, and again, Abby felt her body relaxing against his. How was it possible that dancing with Trace felt so natural? Somewhere deep inside, blurred by the champagne, the exhaustion, and the post-wedding partying, Abby's rational side blinked drowsily awake and mumbled something about this being a terrible idea. The new, romantic side of Abby, fueled by all the same things that put her rational side to sleep, shook a fist and said, *But this is nice. And, after all, sometimes the worst idea is the best idea.*

———

TRACE

TRACE COULDN'T EXPLAIN to himself or to anyone else, what was happening. If someone had asked him five minutes before whether he'd ever find himself dancing with Abby Flores — a private, front-porch dance, no less — he would've laughed himself silly. In the past couple of months, he had caught glimpses of her softer side, but in his stubborn way, he'd written them off. In the past hour, though, he learned more about Abby than he ever imagined he would.

And he liked her. Heck, he *respected* her.

Where he'd once thought she was cold and unfeeling, a calculating developer out to make a killing off crushing his dreams for his child-hood home, he now saw her as someone's daughter, an independent woman making her own dream come true while honoring her father's legacy.

Being there with her, holding her in his arms, felt so good. It also made him feel like a jerk. He sighed.

"Everything okay?" she asked.

Her body had stiffened, the tiniest bit. She was probably antici-pating that he was going to say that the evening — the talking, the dancing — was a mistake.

When he didn't answer right away, she stopped moving. Some-thing broke inside him. He knew she was bracing for him to hurt her again.

He might as well come out with it. "Abby."

She took a step back, but didn't release him. "Yes?"

"I owe you an apology. Almost from the moment we came into contact with each other, I … "

"You despised me?"

Something like humor flashed in her eyes, but in the lift of her chin, he saw a challenge.

"Not exactly. I've never *despised* you. I guess you could say I despised what I thought you stood for. But after spending time with you the past few months, after talking with you tonight, I see that I was wrong. You are so much different than what I thought. And I'm sorry for jumping to conclusions before I got to know you."

Trace hadn't even realized he was nervous, but even once he'd stopped talking, his heart pounded hard. His mouth felt dry.

Abby's entire body relaxed, then, and she started to sway again. "That is so not what I thought you were going to say," she said.

Before he knew it, she was laughing, a loud, unrestrained laugh that had him chuckling, too. Once again, they settled in a comfortable rhythm. Still smiling, Trace asked, "What did you think I was going to say?

"Oh, I don't know," she said. "Something about how, even though we had a very nice conversation and a very nice dance, we should probably never speak again."

Just as he'd thought.

"You thought our dance was very nice?" he asked. Trace was surprised to find himself holding his breath as he waited for her answer.

"Well, yes. Didn't you?"

He exhaled. "I did, yes. I was hoping you would say that."

"It's something I thought I would never say, but it is what it is."

It was Trace who laughed then.

When his laughter subsided, Abby said, "Thank you."

"For what?"

"The apology. It means a lot. I hope you know that it's not my intention to change the way things are here. I love Prescott."

"I know you do. And I hope you know that it's my love for this place that made me act that way. However misguided I was."

"Understood."

The fast song ended, and another slow one came on.

Abby sounded disappointed when she said, "I suppose we should get back to the reception before someone misses us."

"We probably should," Trace said, but he didn't stop dancing.

"After this song?"

———

ABBY

WHEN THAT FINAL SONG ENDED, Abby and Trace stopped dancing and simply looked at each other. As reluctant as she felt to head back to the reception, the last thing she needed was anyone asking questions. In this town, any sort of romantic relationship, especially with one of the main players in city development, was a bad idea, and not the kind that could be a good idea.

Before she could come up with something clever, or even coherent, to say, Trace brought his mouth to hers. The kiss said everything. It said, *I'm sorry, I was wrong about you, I like you.* And maybe even, *I would really like to take off that dress.* In response, all the nerve endings in Abby's body tingled in anticipation. She felt desire pool between her legs, and when she grasped his waist and pulled him closer, he didn't try to fight it. As she kissed him back, she hoped she conveyed everything she was thinking: *I'm sorry, too. I like you.* And *I want you to take off my dress.*

His hands cupped her face, and she let herself lean into him.

This was different from anything she'd ever felt before. Never had she completely lost herself in a single kiss. The temperature cooled, from insanely sexual to tender and sweet. Abby felt weak in the knees, and she clung to Trace like her life depended on it. And in the moment, it felt like that was true. When they broke apart, Abby felt a deep sense of loss. Trace ran a hand through his hair. Abby had to force herself not to reach up and smooth it out.

"Well," he said.

"Yeah."

He reached out, put his hand on her cheek again. "Do we have to go back?"

Her breath shaky, Abby said, "I'm afraid so. Do you think we should —" she started. She regretted it right away, but it was too late.

The words were already out of her mouth, the idea hanging in the air between them, invisible but tangible.

"Don't worry," he said. "Your secret is safe with me."

Abby was almost positive he looked hurt. There was a tightness around his eyes and mouth that hadn't been there before. Maybe regret? Abby couldn't be sure.

Ever the gentleman, Trace smiled again and held out his hand, palm up, gesturing for her to go ahead of him. "Shall we?"

Abby swished by him, her body hyper aware of his as she passed. Even while she regretted starting to say what she was going to say — that maybe they should keep their evening a secret — she felt herself tempted to suggest that he give her a few minutes' head start so no one would know they'd been alone together. But she didn't have to. When she reached the edge of the crowd standing around the dance floor and turned around, he wasn't there. Relief and disappointment mixed, a dangerous cocktail in her mind.

"I need a cocktail in my hand right now," she muttered. She wove through the crowd to the line at the bar. A hand on her shoulder startled her.

"Where'd you go?" Montana looked so happy, so at ease. Abby was jealous. Why couldn't she be that comfortable in her own skin?

"Oh, I was taking a quick break. My feet are killing me. These sandals are nothing like the work boots my feet are used to."

"What about those pink snakeskin heels?"

"Touché. I guess those are broken in, though."

"Didn't you bring a spare pair of flip-flops like I recommended?"

"I did, but I haven't had a chance to change into them."

Montana looked a little suspicious. But she had the grace, or the sense of timing, not to question Abby.

When she got to the front of the line, Abby ordered a cosmopolitan. "And make it a double," she told the bartender, tucking a five-dollar bill into the tips jar.

Ten minutes earlier, she might have found an empty seat and nursed the drink. But the only way she was going to get that kiss out of her mind (which she absolutely must do, as soon as possible) was to throw it back. So that's what she did, while still standing at the bar. She ordered another one, added, "Make this one a double, too," and tossed it back just as fast.

The rest of the evening, she stayed on the dance floor, moving to the music, pretending to be oblivious to everything around her. She told herself she wasn't thinking about Trace, and certainly not about dancing with him or kissing him. But she knew she was lying to herself. Even as her body swayed to the beat, her eyes searched the space. Every time they found him, settling on his rugged jawline, moving over his muscular chest, checking out the fit of his jeans from behind, she felt a little thrill. Finally, the DJ announced the last song. Even though Abby groaned along with the rest of the guests, pretending she was sad it was almost over, she couldn't wait to get out of there. She couldn't wait to get home and sleep like the dead.

CHAPTER EIGHT

TRACE

THE MORNING after Cody and Tessa's wedding, Trace woke up feeling ... exhilarated. He couldn't remember the last time he'd felt that way first thing in the morning. He found himself whistling — whistling! — as he went to the kitchen to get his coffee. Usually, the morning after any wedding, he felt a million tiny guys with hammers inside his skull, but not at the moment. Switching to sparkling water during the reception had been a good idea, apparently. And maybe sneaking those dances (and that kiss) with Abby had, too.

Coffee in hand, he made his way out to the porch. His watch read six-thirty. Well, he'd slept in. He couldn't remember the last time he'd done that, either. The horses were waiting. Even on a Sunday, they had to eat. So he wouldn't linger too long over coffee. Besides, his mom would be calling soon, like she did every Sunday. He decided he could spare a few minutes to think about what transpired the night before.

He settled into his favorite chair and propped his feet up on the ottoman. Below, Mint Creek danced by. The sound was like music. As he sat there, a different sound startled him. Humming. *He* was humming. First whistling, then humming. What was going on?

Then it hit him: Abby. The movie reel from the night before

paraded across his mind. From finding her on the Davises' front porch to watching her face while she talked about her passion for building houses to dancing with her, her body against his. Kissing her.

At that, his mood shifted. What was he thinking? Trace shook his head.

"Playing with fire, boy," he said.

Getting tangled up with Abby Flores wouldn't be prudent. He knew that. But wasn't Trace *always* the prudent one? Yes. Yes, he was. Maybe it was time he do things differently.

His coffee cup was empty, so, with a spring in his step, he headed out to feed the horses. As he went through the motions, an idea started to form.

———

ABBY

ABBY'S PHONE rang in the middle of her Sunday morning ritual: spa day. She had a cooling cucumber mask on her face and her electric massager draped over her shoulders. Her skin was soft and glowing from a long bath, a good sugar scrub, and an ultra-hydrating coconut oil body cream. The sound of her ringer cut through the relaxing music. She jumped. She didn't recognize the number on the screen, but it was local, so she picked up.

"Abby?"

She might not recognize the number. But the voice? She knew it immediately. "Trace."

She wondered if he could hear the smile in her voice. Even as she thought again about the night before, she wanted to say, *I wasn't expecting to hear from you. To what do I owe this surprise?* Fortunately, he spoke first. "How are you this morning?"

Abby thought for a minute. How *was* she? "Relaxed. This is the best I have felt after a wedding in years."

His chuckle came through the earpiece, rumbly and — well, sexy, if she were being honest with herself. "I was thinking the same."

"I usually sleep 'til ten, at least, and then wake up wishing for another few hours in bed."

"Me, too. Well, I'd like to. But the horses wouldn't have it. I usually drag myself out to feed them at six and then go straight back to bed."

She could tell Trace was nervous. And he didn't seem like the kind of guy who got nervous very often. It would probably do him some good to sit with that feeling. Still smiling, she waited for him to speak again. After a couple beats of silence, he said, "Right. Well, not this morning. I've been up since the crack of dawn. And I got to thinking. Do you have plans today?"

Abby looked at her toenails. She refrained from saying, "Getting a pedicure," and instead answered, "Nothing that can't be rearranged."

"Would you like to go for a ride?"

"Like, in your truck?"

Another laugh. "On a horse."

Abby felt her lips twitching. "Actually, that sounds like a lovely way to spend the day."

Her toenails could wait. She could really shake things up and paint them in the evening. No one saw them anyway. The ritual was for her — had been for a long time.

"Well, okay," he said, surprise evident in his tone. "We can go from here, if you don't mind driving over."

"Not at all."

Still grinning, Abby peeled the mask off her face and rubbed in the rejuvenating gel. She had a feeling it was about to turn into a very interesting day.

The sight that greeted Abby when she pulled up at the Mint Creek Ranch two hours later gave her goosebumps. It also gave her a warm, tingly feeling, one that settled below her belt.

Trace stood with a horse, his forehead against the horse's, his palms flat on her cheeks. Eyes closed, lips moving, it looked like he was telling her a secret. That would have caught Abby's attention. But the way the horse leaned into Trace, the way it seemed like she was really listening, is what got her. For all the times she'd seen this man be brusque, short, and moody, she couldn't remember ever seeing this side of him. *Well, maybe last night,* a little voice chimed in from the back of her mind.

For a man to have a relationship like that with his horse really said something.

He must have heard her drive up. The tires would have crunched on the gravel. But he remained where he was, talking to the horse, until she got out and shut the door of her truck. Then, he straightened up, ran one hand down the horse's neck, and turned to Abby with a dazzling smile.

If she were any other woman, she would've gone down cold. Had a good, old-fashioned fainting spell on the spot. As it was, she couldn't help but smile right back at him.

"Hello there," he said. "Right on time."

"My dad always quotes King Louis of France: 'Punctuality is the politeness of kings.' Or queens."

"I like that. Well, Louise and I were just having a little talk. I was telling her how she'd better treat you nice."

"Doesn't she usually treat people nice?" Abby wanted to know. "You're not putting me on a mean horse, are you?"

"She's the nicest. This ride means a lot to me."

At that, Abby's stomach fluttered. Trace added, almost as an aside, "No pressure, Louise."

Something about the last sentence made Abby blush. "Where are we going?"

"I thought we need to do a little trail ride, start from here. Make our way around the ranch. Maybe take a couple of hours? How does that sound?"

Abby took a minute to look around. She knew from looking at property maps that Mint Creek Ranch extended more than a hundred acres. They could probably ride all day if they wanted to. "That sounds lovely," she said on exhale, in a voice so breathy it sounded sexual.

She didn't have to wonder whether Trace picked up on it. His eyes were twinkling when she looked back at him.

"All right, then," he said. "We may as well head out."

TRACE

FROM ALL THE time he'd spent around Abby the past few months, Trace knew she'd ridden before. He'd never seen it for himself, but she talked about riding as a kid.

"How long has it been?" he asked, and then he almost laughed out loud at the innuendo.

She answered, smoothly, "Not long enough that I don't remember how to do it."

As she walked past him, she winked at him — actually *winked* — and then she mounted Louise in one fluid motion.

"I guess I don't have to ask if you need any sort of refresher."

She smiled down at him. "It's like riding a bike, right?"

"Close enough. Except, a little more interactive."

When she threw her head back and laughed, the sound musical, Trace literally felt his blood heat up. What was it about this woman that got him so aroused, over and over again?

He mounted his horse, Heidi. "Ready?"

"Ready." He started off slow. Taking things easy seemed like the best idea. The horses walked side by side, obliging their riders, but pulling at the reins. After a few minutes, Abby said, "I think these ladies want to run."

"Do you?"

"I do," Abby said. He looked over at her and couldn't help but notice how relaxed she seemed. Her grip was loose on the reins, her heels were nice and low, and her expression looked peaceful.

No matter how many years had passed since the last time Abby rode, Trace was confident she could handle a good run. "Well, should we let them have their way?"

Abby nodded, leaned forward. Trace gave Heidi a little nudge with his heels, and that was all she needed. She took off, and Louise, not to be left behind, did the same.

Trace had ridden the Mint Creek Ranch property thousands, even tens of thousands, of times. But never before had he felt like this.

Well, maybe once. That first time he got to take his own horse and go out alone, and, when no one was watching or telling him to be careful, he opened her up full throttle. The pure exhilaration of that moment was never far from his mind. Any time he recalled the memory, shivers rushed over his skin. It was like he was there, in the golden sunlight, the wind pushing against him, blowing his hat off his head. He still remembered that excitement bubbling up inside him, so big, he had no choice but to laugh out loud (before he got lost).

He felt the same way on the ride with Abby, a couple of decades later. The two horses matched each other's strides and ran in sync, necks outstretched, hooves kicking up dust. Trace looked over at Abby, and he could tell she felt it, too. Her smile was as wide as his must be. He felt that excitement again, bubbling up inside. He couldn't contain it, and he laughed, the unbridled laughter of childhood. And then, Abby was laughing, too, glancing over at him, looking forward, laughing.

Trace found himself thinking, *This. This is perfect.*

At that sober thought, he felt his own energy shift. How was it possible that he experienced that moment with Abby Flores, who a day earlier he'd thought of as his sworn enemy? Heidi must have felt his mood change, because she slowed to a trot.

Half dazed, Trace looked over at Abby. And there she was: the most beautiful woman he had ever seen.

"Whoa," he said, and although the word was barely audible, Heidi slowed to a walk. Abby slowed her horse, too, with a gentle pull on the reins.

"You okay?" Trace asked her.

"I'm more than okay! That was so much fun!"

Abby's voice held the same excitement Trace just experienced. He couldn't believe any of it. Sure, he'd ridden with women before, but it had never been so … perfect. From the moment she arrived, Abby simply fit. She handled the horses like she knew them. She rode as naturally as she walked, and being around her felt easy. Except the part where he had to restrain himself from touching her at every opportunity.

"Are *you* okay?" she asked. She looked genuinely concerned.

"Yes," Trace said. "I think I'm in shock. I mean, I really enjoyed our conversation last night. And our dancing." He offered her a little smile. "And obviously, I expected to enjoy spending time with you today. That's why I invited you."

"Obviously," Abby said, slowly.

"I can't believe you're so … fun."

"You know," she said, wrinkling her nose in a way that made her even more irresistible, "I'm going to go ahead and take that as a compliment. And then I'm going to say that we should keep riding."

With that, she gave Louise a nudge, and they were off.

They hit the creek, and the horses went left. When Trace thought about the fact that they'd have to ride across the back of Abby's property to get to the swimming hole, he didn't feel the usual surge of anger. A new kind of calm replaced it. He slowed Heidi a little, so Louise could take the lead.

He'd meant to be a gentleman, but the thoughts he had while taking in the view were anything but gentlemanly. He shook his head, called himself a couple of rude names, and looked right, toward the creek. The horses knew the trail, and they sped along.

The midday sun burned hot. Despite the air rushing over his body, Trace could feel himself sweating. The swimming hole sounded mighty nice. The swimming hole with Abby — and that tank top — sounded more than nice. In fact, it sounded downright sinful. He hadn't planned to go there, but he couldn't think of a more perfect turnaround spot.

The horses could get a drink there, and he and Abby could cool off, too.

He wondered what Abby would think of it. Although he'd never taken a woman there before, he'd imagined doing so countless times. He had pictured how a woman would react. Some of the women he dated would probably love to take a dip, but the sad truth was that most of them would probably feel squeamish about getting in a natural body of water.

It looked so pretty and serene from horseback. The trail led right to an opening between a couple of the boulders that surrounded the swimming hole. Vines cascaded over the tops of them and down toward the water, and giant cottonwood trees shaded the whole area. Reeds grew along the edges, and some years, lily pads grew on the surface, their delicate yellow flowers peeking up.

When a person got off her horse though, she stepped in mud. And the edge of the lake could be slimy with algae. When it came to women, Trace had a certain type. And when he imagined any of his typical female companions putting their toes in the mud or algae — and squealing in disgust — he had to laugh. Somehow, he knew Abby would be different. She didn't strike him as the squeamish type. Not even when it came to algae and mud.

Again, he looked at Abby in front of him. And again, desire sliced through him, guilt on its heels. The images his mind conjured up were not innocent or pure.

Out of habit, Louise stopped at the entrance to the swimming hole. Trace pulled Heidi in beside her, and the horses moved together to walk toward the water. As soon as Abby saw the swimming hole, she gasped. She turned toward Trace, both hands over her heart. "You didn't tell me there was a swimming hole!"

Her reaction was priceless. "I wanted it to be a surprise."

She looked at the water, then back at Trace. "This is a lifelong dream of mine! A total bucket-list item!"

"The swimming hole?"

"Don't wrinkle your nose at me! Yes! I've always wanted to go to a swimming hole. I've never had the chance."

"Then today is your lucky day!"

"Can we go in?"

Her rapid-fire words reminded Trace of his childhood. "I was hoping you'd ask."

Abby offered a little squeal, and Trace said, "I admit, I didn't take you for a squealer."

"I'm so excited! I've waited my whole life for this!"

"I should warn you —"

"Unless it's leeches, you don't have to warn me about anything! I want the whole experience!"

Trace shrugged. "Okay. There's algae. It's slimy."

Abby was already dismounting. She led Louise over to the place where Trace normally tied them off. Again, he thought how naturally she fit there.

She looked back at him. "Are we going in?"

Trace dismounted and followed Abby to the water's edge. And then, much to his surprise and delight, she started stripping down. She stepped out of her boots and set them aside. Then, she started to undo her belt. Trace's heartbeat thrummed in his ears. He'd never wanted so badly to see what was under someone's jeans. The only reason he was able to tear his eyes away was because he didn't want her to see him gawking. If she did, he might never get the chance again. She must have sensed him looking at her because she froze and turned around.

"You getting in? Don't make me go alone!"

Trace literally sprang into action. He removed his own boots, and then his long-sleeved shirt. He needed to take his time removing his pants — there was definitely some evidence of his arousal — and, thank the heavens, she turned away. Without a warning or a count-down or anything, she jumped right into the water. By the time she emerged, shouting, "Well, *that's* refreshing!" he was waist-deep, too.

Her bra, an engineering feat way lacier than what he would've imagined for her, hugged her full breasts in the best possible way. Her underwear, low-cut bikini style, matched the bra, lace and all. It was a good thing his lower half was submerged in the chilly water.

"The water's nice, right?"

His voice sounded tight. He gulped, hoping to loosen his throat muscles. "Oh, it's perfect!"

Whatever he had expected of that woman in that place, it wasn't bubbly excitement. But Trace found that he liked that side of Abby. She was fun. And sexy. Sinking back down into the water, Abby came toward him. He lowered himself too, so they were eye to eye, their chins above the water's surface. Her grin wide, she said, "Thank you so much for bringing me here!"

"Don't thank me. Thank the horses! They love coming here."

At the edge of the swimming hole, the horses stood still, watching the humans with interest.

"Riding was your idea. You get all the credit."

For some reason, Trace felt a rush of pride at her words.

"What do you guys do when you come here?"

Remembering all the fun they'd had here as kids, Trace laughed. "Well, it's been a long time since the four of us came here for fun. As kids, we'd catch frogs. Have contests to see who could hold our breath the longest. Race."

"Race? As in, across the swimming hole?"

Trace nodded. "Yeah. Or across and back. Or, three laps, whatever."

"Want to race now?"

Laughing, Trace shrugged. "Sure. As long as you don't mind losing. I'm not going to take it easy on you just because you're a girl. And I've been known to win."

"I would think less of you if you let me win because I'm a girl. I've been known to be pretty fast, myself."

Charmed, Trace pretended it was no big deal even though he felt a magnetic pull toward her unlike anything he'd ever experienced. "You're on. We usually start over there, by the horses."

The two of them moved to the edge of the swimming hole and clung to the rock there.

They looked at each other. Abby's stare was intense. "Give us a count," she said.

He nodded, tried to match her intensity despite the fact that he was having so much fun, he wanted to laugh. "On your mark, get set, go."

True to his word, Trace swam as fast as he could. His arms churned through the water, and his legs kicked it up behind him. He could sense Abby right next to him. He felt the water tugging on his own boxer shorts, and wondered what it was doing to those lacy undies she had on.

They reached the other end of the swimming hole at the same time, their heads emerging simultaneously. If Trace had been racing Cody or Sawyer, he would have spent the next several minutes arguing over who'd won. But when Abby called, "Tie!" and slapped the water like an Olympic swimmer, Trace held up a hand for a high-five. When their hands touched, he wrapped his around her and pulled her close. Now that his blood was pumping, his arousal was once again evident, and he was certain she could feel it against her. They were eye to eye.

"I was sure you were going to beat me by a mile," she said, her smile fading.

A strand of her dark hair had fallen across her forehead, in front of her eye, and he brushed it back. "I thought I was going to beat you, too."

She laughed, and her gaze drifted down to his mouth.

For a fraction of a second, Trace felt nervous, uncertain. But only for a beat. Certainty took over, and he brought his lips to hers. She made a little sound, satisfaction, and her arms came up and around his shoulders as she kissed him back.

As he had earlier, Trace thought, *This is perfect.*

That was what a kiss should feel like. Now her fingertips were running through his hair. She deepened the kiss. A satisfied sound escaped Trace's throat. Suddenly he remembered she was wearing nothing but a lacy bra and panties. He let his hands roam from her waist to her stomach to her breasts.

"Trace Nelson," she said, her mouth still against his. "Did you bring me here so you could get me in my underwear and kiss me?"

"No," he said, as he ran his thumbs over her nipples. "I came here so I could see you in your underwear and get to second base."

She groaned, and he pulled down one side of her bra before taking her nipple in his mouth.

She ran her hands down his torso and grasped him.

"Nice," was all she said, and for some reason it drove Trace absolutely crazy. It was all he could do to stop himself from tearing off those panties and sliding himself inside her.

He didn't, though. Not yet. No, he thought as she continued to stroke him, their first time was going to be special.

———

ABBY

ABBY COULD NOT GET ENOUGH of Trace. A moment before, the water felt chilly, almost too cold to swim in. But with his hands and his mouth on her breasts, she didn't even notice the temperature.

In fact, all she noticed was the pressure building inside her. She could feel him, how aroused he was. And that made her even more aroused. His mouth on her breasts, his hands began to work below her waist. One hand slipped into her panties, and not for the first time that day, she was grateful she'd had the foresight to put on something nice. His fingers went to work, stroking, teasing. He kept at it, speeding up as she pressed against him. The pressure built even more, and she arched back, her hand still wrapped around him. He brought her closer and closer, the intensity rising and rising. She did the same for him, and they both cried out with release.

———

TRACE

THEY CLUNG to each other for a few minutes, gasping, before Trace felt Abby shiver.

"Cold?"

"Yeah," she said. "I forgot for a minute how cold the water is."

Trace took a step back so he could look at her. "You forgot how cold it is because you enjoyed that so much."

A glint in her eye, Abby responded, "No, I forgot because *you* enjoyed it so much."

Before he could answer, she shivered again, and he said, "You know what will warm us up? A race back to the other side. Then we can get out, put on dry clothes, and ride home. Are you hungry?"

"I may or may not have worked up an appetite."

God, why did everything she said make him feel even more turned on? The next words were out of his mouth before he had a chance to think better of them. "I could make soup."

She didn't answer right away. He saw her consider, held his breath. "That would be nice," she said, finally.

Trace grinned and then counted down for the race.

ABBY

AS THEY RODE BACK to Mint Creek Ranch, Abby tried to keep a gloating smile off her face. She won the second race — not by a lot, but fair and square — and even though Trace was a good sport, she could see he was surprised.

The horses ran a little easier on the way back, and Abby supposed going home wasn't as fun for them as going to the swimming hole.

She wasn't sure why she accepted Trace's invitation. She *was* hungry. But also, she was having so much fun with him, and she didn't want the day to end. When they got back to the ranch, they rode right into the barn.

"You can dismount if you like, and hook the reins on that post there," Trace said, pointing. "I'll take care of her saddle and every-thing as soon as I'm done with Heidi."

Abby dismounted and went to stand next to Louise's head. She stroked the horse's neck, and she whickered in response. "I think I can handle all that," she said. "I'll watch you, and do what you do."

If she wasn't mistaken, Trace looked surprised. Or impressed. Maybe both. He began to lead her through the steps. She took off the saddle and blanket and hung them up. Next, she removed the bit and reins, replacing them with a soft halter. Louise stood calmly, appar-ently not opposed to a stranger taking care of her.

"She's a good horse," Abby said to Trace.

From the other side of Heidi, he grinned at her. "The best."

"You know I always wanted an —"

"Appaloosa," they said at the same time.

"I remember. You talked about that rodeo clown family and the painted wagon."

"Pulled by Appaloosas."

Trace handed Abby a brush, and she ran it over Louise's body, copying the way Trace brushed Heidi.

"I thought you were so busy bristling at me for being alive that you didn't hear a word I said."

Trace stood up. "Abby," he said. "I'm sorry. I really am. I should've gotten to know you, before, you know."

"Before you decided to make my life miserable?"

"I didn't make your life miserable, did I? You wouldn't let one dumb sucker like me bring you down."

"Well, you're right about that. No, I guess you were more of an irritation." She offered him a little smile. She could speak lightly about it, but his disdain for her had stung at the time.

"You were irritating," he said, his smile broadened. "Coming to Prescott like you own the place."

"I own a hundred acres of it."

"That you do."

They finished with the horses and then drove over to Trace's house. The first time Abby saw it, on the day of the flat tire, she hadn't paid much attention. Since then, she'd been to the Mint Creek Ranch several times, but never near Trace's house.

Meanwhile, based on his behavior (a bit uppity, really) she'd built up a vision of Trace's home as grandiose and fancy. But it was the opposite: cozy and plain. She looked it over with a contractor's eye. It was older, probably built in the fifties or sixties. It was a typical ranch-style house, with a wide front porch. Trace had kept up the place. The paint was fresh, and the yard was tidy.

He'd obviously renovated the interior. High-quality, real hardwood floors, granite countertops, open space. Whoever designed it had considered window placement and made good choices. Afternoon was giving way to evening, and the whole house was filled with golden sunlight.

"Nice place," Abby said. Trace set his hat on the countertop, upside down.

"Thanks," he said. "I lived here with my parents until they moved away a few years ago. As you can see, I'm not as concerned with my indoor setting as I am with my outdoor setting."

Abby laughed. "That's true. I see you've got the obligatory horse painting above the fireplace. No family pictures?"

"I live with the only family I've got. Well, except my parents. My mom always jokes that she's going to get me a framed picture of her and my dad to put next to my bed. But I always tell her that'll scare away the ladies."

Abby smiled. "Yeah, if you kept the picture on your nightstand, it might."

"I'm just kidding, you know. I don't bring women home."

Abby gave him a look.

"Really. I don't make a habit of it."

"Huh," Abby said, but she was thinking that if he were telling the truth, him bringing her there was huge. And she didn't know how to feel about it.

"When I first saw you — that day you were driving the Mustang — my first thought was, 'Wow, that's the most beautiful woman I've ever seen.'"

"You're making me blush," Abby said, putting her palms on her cheeks. "Please stop."

"No, really. That was my first thought. And it was quickly followed up by, 'That woman does not belong here.'" He opened the fridge and pulled out two beers, holding one out in an offer. Abby nodded, and he opened hers before handing it to her. She took a sip, and the piney IPA bubbled on her tongue, refreshing.

"Was it the car?"

"It was. And then, when I saw you at that first City Council meeting, it was those high heels. Tell me those are not snakeskin. I can't think of any snake that would not be mortally offended at having its skin dyed pink and turned into a pair of high heels."

Abby shook her head. "No, not real snakeskin. One hundred percent synthetic. Those are my confidence heels."

His own beer open, Trace gestured to the kitchen door. He opened it for Abby, and she stepped out onto another deck. This one was small, maybe about eight feet square, and low to the ground. Beyond the deck on one side, the ground sloped toward the bank of Mint Creek. On the other side, several raised garden beds stood, full of leafy green plants, which Abby assumed were vegetables. Beyond those were three rows of trees, their green leaves catching the sunlight.

"Wow," Abby said. "You said you're more into the exterior, and I guess this is what you mean. This is incredible. I assume those are vegetables? And those must be fruit trees."

"Yes," Trace said. "I started growing vegetables as a kid in 4-H. It came easy to me, even though my mom could never grow a single tomato."

"Trace, that's really impressive. I can barely keep a houseplant alive. Not even a cactus."

"Now *you're* making *me* blush," he said. "Anyway. I know we're both hungry. I thought we could pick a few vegetables, throw together a salad."

Something funny happened then. Abby had a flash, almost an instant daydream, imagining what day-to-day life would be like if she and Trace were … together. In the briefest span of time, she saw one hundred images: the two of them picking tomatoes, slicing them, tossing together a salad. Enjoying a glass of wine on the front porch, greeting Cody and Tessa and Sawyer and Montana. Saddling up horses first thing in the morning, smiling at each other as they did. Kissing good morning and goodnight. Making love. Abby took a healthy swig of her beer. Gulped.

"You okay?"

She laughed, a little too loudly. "I'm in shock. I can't believe you're so much better than I am at growing plants. I would love a fresh salad."

CHAPTER NINE

TRACE

THE NEXT MORNING, Trace could actually feel the contentment as he went about his chores. Cody walked into the barn when Trace was mid-song, whistling "Clementine."

Cody froze and looked around the barn as if he were searching for someone. "Where is the real Trace Nelson? Is he around?"

Trace knew what he was getting at, but he wasn't going to bite. "It's a beautiful morning, man."

"Yeah?"

Oh. Trace recognized the edge in Cody's voice. It was more than curiosity. He was getting into predator mode. Thinking about how he was going to attack. Which questions he was going to ask to get the answers he wanted. Trace braced himself, and then went on whistling.

"What did you do last night?"

"What did *you* do last night?" Trace countered.

Smiling, Cody moved closer. "Let's just say I enjoyed that thing people refer to as the honeymoon phase."

Trace covered his ears and squeezed his eyes shut. "Don't even go there, man!"

"So?" Cody said.

"Wait, what are you doing here? I thought you and Tessa were leaving for your honeymoon today."

"Nice try. What were you up to last night?"

Trace considered himself a smart guy. He could recognize when he'd been beat. "I enjoyed a nice dinner."

"It wasn't with a certain Abby Flores, was it?"

He knew.

"More importantly," Trace said, "why are you asking?"

Trace thought back to the day before, when he and Abby shared those intimate moments at the swimming hole. Had someone seen them? It wasn't out of the question. Any one of the Mint Creek Ranch residents could have ridden over to the swimming hole. And Trace was so wrapped up in Abby, he wouldn't have noticed.

Cody pointed at Trace, eyebrows raised. "Guilty! It's written all over your face. Eating dinner wasn't the only thing you did, was it?"

So. Cody had outsmarted him, like a rattlesnake waiting to strike a rabbit. Normally, this would make Trace irritable. But that day, it made him laugh. He held up his hands in surrender. "You've got me. I spent a very nice afternoon with Abby."

"'A very nice afternoon'? What does that mean?"

"I never kiss and tell."

Cody offered a sharp bark of laughter. "Yes, you do! You always kiss and tell! The fact that you're not doing it now …"

Lifelong friends could be a blessing and a curse, Trace thought.

"Interesting," Cody said as the two of them began to work together to feed and water the horses.

"Okay, fine," Trace said. "We kissed. Fooled around a little." The thought of her hand on him made Trace squirm. "But that's it."

Cody didn't answer right away. When Trace looked over at him, he saw Cody's eyebrows were raised again.

"I'm serious, man. She didn't stay the night."

"I believe you," Cody said. "I just don't believe *it*. Have you lost your touch?"

Out of nowhere, Trace felt himself blush. He couldn't remember the last time he actually blushed.

"Well, well, well. What do we have here?"

"Sawyer," Trace and Cody said as their friend walked in.

"Morning, my bros."

"Morning," Cody said.

Sawyer jumped right in, measuring food and scooping it into the feed buckets.

"I can't help but get the sense I just walked in on something juicy. What did I miss?"

"Well, Trace here —"

Trace interrupted before Cody could finish. "Show up on time next time, and you won't miss out."

His friends hooted with laughter.

"Our man Trace spent almost an entire day with Abby Flores yesterday. When I came in this morning, he was already here, *whistling*."

"Whistling?"

Oh no, Trace thought. *Here it comes.*

"That's right. Our man Trace has a little spring in his step this morning."

Sawyer clicked his tongue. "No kidding, huh?"

"Says all they did was kiss, mess around a little."

Even though Trace busied himself looking for the tools to muck out the stalls, he caught Sawyer's expression out of the corner of his eye. His friend's mouth had dropped open, and he was looking from Cody to Trace, then back again, his face lit up with mock surprise. Trace shook his head and tossed each of his friends a shovel.

Good naturedly, Sawyer said, "What's the matter, man? Lost your touch?"

Trace went into one of the stalls and started removing the soiled hay. "My touch is just fine, thank you very much."

"That's what she said," Cody and Sawyer said, before they both guffawed with laughter.

Trace found himself smiling

"You two are as bad as a couple of teenagers," he said.

"And proud of it," Sawyer said, his voice coming from the other side of the wall.

"As a matter of fact, gentlemen," Trace said, "we had such a nice time that I didn't want to rush things. I guess I couldn't believe my good fortune. We actually talked and laughed and cooked together. It wasn't a typical first date for me, so I thought I should treat it differently."

Crickets. Neither of his friends responded. He could hear them, shoveling hay in the next two stalls. Deciding to wait them out, he shoveled, too.

Finally, Sawyer said, "Well, I'll be."

They worked in silence for a few more minutes. Trace realized it was too silent, and looked up to see Cody and Sawyer standing outside the stall where he was working, both of them wedged into the tiny space above the half-door, their elbows resting on top.

"Go ahead," Trace said. He could hear the dread in his own voice.

Sawyer went first. "Be careful, all right? I mean, I know she's a strong, independent woman, but I think she has a gentler side. I know how you felt about her at first, and I don't want you to hurt her. She is building my house, after all."

Still shoveling, even though he'd removed most of what he needed to, Trace nodded. He felt himself starting to bristle at Sawyer's comment, but he knew his friend was right.

"Trust me, man. I'm not out to hurt her. I feel like we've actually gotten to know each other a lot better over the past few days. And you?" He turned to Cody, who grinned.

"I don't know. I was going to say, there's something different about this one. Don't let *her* break *your* heart."

"Ain't never met a woman who could break my heart," Sawyer said, in a deep voice Trace knew was meant to mock him.

Trace switched to putting clean hay on the floor of the stall. He realized he couldn't resist asking, "What makes you say that?"

Cody and Sawyer looked at each other, and Cody said, "I've never seen you like this, man."

His smile was so big, like he was overjoyed.

Trace rolled his eyes. "Don't be getting any ideas just because the two of you are going off and getting hitched."

More laughter, and the two of them turned away.

It was exactly like that moment a few months before, when Trace and Sawyer had laughed at Cody when he fell off a horse and dislocated his shoulder. They hadn't been laughing because he was injured, but because of the reason he got injured: he was distracted ... because he'd fallen hard for Tessa. His friends knew it before he did.

Trace shook his head. "Shit."

———

ABBY

FRIDAY MORNING, as she rushed to get through her routine so she could get to Utah, Abby found herself thinking about Trace.

Again.

Almost an entire work week passed, she thought while she stirred milk into her coffee, and she hadn't made much of an effort with Trace at all. Strangely, she regretted it.

Those days had flown by, though. Her projects were coming along nicely, she thought. She sipped her coffee, which was still too hot, and carried it to the bedroom, reviewing where everything stood.

Windows were going in over at the retail space, and the next round of paperwork for inspections was done and turned in. She was putting in bids for a couple of new commercial projects. And although she knew nothing was set in stone until she finished building the houses, the Sunset Valley subdivision — her dream project — was unfolding according to plan.

Things with Trace ... well, those weren't really coming along at all. She selected her outfit with him in mind: jeans she knew flattered her figure, and a button-up shirt that made her waist look trim.

The two of them had texted a few times, but they certainly hadn't seen each other since the night they enjoyed soup together at his house (and what an afternoon *that* had been — Abby's ears still turned pink when she thought about it).

The coffee had cooled enough for Abby to take a full drink before she got in the shower.

A week before, Abby would have said she was too busy for romance. Between swinging her hammer, adjusting bids, answering emails, picking up supplies, and managing deliveries, she'd never been anything aside from focused. But things had changed.

She was still busy ... downtime was a mysterious, elusive concept, but for the first time, she wanted to change that. Toweling off, she considered how she could shift her schedule to accommodate someone. Trace, specifically.

For all the time she spent thinking about him, she very well could start a relationship.

But her relationship with her work required so much. She was at it from before dawn until after dark, every day. By the time she fulfilled her obligations and checked off all the items on her to-do list, she had no energy left to have actual conversations with other humans. It was why, since her dad stopped working, she spent almost zero time socializing. Sure, Montana helped to change that — on a small scale. Abby loved hanging out with her and Tessa. But a romantic relationship? That was different.

While good friends (and Montana and Tessa were the definition of good friends) generally accepted as much as a girl could give, romantic partners wanted reciprocity.

If there was anyone with whom Abby would want to experience reciprocity, it was Trace.

Yet, their communication illuminated the fact that Abby wasn't ready for a real relationship.

He'd texted her Monday, mid-day:

How's your day?

Because she wasn't in the habit of checking her phone, she didn't see it until she'd already dozed off on the couch that evening. It was simple enough, a conversation starter. But she barely had the energy to read it before going to bed, much less respond to it. She answered the next morning: *My day was great. Definitely a Monday. So much so that I was already sleeping by the time you texted.*

When she mentioned to Montana that Trace had texted her Monday and she felt bad about taking so long to respond, Montana raised her eyebrows. Abby thought maybe Trace had broken some unofficial rule about how soon to text someone after making soup with her.

By Wednesday, he was commenting on how busy she seemed: *Geez, woman. Do you ever get to relax?* (To which she responded, *What's that?*) By Thursday, she was telling him she'd be gone that weekend.

And then it was Friday. Because she had a flight to catch that afternoon, she made her rounds to the job sites early, coffee in a travel mug.

At the retail site, she practically sawed off her thumb when the board she was cutting slipped.

"Gosh, boss," said Sam, one of her best framers, and so familiar with circular saws she doubted he ever nearly cut off one of his fingers. "You okay? I've never seen you do something like that. You seem real distracted."

Abby looked up at him with a smile, one she hoped was reassuring. "I'm fine. A little tired, that's all. TGIF, right?"

"That's right. Going to see your dad this weekend?"

Abby nodded. "It's always so nice to see him. But I can't wait until we both live in the same town again."

"Listen, boss, why don't you get going? I can finish up here."

Abby glanced at her watch. "I wasn't supposed to leave for another —"

"For another couple of hours, I know. But we've got this. Give yourself a break. Go do something nice for yourself before you head over to Utah. I know manicures aren't really your thing, but get a massage or something. That's what my lady does."

Abby found herself smiling at the gesture. For some reason, she loved the thought of Sam calling his partner his "lady," and she wondered how she'd feel if she ever heard someone refer to her that way. It was a little possessive, yes. A little old-fashioned, maybe. But still. The idea of belonging to someone suddenly seemed so … nice.

So did cutting out early.

"I'm sure your lady appreciates having a guy like you, Sam. And I appreciate the offer. You know, I think I will take off. I see the job is in capable hands."

Truthfully, a massage would be nice, she thought as she walked out to her truck. Heck, she would even go for a manicure. Let the manicurist rub lotion into her dry, calloused hands. Her body nearly melted at the thought.

Still. When she considered what would feel refreshing to her soul after such an ultra-busy week, she wasn't thinking about pampering. She was thinking about Trace. And that was a problem. It would be good to get out of town for a couple of days. Maybe she would stop thinking about him. She buckled her seatbelt, started the truck, and put it in gear.

Immediately, though, she considered calling him, right then, at ten o'clock on a Friday morning, and inviting him to brunch. No. She couldn't do it. She *wouldn't* do it.

With the feelings she was having, she needed to be careful. Very careful. Before she could talk herself out of not calling him, she put the truck in park again and used her phone to book a massage at the parlor around the corner.

She fell asleep mid-massage, thinking about brunch with Trace. When the massage ended, she retrieved her phone from her bag and found that he had texted her: *I know it's technically still a work day, but would you be interested in getting away for brunch?*

Abby's heart stuttered. She wanted to write back, to tell him she'd thought of inviting him to brunch, too. They were on the same wavelength. Their stars were aligned.

For a long moment, her thumbs hovered over the keyboard on her phone ... until she realized the massage therapist probably had another appointment.

Without responding to Trace, she dropped her phone back in her bag, got dressed, and left.

———

TRACE

FOR TRACE, the week after he and Abby spent the day together felt agonizing. Time hadn't passed so slowly for him since he was a teenager waiting for Friday afternoon so he could head out for a weekend camping trip with Cody and Sawyer.

As an adult, though, all he could think about was Abby. Riding next to him, hair flying behind her. In the barn with him, brushing the horses. In his garden, picking tomatoes. In his kitchen, making soup. Every time he had a free moment, he wanted to call or text her. Most of the time, he stopped himself. A guy couldn't seem too eager, too desperate.

The fact that they'd shared one particularly erotic make-out session in a swimming hole and a surprisingly intimate afternoon and evening cooking and eating didn't mean they were together. Or that she wanted to do those things again. When he did give in to the urge to reach out to her, her answers were delayed and short. He wasn't sure whether to chalk that up to regret or busy-ness. Or both.

Finally, it was Friday. The end of the week. He thought it was safe to ask to see her again. He wouldn't come off as too needy. He knew she planned to leave in the early afternoon to go back to her dad's house, but maybe they could catch a meal. Mid-morning, he invited her to brunch. Kind of a strange move, maybe, but it didn't matter. She didn't respond until four p.m., as he was sitting down on his front porch, a glass of iced tea on the table beside him.

His hopes lifted when he heard the alert on his phone. Maybe she wasn't going out of town after all. Maybe she was writing back to say that she decided to stay, and why didn't they have dinner? But no, it was: *Sorry I missed you. Brunch would have been nice. Today was a whirlwind. This whole week, actually. Getting on the plane now. Be back Sunday, early evening.*

Did that mean, *Let's do something Sunday? I'd like to see you?* Or did it mean, *Don't bother asking again?*

Trace sighed and rubbed his hand over his face. He never second-guessed his interactions with women that way. The Sunday before had been so perfect, he hadn't wanted to ruin it by asking then and there if they could see each other again.

But he wished he had. He couldn't tell if she was putting him off or genuinely busy. The way she talked about her work, he suspected the latter. She had several different projects going, and she said she really enjoyed being hands-on. Besides, he thought as he took a sip of his iced tea, she didn't owe him anything.

Normally, he wouldn't overthink things. But something about Abby made him question himself. So, there he was, looking forward to a weekend alone. Surely, Cody had plans with Tessa, and Sawyer had plans with Montana.

Trace tensed when he heard the sound of tires crunching on the gravel driveway. He experienced a brief moment of childlike hope: maybe Abby was there to surprise him, and she wasn't going to Utah after all. But no, it wasn't her. The truck coming around the corner belonged to Hector Inman, the owner of Bright Moon Ranch. Trace could see his giant, gnarled hands on the steering wheel. He stood up to greet the old man, who parked the truck and tipped his hat as he got out.

"Mr. Nelson."

"Mr. Inman. To what do I owe the pleasure?"

It wasn't really a pleasure. The old farmer almost always stopped by to rustle up some drama.

Trace didn't know what to make of Hector's arrival. He looked a little crazed. The grizzled white stubble on his face couldn't decide between being a five o'clock shadow or a scraggly beard. His eyes were bloodshot, and his shirt was buttoned improperly, so that it sat higher on one side than the other. Trace would have laughed if it wasn't for the wild look in the old man's eyes. Those eyes darted back and forth, as if he were suspicious of someone hanging around. He took so long to answer, Trace thought maybe something was wrong. "Everything okay, Hector?"

Hector cleared his throat and then offered Trace a forced laugh. "Fine. Everything's fine. Oh! I forgot my clipboard."

He turned around and shuffled back to his truck. A visit from Hector, clipboard in hand, wouldn't classify as unusual. He often involved himself in city politics, and always had some scheme going. He returned, and thrust his clipboard at Trace, who couldn't help but notice it shaking in Hector's hand.

"What have we got here?" Trace recognized it as a petition. As he read the paragraph describing the reason behind a signature collection, his mouth went dry.

"You're trying to get Abby Flores's property reclassified?"

"Smart man," Hector said, tapping his own temple with a pointer finger. "It's what we all want, isn't it?"

Several weeks before, it was what Trace wanted. He would've signed any number of petitions to get that land back to its original agricultural zoning. But after spending some time talking to Abby, and actually getting to know her, hearing about her vision, Trace had changed his mind. Her parcel was large. At one hundred acres, splitting it into five-acre parcels meant the lay of the land wouldn't change much. Even though Abby's Sunset Valley subdivision was adjacent to the Mint Creek Ranch, Trace was pretty sure he wouldn't even notice the comings and goings of his new neighbors.

"I don't know, Hector."

"But you — at that City Council meeting, you were one of the biggest opponents of her development. What's changed?"

Trace scratched the back of his neck. "I don't know. I guess I've done some thinking. The parcels will be large. I don't think it's going to have a negative impact on us."

Hector put his hands on his hips. He nodded at the clipboard. "Well, I'm not asking you to make a vow or take a stand. All I'm asking for is your signature. Let the voters decide."

Trace considered. Petitions were public documents. If he signed it, there was a pretty good chance Abby could see it. There was an even better chance she *would* see it. The thought of Abby seeing his name on that petition — the first step in an effort to rob her of her dream — made Trace's stomach curdle. And that was before he thought about how Montana and Sawyer would feel if they saw it. They were set to buy two of the lots in the new subdivision. Trace wondered if Hector was aware of that.

"I'm not going to sign it, Hector."

"You're not going to sign it?"

Trace held out the clipboard. Hector snatched it out of Trace's grasp, his face red, spittle collecting at the corners of his mouth. "Suit yourself. But you should know I won't stop until I get all the signatures I need to get it on a ballot."

"Well, Hector, I'm confident you can get all those signatures without mine. Have a nice day."

With that, Trace took his iced tea and went inside. He closed and locked the front door behind him, leaving Hector spluttering in the yard.

CHAPTER TEN

ABBY

AS SOON AS her dad saw her, he said, "Something's different."

She started to smile, then tried to replace her smile with a surprised expression.

"Fail!" he said, laughing. "Did you meet someone? The feeling I'm getting from you now is reminiscent of when you first decided you liked that boy. Your first crush. What was his name? Stewie, or something like that?"

It was an old joke. Ernesto was always messing up the names of the boys Abby liked. She suspected he believed that somehow, if he made light of it, he wouldn't have to worry about his baby girl getting her heart broken.

"His name wasn't Stewie, and you know it. His name was Robert." She smiled. "And this is nothing like that."

"So, there is a 'this.' What is 'this'?"

Abby realized too late that she'd slipped. "It's nothing."

"Yet."

Abby shook her head.

"Tell me what it is, so far. I know it's something. You're grinning from ear to ear."

"It was one nice day. A horseback ride, an early dinner." She left out the part about the swimming hole. If she even thought about it in her dad's presence, she would feel supremely uncomfortable.

"Tell me more about this young man." Resistance was futile, so Abby didn't even try. "His name is Trace Nelson. He's not quite a Prescott native, but as close as a person can get without being born there. He grew up on the property adjacent to ours. The Mint Creek Ranch."

At this, Ernesto's eyes went round. "No! This isn't the guy who —"

She held up a hand. "One and the same. But don't worry, Daddy. I think I've given him a change of heart."

"Abby! I raised you better than that! You —"

Again, Abby held up her hands, laughing. "No, Dad! Not like that. I *talked* with him."

"This isn't like those times you *talked with* boys when you stayed out past your curfew, is it?"

Again, Abby shook her head. "I'm surprised you think so little of me."

"I don't," he said, his smile as wide as hers. "I'm just giving you a hard time. Mostly. So, you talked things through, eh?" He winked.

Abby rolled her eyes at her dad's good-natured teasing. "Yes. About a week ago, we had a nice conversation during which I explained our dream for Sunset Valley."

"And?"

Abby set down her drink and stood up to pace the length of the porch. "And, he invited me over for a ride. After that, we were both hungry, so he invited me over for some soup."

"Soup?"

Still walking, Abby dropped her forehead into her hand. "Dad," she said. "Soup. Yes, we had soup."

"Well, as long as it wasn't from a can."

"You expect all the men I date to be Renaissance men."

"I sure as heck do. For you, I want a man who can take care of you. I expect you to take care of him, too. But that's neither here nor there. Yet."

"And it probably won't be," Abby said. "I don't think I'm his usual type." She gestured at her jeans and boots. "We had a nice time together, but it's my guess that it was a one-time deal."

Ernesto rolled his wheelchair to the deck railing so he could look out over the red rocks.

"But somehow, I suspect that you really care for this man. And that you're telling yourself it was a one-time deal to protect your heart."

Abby walked over to stand next to her dad. She put a hand on his shoulder. "You might be right. We didn't just have a nice time. We had a lovely time. He made the soup. From scratch. With ingredients from his garden. It was, like, the perfect day. And — I can't believe I'm going to admit this to my dad — before I left, I had the weirdest vision of us spending day after day together. Just living."

Ernesto turned to look up at Abby. He put his hand over hers. "Monkey, you know I rarely give advice in these matters. But I'm going to give you some now. If you find yourself falling for someone — really, truly falling — that's special. That's rare. I've seen you in relationships before, and I am almost positive you have never really truly fallen for someone. Whatever you do, don't guard your heart. That's how people end up getting hurt."

"Wait. Did you mean to say, 'Guard your heart'?"

"No." Ernesto wasn't smiling now. A fierce look in his eyes, he said, "If there's any chance this is the man for you, don't hold back. Go all in. You don't know how much time you have with someone. Understand?"

Abby understood. Ernesto lost the love of his life when they were in their forties.

"I understand. Anyway. I'm almost sure that he's all wrong for me, dad."

"What do you mean? Because he opposed your development?"

"Our development. And yes. Pretty much. I mean, once we got to talking, we realized we want all the same things. But before this, he seemed so opposed to what you and I do."

"Then it's up to you to enlighten him."

Feeling edgy, Abby gave her dad's shoulder a squeeze before starting to pace again. "Maybe it is."

———

ABBY AND ERNESTO spent Saturday relaxing, working on a jigsaw puzzle that pictured about a million candy bars. It was a hobby they'd developed after Abby's mom died, in those days when the grief still settled over them like a heavy blanket, muffling out any joy.

They sat across from each other at the small card table in the living room, silently placing pieces. The activity was so soothing, so meditative. Together, at that card table, they began to heal. Neither of them particularly loved puzzles before, but they found that while they placed the pieces, they were able to speak again, at first about small things like the weather, Abby's track practice schedule, or what they would eat for dinner that night. As the years passed, the two of them worked on puzzle after puzzle, the pictures increasing in difficulty. And then, over time, they were able to talk about Abby's mom.

In present day, as Abby placed an orange piece onto the puzzle — part of the wrapper of a peanut butter cup — she smiled up at her dad. "Remember that time Mom sneaked a peanut butter cup into my sandwich? She knew we weren't allowed to have candy, and I was heartbroken because —"

"Because that Maria girl refused to sit with you at lunch the day before. Yes, I remember."

His eyes filled with tears, and he blinked several times before picking up another puzzle piece: the corner of a box of malt balls.

Ernesto had put on music, a country station. He tapped his foot and whistled while they worked on the puzzle.

Abby itched to tell him about the retail space, about the businesses clamoring for lease agreements, even though the building wasn't complete. But business would wait until tomorrow. They always spent Saturday enjoying each other's company, and Sunday morning talking business. Kind of unconventional, but for them, it worked.

"So tell me more about this rancher."

While Abby had been thinking of Trace practically nonstop since arriving in Utah, she hadn't really been expecting to talk with her dad about him. She should have known he would bring it up if she didn't. He was never one to let an important subject lie. She picked up a red puzzle piece with an unidentifiable part of the picture on it and looked for more red.

"Trace."

Grinning, Ernesto held his hands up next to his face and wiggled his fingers. "I can see the little cartoon hearts coming out of your eyes."

Blushing, Abby said, "No, you can't."

Ernesto motioned for her to keep talking. He chose another puzzle piece.

"Well, at first I thought he was a real jerk. Actually, let's back up. I never did tell you about the flat tire I got the day we made the offer on the Sunset Valley property, did I?"

"No, you didn't. I'm sure you didn't want to worry your old man."

"True," Abby said. "I was so stressed. I'd already hit a bunch of snags that day, including getting lost looking for the place. Which Trace helped me with. The last thing I needed was to miss my flight back home. As I was cursing my bad luck and that fancy rental car, a guy from the neighboring ranch came over and offered to help me change the tire. I thought that meant our neighbors would be friendly."

"Right. Small town. Western hospitality."

"Well, I thought he was a gentleman then."

"That was Trace."

"One and the same. Anyway, I thought he seemed pretty nice. If not a little standoffish when I took a wrong turn and ended up in his yard. But that was before he realized I planned to move here. You know the next part. He showed up at the City Council meeting, trying to get them not to approve the rezoning. So then I spent a few months thinking he was a jerk."

"So did I."

They both chuckled.

"Unfortunately — and I didn't mention this, either — he was part of the friend group I made. So I spent a lot of time with him over the next few months."

"And?"

"And I saw that while he could be a jerk, he could also be thoughtful. Kind. There were many instances where he put his friends ahead of himself."

"Unexpected," her dad said. It wasn't a question.

"Unexpected."

"And?"

"And, we were both in the wedding party at that wedding."

"The reporter and the bull rider."

"Right."

"And?"

Abby laughed. "And neither of us is much for being in the spotlight. So during the reception, we both found each other taking a breather in the same place."

"Out of the spotlight."

Abby nodded. "Out of the spotlight."

Abby held up a finger before her dad could ask. "*And*," she said, "we shared a nice conversation. And a nice dance. And I think we found an understanding. That was the night before he invited me over. I don't know why I accepted, but I did. And when I pulled up at his house, I saw him standing there, talking to his horse. The two of them were practically having a conversation."

Ernesto inclined his head. "You can tell a lot about a man by the way he handles his horses."

Again, Abby nodded. "I know. And then we had the nicest day."

"And?"

"And here I am. Wishing I'd called him this week."

"But?"

"But I didn't. I was guarding my heart."

"Make me a promise?"

"Depends."

He chuckled. "Call him when you get home."

Abby pursed her lips, thoughtful. "I'll think about it."

———

SUNDAY MORNING, Abby and Ernesto cooked a breakfast feast. He mixed muffin batter while she chopped vegetables. The two of them made omelets while the muffins baked. Then, as was their custom, they sat at the old kitchen table, food and hot coffee alongside blueprints and spreadsheets, and talked business.

That ritual had become Abby's favorite part of her weekend visits with her dad. She loved running her ideas by him, getting his advice, seeing the approval in his eyes. Even better: the way he lit up when they discussed their work.

Sometimes, she felt a twinge of sadness when she thought about how he couldn't work anymore. He could still use his mind. But he'd always taken pleasure in working with his hands, bringing his vision to life, one board at a time. She could see the grief creep into his expression, too, every once in a while.

They never talked about it. He would hate the idea that she felt sorry for him, and she didn't want him to think she carried on out of pity. The truth was, he inspired her.

Later that afternoon, Abby packed her suitcase. She and her dad said their goodbyes at the front door.

"What you've done, with the business," he said, still clasping her by the shoulders, "it's wonderful. It may not be the same vision I had when I started, but it's turning out better than I could have imagined. You're making a real difference, for real people. That's the best any of us can hope."

Abby's throat tightened at his compliment.

"And the boy — man — I hope you won't guard yourself so carefully that you miss out on one of life's greatest blessings."

"Romance?" Abby said, wrinkling her nose. She was half-joking, but Ernesto didn't crack a smile. "No. True love."

His parting words still fresh in her mind, Abby headed to the airport, turning the situation over in her mind.

Did her relationship with Trace have the potential to become true love? Her father had never steered her wrong. And, he and her mom had experienced true love, for sure. She'd seen it.

As a child, Abby had never been a great sleeper. She often woke up in the middle of the night. Most of the time, her parents were already in bed, and she would climb under the covers on her mom's side and snuggle up close to her body. But sometimes, Abby would find her parents sitting on the couch, hand in hand, talking. She would peer around the corner from the hallway, and hear words or phrases, snippets of their conversations. It seemed they talked about everything: her dad's business, her mom's teaching career and latest sewing projects. They talked about Abby: how she was doing in school, whether they liked her friends, what they thought she would do for a career, what kind of man she would marry, whether she would have kids, whether she would be happy.

Some nights, they sat at the kitchen table, cards and poker chips between them, laughter filling the house. Other nights, they played Speed, facing off in fierce competition.

It was on those nights, when Abby saw them interacting in the quiet hours when she was supposed to be asleep, that she could *feel* the love. On those nights, she didn't want to interrupt the connection. She would watch them until her eyelids got heavy before she tiptoed back to her bedroom, climbed into bed, and feel as content as if she were in her mom's arms, because she knew that her parents' love wrapped around her, too.

———

DRIVING up the hill from Phoenix to Prescott later that evening, Abby was pretty sure she embodied the phrase, "So tired she can't see straight."

The time with her dad had been restorative, but the breakneck pace she'd kept for the past several weeks had caught up with her. She could barely keep her eyes open while she drove up the winding interstate.

As she finally squeezed her giant truck into the tiny parking space allotted to her apartment, she cursed her own thriftiness. If she had been willing to spring for a rental house, she could have had a garage. Even a driveway would be better than this postage stamp of asphalt.

After backing up, turning, pulling forward — and repeating — several times, she finally achieved a parking job she considered borderline acceptable.

"Stick a fork in me," she said, the words echoing through the empty cab.

She was glad she'd taken the early-afternoon flight. It was just after eight — an acceptable bedtime, certainly. She couldn't wait until she moved her dad to Prescott. As she climbed the stairs to the second floor of the apartment building, her stomach growled, reminding her that she'd skipped dinner.

Her throat clogged with emotion at the thought of another frozen meal. They weren't so bad, really, but she was having a rare experience: she yearned for company.

It would be so amazing to get home from the airport to a freshly cooked meal and a friendly face. The first friendly face that came to mind was Trace's. God, he was so handsome. Even though she knew it was foolish, she imagined him greeting her at the door, arms open, smile wide, a glass of wine in hand. She laughed at herself. That was pretty cliché. Still. Clichés existed for a reason. She reached the top of the stairs and took a left. It was barely dark, but the way her footsteps echoed against the concrete gave her an eerie feeling. The hairs on the back of her neck stood up and she felt a chill pass over her arms. She looked behind her, but didn't see anyone.

Her mom used to talk about this feeling. "Passing through ghosts," she called it. Continuing to walk, Abby shook herself to clear her nerves. She looked back a couple more times, but the hallway looked like it usually did. As she approached the door to her apartment, though, she could see something on the ground. She couldn't quite tell what it was. Maybe it was a gift from Trace. No, that would be silly. He probably felt like she had blown him off all week. Maybe something from Montana? The eerie feeling returned as Abby drew closer. Again, she shivered. Suddenly, the hallway seemed a lot longer than it actually was. Finally, she reached her door. She gasped when she realized what lay on the ground, right in the middle of her doormat. It was a little cottontail rabbit. And it was dead. Recently, from the look of it: blood still pooled around a spot where its neck had been cut. It was a fresh kill. Which meant that whoever left it there wasn't far away.

CHAPTER ELEVEN

ALTHOUGH HE TRIED NOT to get his hopes up, Trace sort of expected Abby to call or text him Sunday afternoon when she got home from Utah. But she didn't. The later it got, the lower his hopes fell.

At six, he took a beer out of the fridge. Before he opened it, though, he switched it out for a sparkling water. If she did call, he wanted to be able to drive over to her place. At seven, he opened the refrigerator, looked at the beers, and closed it again. Not that he was desperate for a drink, but it would help pass the time. By eight, he'd run out of things to do, having already watched three episodes of his favorite comedy and scrolled through his social media apps.

All the while, his eyes flicked up to check the time every thirty seconds.

"I give up," he said as the minute hand hit the twelve. "If she were gonna call, she would've called by now."

In the short time they'd been talking, he realized that she went to bed pretty early. The chances of her wanting to meet up after eight p.m. were slim to none, so he grabbed a beer. Then he walked on down to the barn, where he knew he could always find a listening ear.

Sure enough, even though it was late, Heidi's ears perked up when she saw him coming. She made a soft noise in greeting.

"Hey, girl," he said. "How are you doing?"

As always, Heidi relaxed her cheek into Trace's open palm as he pet her. "I've been waiting all afternoon for Abby to call. But nothing."

The horse nodded, as if she were sympathetic. Then she took a step back, and Trace laughed. "No, you're never second-best to me. I needed to get out of the house. And you're the first one I wanted to see."

Trace jumped when he heard a voice behind him.

"Hey, bro," Sawyer said, ambling over.

"What are you doing down here? I thought you were shacking up with Montana every night."

Sawyer gave him a cocky smile. "I decided to give her the night off."

Trace rolled his eyes. "I don't know what she sees in you. You're a pig."

"I'm kidding, you know that. Montana's back at my place. To tell you the truth, I got a weird feeling. Something off. Then I saw movement down here. That sixth-sense factor was so strong, I didn't even think it could be you. But here you are."

Sawyer reached up and combed his fingers through Heidi's mane. "What are *you* doing out here, anyway?"

In the old cottonwood tree on the other side of the barn, a cicada started singing. Another joined it, and within a few seconds a whole chorus rose. The sound was almost deafening.

"I don't know," Trace said, not wanting to admit he'd come to the barn because he was pining away after a woman who hadn't shown him as much enthusiasm as he would like.

"Abby was gone this weekend, right?"

Trace closed his eyes, only briefly. That was the thing about friendships as old as theirs. Sawyer knew Trace as well as Trace knew himself.

"She was, yeah. I hate to admit it, but I was hoping she would call when she got home."

"But nothing."

"But nothing."

"She's got a lot going on, man," Sawyer said. "I'm sure it's nothing personal."

"That's what they all say," Trace said. "But thanks for trying to make me feel better. It's weird because we had such a nice time last weekend. And then, it's almost like —"

"Crickets."

Trace nodded, laughed. "Exactly."

"You know what would make you feel better?"

"Don't say what I think you're going to say."

Sawyer backed away, hands up. "I wasn't going to say anything like that, man. I swear. I was going to say, a night ride."

Trace felt the heat creeping up his neck and into his cheeks. "Right. That's what I was thinking."

Sawyer slapped him on the back. "Right. Anyway. Want to? Montana's expecting me, but I can text her real quick."

Sawyer didn't even wait for Trace to answer. He already had his phone out and was presumably sending Montana a message.

Trace knew his friend was right. Going for a ride would get his mind off Abby — temporarily, at least.

Sawyer's phone made a sound, and Sawyer said, "She said she hopes you feel better. And if she doesn't hear from us within an hour, she'll assume we decided to camp out on the creek, like the old days."

The night air was soft and humid. As Trace and Sawyer rode out, side by side, Trace inhaled deeply.

"So what's got you all discombobulated?" Sawyer wanted to know.

"It's just — Abby's different than I thought she was."

In the silence, Trace could hear the horses' hooves plodding along. He knew exactly what was going on. Sawyer was thinking, *I told you that from the beginning, you dummy.* And then he was thinking, *But I don't need to tell you that now.*

When he spoke out loud, he said, "She's pretty great, isn't she?"

"Thanks for not saying all that other stuff you were thinking."

Sawyer chuckled. In the distance, from somewhere near the base of Granite Mountain, a coyote howled. It yipped a few times, then howled again.

"I know, I haven't spent much time with her. There was the wedding night. And then we hung out on Sunday."

"Wait," Sawyer said. He brought his horse to a stop. Trace did the same. "The wedding night? What are you not telling me.?"

Caught.

"Nothing. We had a conversation, that's all."

"A *conversation*? Like the conversation you had with Sally Jensen after prom junior year?"

Trace shook his head and gave Heidi a little nudge. The moon was low enough in the sky that their shadows looked huge. Trace had the urge to make a few shadow puppets, like they used to when they were kids. But this was an adult conversation. "No, not like that."

"I don't remember any moment that it was quiet enough for conversation. So, the two of you must have slipped away," Sawyer said.

"Well, if you want to put it that way."

"Oh, I do."

"Well, if you must know, we did sneak away, together. But not on purpose. I was bone tired, you know? That storm that rolled through right before the wedding —"

"The storm that brought Montana and me back together."

Trace nodded. "I guess it had a role in creating my conversation with Abby. All the work we did to make things right for the wedding after that wore me down. And when the DJ started announcing Cody and Tessa's first dance, I knew I was going to have to dance with Abby, too. They always do that stupid thing where members of the wedding party dance together."

"It's stupid." Sawyer's voice was pouty.

"Don't mock me."

Sawyer clicked his tongue and Whistler picked up his pace. "I wasn't. I was making fun of you."

Trace ignored him. "So, I went around the corner of the Davises' house. I thought I would take a little break on the front porch. To my surprise, my spot was occupied."

"By Abby."

"By Abby." Naturally, the events of that conversation, including the dancing, began to replay themselves in Trace's mind. His heart rate picked up at the memory. He was grateful for the dark, because he was pretty sure he was grinning. Or blushing. Or both.

When Sawyer interrupted the film reel with, "Well?" Trace laughed. "So, believe it or not, I didn't hightail it. I offered to bring her a water. And then we sat and talked."

For a few long seconds, Sawyer didn't speak. They were riding along the creek now, and over its cheerful babbling, Trace heard a bull frog croak. Again, he knew what Sawyer was doing: waiting him out. Two could play at that game. The coyote started up again.

When Sawyer spoke, Trace clenched an imaginary fist in victory. "I don't suppose you're going to tell me what the two of you talked about."

Casually, Trace said, "Oh, just our hopes and dreams for the future."

"Abby shared that with you?"

"I don't know why you're so surprised, my friend. I've been known to charm a lady or two in my life."

Sawyer whistled, long and low, through his teeth. "Apparently, you've taken your skill to a new level."

"I have. And then I invited her to go for a ride yesterday." He cleared his throat as he remembered the swimming hole. "And we had the best time. But since then, she's been distant."

"So what did you do?" Sawyer asked. "Fart at the dinner table?"

Trace gave him a sideways glance. "I only ever did that when I was a kid. I wouldn't do it in front of a woman."

"Ha! 'I can't help it,' is what you always used to say," Sawyer said, chuckling.

Trace tilted his head back and looked up at the stars.

"So what are you gonna do about it?" Sawyer wanted to know.

"What do you mean?"

Sawyer's punch came fast and hard, and pain seared Trace's shoulder. "What do I mean? Trace Nelson, you've never waited around for anything to happen. Last year, when Cody decided to go back on tour, you headed up the whole process of making sure we got a great reporter."

"And look how that turned out."

Sawyer laughed, a hooting sound that always reminded Trace of a hyena. "You bet your ass I'm looking at how that turned out. Not quite like we expected, Tessa being the great person she is, but it turned out pretty damn good."

Trace shrugged.

"And," Sawyer went on, "when it was time to build the head table for their wedding, you took over, captained that ship."

"True. But you guys always say it's because I'm a control freak. You've never acted like it's a good trait."

"Aw, man. Come on. You know we like giving you a hard time.

Remember when you raised that pig for 4-H? The first one, what was her name?"

"Lucy."

"That's right. Lucy. Anyway. You were going to be the best damn hog raiser in town. Remember that? You wouldn't let anybody do anything for you. You went to the library and got all the books on hog raising. You followed about twenty different methods. And by golly, Lucy was a great hog."

"That she was."

"You got top dollar for her, if I remember. More than Cody or I ever got for a hog."

"I did."

"So, what are you going to do about Abby? I fully expect you're going to treat her like you did Lucy."

The laughter was barely contained in Sawyer's voice, and Trace was laughing too, as he said, "You're right. I guess I'll have to treat Abby like a hog."

They turned the horses around then, and as they rode back toward the barn, Trace thought about what Sawyer said. His friend was right. Most of the time, when Trace wanted something, he went for it. He stopped at nothing to get it. So why should this, of all things, be different?

It shouldn't, Trace decided.

The smell of smoke interrupted his thoughts.

"Smell that?" he said to Sawyer.

They'd reached the barn, and they dismounted before going inside.

"Smell what?" Sawyer said.

"I thought I smelled smoke."

"Oh," Sawyer said. "I don't smell it, but the fire department's always doing some prescribed burn or another, this time of year."

"True."

As they put up the horses, Trace's thoughts went back to Abby. Starting tomorrow, he would go after her like he really, truly wanted her. Because he did. About as much as he wanted anything in his life.

———

THE NEXT MORNING, Trace began to develop a plan. Contacting Abby by phone had proven unsuccessful. She rarely answered her calls or texts. So, he would have to get her in person. Showing up at her apartment first thing in the morning would cross the line right into creepy territory. But if he just so happened to be driving by one of her jobsites, that was coincidence. Luck.

Montana had mentioned being excited about the new retail building Abby was putting in. And, during their conversations the weekend before, Abby talked about how much time she spent there. It only made sense to head that way first.

Trace hurried through his morning chores and made a quick stop at the convenience store on his way to the jobsite. His heart beat faster when he saw Abby's truck in the empty space that would become the parking lot. Good. She was there. He pulled his truck up next to hers and realized how nervous he was when he got out and shut the door. *Really* nervous. Hands-shaking nervous. Mouth-dry nervous.

He swallowed. "What was I thinking?"

The place was busy. Trace could hear all the sounds of construction: saws buzzing, hammers pounding, people shouting. The exterior walls were up, so he couldn't see much of the action until he walked through a set of double doors on the first floor. Inside, the framing was about done, although he could see through to the other side of the building in the space between the two-by-fours. He could also visualize the shapes of the different spaces. On one end of the building, an electrician worked, running wires inside the walls. At the other end, a framer put the finishing touches on some window frames. And, straight in front of him — God, she looked so good in jeans — was Abby. She walked toward him, moving purposefully. Even though her eyes were on the doorway, and even though Trace stood inside, he could tell she hadn't noticed him yet. Which was strange, because he had seen how observant she was. It almost seemed like she was under some kind of spell.

"Hey," he said. Despite all the noise in the building, Abby jumped, obviously startled.

"Trace!" She put a hand on her chest, and he could tell she was breathing hard. "You startled me!"

His first instinct was to reach out, touch her arm, pull her into an embrace. But there was something about the way she looked. Spooked.

As hard as it was, he kept his hands at his sides. "I'm sorry," he said, and he meant it. "Everything okay?"

"Just recovering from a heart attack."

In normal situations, they would both be laughing by now. But something told Trace this wasn't a normal situation.

"What are you doing here?" The lack of warmth in her tone poked a hole in Trace's confidence. It started to deflate.

"Well, I just —"

"I'm sorry," Abby rushed to say. "That came out wrong. It's actually —" she scrubbed her hands over her face and made real eye contact with him — "it's actually really nice to see you."

In that one sentence, her demeanor changed from on edge to ... was she relieved?

"It's okay," Trace said, knowing that when someone was spooked, the best — the only — option was to remain calm. Normally, a blow to the ego like the one he just received would produce an angry reaction. He would turn around and march right out of the situation. But something felt different.

"I shouldn't have showed up without letting you know. But I really wanted to see you. It seemed like texting wasn't working, so ..."

"So here you are."

"So here I am."

Trace immediately second-guessed his honesty. It might come across as contrived. But, it might not. When he looked into Abby's eyes, he thought he saw the shimmer of tears. But she smiled, warmly.

"Trust me, it's good to see you. Really, really good. I'm so sorry I've been kind of MIA. It's been a whirlwind of a week."

"I get it," he said. "And I figured that if I showed up in person, you wouldn't be able to turn me down when I asked you out to dinner."

Abby glanced around, then, as if checking to see whether anyone was listening. Trace found himself doing the same. And he smiled when he realized several of the men in the building had stilled. Things had gotten a lot quieter.

"I'd like that." Her tone held confidence, even as her cheeks flushed.

"Good. How about tonight?"

Abby straightened her shoulders. "Tonight sounds perfect."

She looked at her watch. "I have a couple of things I have to check on after lunch. Would six o'clock work?"

"You got it. I'll pick you up."

For the rest of the day, Trace kicked himself for asking Abby out first thing in the morning. If he'd waited until later in the afternoon, he would have less time to worry about making all the right choices, from whether to show up a few minutes early or right on time, to which restaurant to choose, to (and he couldn't believe he was thinking about this) what to wear.

Trace went back and forth in his mind about a million times before six o'clock finally rolled around. He settled on a few minutes early, his favorite diner, the Horseshoe, because it had a good variety, and jeans with a button-up shirt, untucked, sleeves rolled up. And cowboy boots. Those were still a standard.

He parked across the street from Abby's apartment building at five minutes before six and knocked on her door a minute later. He wondered if, on the other side of the door, she was second-guessing herself, as well. Was she thinking about how long to wait before answering? Had she worried over what to wear? When he finally heard footsteps approaching, saw a shadow pass over the peephole, heard the lock turn, and saw her standing there, he knew it didn't matter whether she agonized over those things or not.

She was perfect.

It looked as though beauty came effortlessly. Her brown eyes sparkled with warmth, and her smile made him want to reach out for her. So that's what he did. He didn't second-guess himself or wait. He simply pulled her into his arms. Her reaction told him it was the right thing to do. Her body relaxed against his, pliable. It almost felt like she was seeking comfort. Her arms wrapped around his waist, and she laid her head on his chest. He inhaled that roses-and-vanilla scent.

"Hi," she said.

"Hi, yourself," he said. "This was a nice greeting."

"I agree. Exactly what I needed."

Even though he could have stood like that forever, Trace took a step back, while still holding her hands in his. "You look beautiful."

She'd chosen a simple outfit, similar to his: a collared tank top that showed off her cleavage and her toned arms, jeans that hugged her curves, and — well, the similarities stopped there. Instead of practical boots, Abby wore a pair of what Trace was starting to think of signature shoes: snakeskin heels. Instead of pink, that evening's pair were black and shiny.

"That's quite the once-over," Abby said.

Not for the first time in recent days, Trace felt himself blushing. He couldn't believe she'd caught him ogling her like that. "I'm sorry," he hurried to say. "You look —"

"Don't be sorry," she said. "I can't remember the last time a man looked at me like that."

That comment had Trace thinking that if he was any less of a gentleman, he would take Abby then and there, right in the open doorway of her apartment. But he was — barely — classier than that.

"Well, that's a shame. Should we go to dinner?"

Smiling, she nodded. "Let me grab my purse."

She left the door open as she walked inside. Trace followed her in. A quick glance around revealed that her apartment was as sparsely furnished as his house. He wondered how much time she spent there. She retrieved her purse from a table in the kitchen, and they went back outside. She pulled the door shut and locked it. Then she tested it, and tested it again. Then she glanced to her left down the hallway, and to her right. She checked the doorknob one more time before taking a deep breath.

Trace thought her behavior was a bit odd, but he supposed a woman living alone had to be extra vigilant. He offered her his elbow as they walked down the stairs, and second-guessed that, too. She was a strong, capable woman who obviously felt comfortable in those heels. She didn't need an elbow. Relief washed through him when he felt her hand encircle his bicep. She didn't let go when they reached the bottom of the stairs, or as they walked across the parking lot. He walked to the passenger side of his truck and opened the door for her. She thanked him and gave his arm a squeeze before getting in. Trace shut the door and cursed himself for feeling so aroused over such an innocent interaction. What was he going to do if they started taking off her clothes again?

"This place is adorable," Abby practically squealed when they walked into the diner a few minutes later. "I've driven by at least a hundred times, but I've only stopped in once or twice."

"It's one of my favorites," Trace said. Even during the dinnertime hours, the diner smelled like pancakes and syrup. The scent immediately transported Trace back in time, to Saturday morning breakfasts with the whole Mint Creek Ranch crew. The sign inside the door encouraged them to seat themselves, so Trace led Abby to a booth in the corner. "This okay?"

"Perfect," she said.

Although Trace would typically take the seat facing the door, Abby rushed to sit there. Again, he considered the behavior a little strange, but figured she was accustomed to being vigilant.

"What do you usually get?"

Trace opened the menu, but he didn't need it. "I alternate. It's either the roast beef or the BLT. With fries, either way."

"This all looks so good," Abby said. "I'm starving."

"I get the feeling you don't take many breaks for eating."

"That's true. I usually eat on the run. I have really good intentions." She laughed, and Trace felt himself leaning forward, drawn to her.

"I'll pick up the best-looking turkey sandwich, or a burrito from that food truck that drives around. You know the one?"

"Mickey's?"

"Yeah, that's it. Anyway, I'll get myself something, and be *so* looking forward to it. I'll eat a few bites and then set it down to do something else. Take notes, make a sketch, put up a quick wall. And before I know it, all this time has passed."

Trace found himself enjoying the conversation immensely. Many of the women he dated were afraid to admit they ate like actual humans. At restaurants, his dates often ordered food he thought was fit for a rabbit or bird. Sometimes he felt like a glutton when he took a woman out for dinner.

"I'm going to have to do it," Abby said. "I'm going to have to order a burger."

Trace felt himself grinning. "You know, I think you're the first woman I've ever taken to dinner who has ordered a burger."

Abby's expression clouded, and Trace wondered if he'd said something wrong. Maybe he shouldn't have mentioned taking other women to dinner.

But then she smiled back and said, "I think you'd better buckle up, Mr. Walker. I guarantee you I don't eat like many other women."

This made Trace feel even more aroused. But that was nothing compared to watching Abby devour a burger, one sinfully sexy bite at a time. She picked that thing up like she owned it, bit into it like she was ravenous. And even though she was ravenous for the food — not him — her appetite turned him on.

After Abby scraped the last of the ketchup off her plate with the last of her French fries, she held up her hands, showing him the traces of grease and ketchup on her palms and in between her fingers. "A napkin isn't going to cut it," she said, laughing. "I'm going to have to go to the ladies' room to wash up. Excuse me for a minute."

He watched her walk across the aisle to the bathroom, his eyes lingering on her waist and the curve of her hips.

Almost immediately after the door closed behind her, their server, Jessica, who'd been the gossip queen since they went to high school together, appeared beside the table. "Are you two dating?"

Her eyes were as round as a full moon. Her eyebrows arched over them, nearly reaching her hairline.

Trace rubbed his chin. He thought about how to answer. "Well, I wouldn't quite say that we're dating — yet. I *will* tell you that I hope this is the first of many more evenings like this. But I haven't told Abby that. So if you could keep it on the down-low, I'd appreciate it."

Jessica gave him an over-exaggerated wink and then nodded. "You got it. Should I bring you a romantic dessert?"

Trace shook his head. "I'm not sure either of us have room for that."

Abby came out of the bathroom and slid into the booth. "Did someone say dessert? I've always got room for dessert."

And that was the moment Trace knew he was in trouble.

"I really enjoyed seeing you in your element this morning," Trace told Abby as they sipped decaf coffee. "I'm not going to lie; I preferred the construction boots and carpenter jeans to the faux snakeskin heels."

Abby raised an eyebrow at him and gave him a look that simultaneously made him squirm in the booth and blush. He could practically read her thoughts: What if it was *just* the heels?

When she spoke, though, she said, "When we first met, and you basically asked to talk to the man in charge —"

"And you told me in no uncertain terms that you were in charge."

"Yes. I almost invited you to come spend the day with me then. So you could see what I do. The way you looked at me, I was afraid if I issued the invitation, you'd show up armed and dangerous."

"I was a jerk. If you had invited me to come spend the day with you, I wouldn't have shown up armed and dangerous. I would have turned you down cold."

"What about now?"

Trace's hopes lifted. "You mean, what if you invited me now?"

Across the booth from him, Abby looked a little uncertain, as if she were thinking about taking back what she'd said.

"Well, are you?" He smiled at her.

She smiled back. "It depends on your answer. If you're going to turn me down cold, then no. I was asking rhetorically. If you're going to accept …" She let her voice trail off.

"I accept. When should we do this thing?"

Pretending to wipe sweat off her forehead, Abby said, "Whew. For a minute there, I thought you were going to say no. I guess I should give you a couple of days to get things done so you can spend the day away from the ranch, right? How about Friday? I try to keep my Fridays light, so I'll have more time to explain things, show you around."

Trace found himself absolutely delighted about the prospect of watching Abby work. Those strong arms, that butt in those jeans.

"And don't sit there thinking you're just going to be watching me. I plan on putting you to work."

With that, Trace's fantasy shifted. So he wouldn't be able to sit back and admire the view. But he would still get to spend an entire day with Abby. And that sounded pretty damn awesome.

CHAPTER TWELVE

ABBY

THE NEXT FEW days were so busy, Abby barely even thought about spending the day with Trace on Friday.

It started on Tuesday, the moment she walked onto the jobsite. Her crew was already there. She spent the first part of her workday immersed in spreadsheets, and her vision was blurry when she finally stepped away from her computer. She treated herself to a cup of coffee on the way into town, and was mentally shifting gears when one of her framers, William, came running up to her.

"Boss! Boss!" He gripped her shoulders, fixing her with a stare that immediately sent her heart racing.

"What's wrong?" The panic in his voice sent her straight back in time, to the day of her father's accident. She could feel William's hands shaking on her shoulders, and her own hands started to shake as well. "What's the matter, William?" Her voice sounded angrier, more demanding than she meant it to.

"My wife!"

Abby offered up a silent prayer that William's wife would be okay. Before William could offer details, his best friend, another one of Abby's framers, Garcia, walked up. "William's going to be a daddy today, boss!" Garcia grinned. His eyes shone with excitement. "Which means I'm going to be an uncle, right?"

"Oh, thank God," Abby said. Her knees started to buckle, but she managed to pull herself together. The next second, it was her gripping William's shoulders. "You scared the heck out of me. But congratulations!"

"Thanks, boss. Do you think I could — you know, it's my first baby and all."

Abby felt her own expression transforming. She couldn't stop herself from smiling. "Of course! I told you that when you found out Melissa was pregnant. Your family comes first. Always. Get out of here! I can't wait to see the little one."

Quite suddenly, Abby found herself wrapped in William's arms, pushed up against his chest. "Thanks, Boss."

His voice sounded thick with emotion, and Abby, her arms around his waist, squeezed him back. "You're welcome. You're going to be a great dad."

As William rushed out of the building to the cheering and applause of the entire crew, Abby thought that her words had been more than lip service. William *would* be a great father. Abby had watched him over the past couple of years. He was always the first to step up, take a new crew member under his wing, share his advice, invite someone to sit down with him for lunch. He was patient, devoted. His wife was a lucky woman. Abby hoped that one day, she could find a partner as devoted as William.

She took his post for the rest of the day, working side by side with Garcia, who kept muttering, "I can't believe I'm going to be an uncle!"

By that evening, Abby's arms and the muscles in her back burned from exhaustion.

She went home, ready to sink into a hot bath. Still riding the high from the day's excitement, Abby pulled into her parking spot and opened the car door before realizing she felt nervous about coming home alone. That was different.

She'd always been a strong, independent woman. Until someone left a dead rabbit on her doorstep. She couldn't shake the feeling that the rabbit was a threat. And that it wouldn't be an isolated incident. She made her way quickly up the stairs and down the hallway, doing her best to be aware of her surroundings without looking like a terrified, preyed-upon rabbit, herself. She scanned the hall and didn't see anyone. The space next to her door looked empty, thank goodness. Moving as fast as she could without getting clumsy, she stuck her key in the lock and turned the deadbolt. She slipped inside and shut the door behind her, turned the deadbolt, then leaned against the door to catch her breath. She really should get another lock.

Feeling calmer, she threw together a salad while reminiscing about the delicious burger she'd eaten the night before on her date with Trace. After dinner, she had that bath.

Wednesday morning, she woke up to several texts from Garcia.

The first one: *My nephew is here! Big strong baby boy, 8 pounds on the dot. A full head of hair just like his uncle.*

Then, a picture. Sure enough, the kid had a shock of white fuzzy hair — exactly like Garcia's in terms of volume, but completely the opposite, in terms of color. Abby found herself smiling.

The third text from Garcia said: *I was thinking of running over there on my lunch break, bringing the happy parents some food. Is that okay?*

Now smiling through a sheen of tears, Abby typed back: *He's beautiful. Congratulations. He looks so much like you.* She added a winking emoji and then typed, *Absolutely you should go see them on your lunch break. I'm sure they'll be grateful for real food they don't have to cook.*

With William off work for at least a couple of weeks, Abby knew she would be doing more of the actual construction labor. She supposed she could hire some temporary crew members — she'd had enough notice to do so — but every once in a while, she liked to get in there, swing the hammer, use the saw. She remembered watching her dad work, even though as the owner, he could easily have stepped into the supervisory role and never picked up another tool.

When she asked him about it once — probably in the throes of long construction days on big projects — he said to her, "I don't *have* to get in there with the crew. For one, I love it. And more importantly, it's a reminder about how every part of this team is important. I could have all the vision I wanted, and even if I could lay every board myself, it would take me months to accomplish what our team can accomplish in weeks. With a great team, this company is a machine. Without it, it's a tiny motor. It works okay; it functions, but it can't do much. Understand?"

Those words stuck with Abby, and she thought about her dad as she sweated through Wednesday and Thursday. By Thursday night, she was more physically tired than she had been in a long time, and she fell into bed and slept like the dead.

Only when she woke before her alarm at five a.m. Friday did she remember she was spending the day with Trace. He'd told her he would be at her place at six-thirty.

She started with coffee and a hot shower, and before he got there, she opened her door a crack to make sure there was nothing sinister outside. By the time he arrived, she felt almost human. She nearly wept when she opened the door to him standing there, a coffee cup in each hand, his face freshly shaven, and a citrusy soap smell coming off his skin.

"I could kiss you," she said. "Coffee. You're my new best friend."

She went to take the coffee cup from him, but he pulled it out of her reach, smiling. "You said you could kiss me. And I wouldn't turn that down as a form of payment."

How amazing it would be to enjoy this sort of a greeting every morning, Abby thought. She put her hands on his waist, her fingers through his belt loops, and pulled his hips against hers. Then she brought her mouth to his, giving him a slow, deep kiss. He made a little sound in his throat, and Abby felt a response below her own belt. Although she could have kept kissing him for hours, maybe even all day, she broke the contact and looked into his eyes. They smoldered back at her, so dark, they almost looked gray.

"Are we even now, or is there a balance?"

He handed her the coffee. "I'd like to say there's still a balance, because I wouldn't mind another payment. But as it is, were going to have to wait a few minutes for things to … settle down."

Feeling a bit smug at her prowess, Abby stepped back and gestured for him to come inside.

"Perfect," she said, "because I usually start my day at home anyway. Come into my office."

She led him over to the kitchen table where her computer was set up. They sat down and she unlocked her home screen.

"So this is where the magic happens, right?"

"If you call a whole lot of brainstorming and arranging and rearranging and second-guessing and scrapping the whole thing and starting over 'magic,' then yes. That's exactly what happens here."

Abby spent a few minutes reviewing her schedule for the day. She showed Trace the project schedule, which outlined when certain suppliers would make their deliveries, when subcontractors would come in and do their work, when the inspections would happen, and which crews would be on which jobs.

"I had no idea you had this many projects going on," Trace said. "This is huge, Abby."

The words filled Abby with pride. She knew she had a lot going on, but only in terms of all the details she kept track of. She'd built the business little by little, piece by piece, gradually. But here, looking at it through Trace's eyes, it did seem pretty impressive.

"I didn't build it from scratch," Abby said, "but thank you."

Trace whistled as he leaned closer to the screen of her laptop. "That project, over on Granite Street — that's yours?"

"That's mine," Abby said.

"I've heard Montana talking about it — she's, *like, so excited* about it — but I didn't realize it was yours."

Abby laughed. "She probably kept that part from you. I'm pretty excited about it, too. People are always stopping by there, saying they're excited for more retail."

"Wow," Trace said. "That's not what I expected."

Abby winked at him. "Well, you may not be much of a shopper, but your fellow Prescottonians are beside themselves. All right. I know what's supposed to happen today. Now, it's time to hit the road and see how my best-laid plans play out."

The two of them walked down to Abby's truck.

"The crews are supposed to be to work by seven," she told Trace. "But I usually don't head out until half-past. You know, there's always chit chat, all that morning gossip, at the start of the day. I like to let the guys have a little time without the boss lady around."

Trace nodded. "Makes sense."

They drove from jobsite to jobsite, doing walk-throughs at each one. Trace stuck close to Abby, walking a half-step behind her as she checked on everything. She watched him take in the sights, his eyes landing carefully on the crew members as they worked, looking over the framed-in walls, the electric wiring, the HVAC work. Between jobs, in the truck, he asked questions and listened intently as she answered.

"If I didn't know better, I'd think you are trying to steal my company secret," she told him at one point.

"You never know," he said. "You'd better keep me real close. Keep an eye on me."

Before she knew what she was doing, Abby reached across the center console and took Trace's hand, intertwining their fingers. "I don't think I'll hate that."

He smiled and gave her hand a little squeeze.

At exactly ten o'clock, Abby pulled into the parking lot of the mall.

"What do you have going on here?"

Abby winked at him. "Shopping."

Abby liked the way Trace didn't ask any questions. He got out of the truck and walked with her into the department store. When he saw they were headed to the baby section, he stopped walking.

"I'm sorry to say this Abby, but I think it's too soon to go baby shopping together."

"Oh, stop," she said. She grabbed his hand and tugged him along. "One of my best guys, William, had a baby Tuesday night. Well, his wife did. I wanted to give them a couple of days to get settled in, but I asked him if I could stop by this afternoon or evening. I thought I'd better bring a present. You don't show up to visit a new baby empty-handed."

"Boy or girl?" Trace asked.

"Boy," Abby said. She pulled out her phone to show Trace the picture Garcia had sent her. "Look at that face," she said. "Doesn't he look alert?"

"He looks like a little old man. Wise beyond his years."

"That's what I thought," Abby said, feeling strangely touched that Trace's reaction was similar to hers.

"So, I don't think we can go all babyish on this guy," Trace said. "You know what I mean? I feel like he needs a good western shirt. Is it too soon for a cowboy hat?"

Trace's expression serious, he pored over a display of miniature Western wear. He held up a pair of cowboy boots.

"So tiny and adorable, and so impressed," Abby said. "Those are the cutest pair of cowboy boots I've ever seen."

They found the baby a plaid shirt and debated over whether to get it in red or blue. When they couldn't agree, they bought both.

Back in the truck, Trace said, "Now, I know I'm tagging along with you for the day, and we're on your timeline. Any chance you have to go to the hardware store today?"

The excitement Abby saw in his expression hadn't waned since they left the department store. His eyes twinkled at her from across the cab of her truck. She glanced at her watch. "I didn't really plan on it, but we have time if there's something you need to do."

"I have an idea. Would you mind if we dropped by?"

On one hand, Abby wanted to press him for details. On the other, she could tell he had something up his sleeve. "I think I could arrange that."

"Follow me," Trace said as they walked through the hardware store's sliding doors a few minutes later.

She could find her way around the place with her eyes closed, and it took only a few seconds for Abby to realize where Trace was going: a little section along the west wall held inventory just for kids. All related to construction and building, there were toys and clothes and work boots. Abby's heart practically melted, then and there.

"I think I might know what you're up to," she told Trace, and was rewarded with a grin.

"Well, I figured we got the kid a bunch of Western wear. Which is perfect for our newest Prescottonian, with this being the Wild West and all. But, seeing as his daddy's in construction, and so are you, it seems only fitting that we get him a few tools of his own."

Abby wanted to wrap her arms around him, give him a good squeeze of appreciation. "That's really thoughtful. I'm sure they're going to appreciate it."

Again, they went a little overboard. The miniature tool belt and toolset, the tiny workboots, they were too adorable to pass up.

"I'm pretty sure we're overdoing it," Abby said.

"That's alright," Trace said. "Welcoming a new baby is one time when that's acceptable."

Abby found herself laughing out loud.

"What? It is!"

"I agree completely. It's just that it's rare to hear a man say so."

"Kids are pretty special. What can I say?"

After successfully purchasing about half of the kids' items for sale at the hardware store, Abby pulled her cooler out of the backseat. "Lunch hour."

She opened the cooler and handed Trace the sandwich she'd made him. He looked at it, then at her, then back at the sandwich. "You eat on the run every day?"

"Yeah." She shrugged. "Like I said, it's the only way I can squeeze everything in. Once I realized I was skipping lunch most days, I started to eat during my drive time. Maximum efficiency, right? Two birds, one stone. It's the only rule of my dad's that I break. He used to take a real lunch. He'd do a sit-down-at-a-restaurant lunch most days."

"First of all, I agree with your dad. I've seen the way you work. You're nonstop. Do you ever cut yourself some slack?"

Abby, who'd already taken a giant bite of her sandwich, shook her head and held up a finger while she chewed and swallowed. "If I took a lunch break, I'd be working further into the evening than I already do. I'd rather do this. Get my hour of quiet time before bed."

"I get that," Trace said. "You said your dad used to take a lunch break. Did he retire?"

Although she tried not to let her sadness show, she could tell Trace noticed. "He didn't retire. He had an accident — took a fall — it paralyzed him from the waist down."

"I'm sorry," Trace started to say, but Abby reached over and put a hand on his shoulder. "Don't be. It's been hard, I'm not going to tell you otherwise. But he doesn't feel sorry for himself, so I'm not allowed to feel sorry for him. And you're not allowed to feel sorry for me. We still run the business together. That's part of why I visit him every other weekend. We go over the finances, blueprints, plans, schedules. Like I said before, I'm the guy in charge now. He still gives me a lot of guidance."

"I'd like to meet him sometime."

Abby was surprised. "You would?"

Trace nodded. "I would."

Abby felt something inside of her shift in that moment. Partly because she had opened up to Trace about her dad and the accident, which she'd never done with a man before. And partly because of how she felt when he said he'd like to meet her dad. He was being so … genuine. As a rule, Abby didn't introduce guys she was dating to her dad. The craziest thing about the whole conversation, she thought, was that she wanted to introduce Trace.

———

TRACE

BY LATE FRIDAY AFTERNOON, Trace was exhausted. Abby ran at a crazy pace all day, and in addition to that, Trace's brain was fried from processing all the new information he took in. Just when he thought they were wrapping up for the day — the crew packed up their tools and Abby sent them home — she said, "One more item to check off."

They drove to the drug store, and Abby said, "Hang tight. I've just got to run in and grab a couple of things. Be right back."

Despite his exhaustion, Trace felt aroused at the prospect of her buying condoms. But when she came back, she wasn't carrying condoms. She was carrying a gift bag and a package of tissue paper. Standing outside the open driver's door of her truck, she pulled out everything they bought earlier. She handed him one of the shopping bags, along with a few sheets of tissue paper. "Here. Would you mind wrapping these up? I'll do the tools, and then we can put everything in this bag."

Trace did as he was asked, careful to make his wrapping job neat and tidy, as he imagined Abby would do. They loaded all the little wrapped parcels into the gift bag, and Abby stuffed a few more pieces of tissue paper in on top of them. She set the gift bag on the center console, and when she headed in the direction opposite of her house, he realized that she was bringing him with her to deliver the gifts they'd picked out.

He didn't know why that made him so happy.

"Wait. If I'm going with you to deliver these gifts, there's one more stop we have to make."

Abby looked at him, an eyebrow raised, before returning her focus to her driving. "All right," she said. "Just say where."

Trace didn't know Abby's crew member — William, the father of the new baby — but he knew, man-to-man, that if he was showing up at the guy's house, he'd better be prepared to congratulate him properly on the birth of his first child. He had Abby stop at the gas station on the corner, where he bought a couple of cigars. When he got back in her car and held them up to show her, he said, "Not what I normally buy, but it was the best they had."

Something in the way she smiled at him then told him he'd made a good choice.

William lived in one of the modest homes that had served as

housing for gold miners in turn-of-the-century Prescott. Trace had always found the neighborhood charming, with its rows of pastel bungalows and their tidy yards. Abby parked on the street and turned off the ignition. She took a deep breath and rubbed her hands on her thighs.

"Are you nervous?" Trace asked.

She leaned her head back against the headrest, and he saw she was gripping her thighs. "Yes," she groaned. "I feel a little like a bull in a china shop when it comes to these social customs. My mom, she died when I was a teenager, so she wasn't around to show me how to behave. Then it was just Dad and me, and we have such a small family, so I didn't really get to observe proper interactions. If that makes sense."

Trace found that he wanted to soothe Abby's anxiety away. "Self-awareness is the first step," he said, before prying her hand off her leg and taking it in both of his. "The best thing you can do is compliment the baby. Compliment something specific. Like his hair, or his eye color, or how smart he looks. Then, compliment the mother. Always the mother. My mom always said that the best thing we can do for families is to let mothers know they're doing a good job."

Abby brought her free hand up to run it through her hair. On an exhale she said, "Okay, these are good tips."

"You're welcome." He gave her hand a squeeze and winked at her. "You can pay me later. Again, I take kissing as a form of payment. Now, let's go meet this baby and shower him with gifts."

He met her on her side of the truck and gave her shoulders a quick squeeze. "You're going to be great. Complimenting babies comes easily. You'll see."

He leaned forward and kissed her on the lips — a no-nonsense kiss he hoped would bolster her confidence. "Let's do this."

He took the gift bag from her. William opened the door, and from the way he was grinning, Trace could tell he'd seen the kiss. *Well, cat's out of the bag.*

"Come on in, Boss, and ..."

"Trace," Abby said. "Trace Nelson."

She was blushing, which Trace loved. William shook Trace's hand, and Trace could tell he was sizing him up. It was evident Abby's crew members liked and respected her, and apparently, that they were protective of her. "I hear congratulations are in order."

William's face broke into the biggest grin. "Thanks, man. Come in, come in. I can't wait to show off the little guy. This is my wife, Melissa."

Melissa sat on the couch in the living room, the baby swaddled and sleeping in her arms. He had a full head of white hair, which looked exactly like a dandelion.

Abby gasped. "Oh my gosh, you guys! He is the cutest baby I've ever seen! That hair!"

Although Abby was following his advice, Trace could tell she meant what she said.

"That's a handsome boy right there," he added. "About eight pounds?"

William beamed at Trace. "Eight pounds on the dot. Came out screaming like he couldn't wait to greet us all."

"What's his name?"

His name! Why hadn't Abby thought to ask that?

"Frederick," William said. "After my dad. We're calling him Freddie."

Abby walked over to the couch. "May I?"

Melissa nodded and patted the spot next to her.

Abby sat and leaned over to get a better look at the baby. She put a hand on Melissa's knee and looked into her eyes. "Congratulations. You did a wonderful job. He's perfect."

Again, even if Trace had supplied her with the words to use, he could see the sentiment was heartfelt.

"Want to hold him?"

Abby gasped again. "Could I?"

Trace's heart pretty much melted.

"I would love to," Abby said. "But I wasn't sure — let me wash my hands."

Laughing, Melissa pointed toward the kitchen. "You can wash up in there. Of course it's okay, I want everyone to admire our little boy."

As much as he'd enjoyed the entire day, the visit was shaping up to be Trace's favorite part. He loved seeing that side of Abby. She came back from the kitchen and sat down next to Melissa and the baby. Melissa placed the bundle in Abby's arms.

Abby settled back into the couch and then looked up at Trace, as if she were thinking, *Isn't this incredible?*

And that was it. That was the moment Trace knew there would

never be another woman for him. He wanted to see Abby holding *his* baby. *Their* baby. That thought shocked him so much, he had to get out of the room.

"Oh, I almost forgot," he said, even though he hadn't. "William, I brought you something."

He patted his shirt pocket, where he'd tucked the cigars. He pulled them out and handed one to William. William smiled at Trace, and then at Abby. "This one's a keeper," he said to her. They were already walking out, but Trace heard Abby say, "I know he is."

After that, he couldn't stop smiling.

CHAPTER THIRTEEN

AFTER SPENDING one full day with Abby, Trace would do anything to spend another with her. And even though he knew he should be able to simply tell her he wanted to see her again, he worried he might come across as too eager. He had to be smart about it.

Saturday morning, as soon as he got up, an idea started to form.

He couldn't call her right away. An early morning call would also seem desperate. He bided his time. Coffee, chores, a nice ride, enjoying the cool morning air. He got back to the barn, put up the horse, and checked his watch. Ten o'clock.

"Still too early," he said to Louise. She put her head over the door of her stall and made a chuffing noise. He ran his palm over her smooth cheek, and she pressed it against him. She blinked, and he felt like she was telling him something. "Are you saying I should go ahead and call her? That no lady could possibly resist the charms of Trace Nelson?"

At this, the horse took a step back, and Trace laughed. "Okay, okay. I guess I'm getting a little carried away. That's exactly what I wanted to hear. But you know what? I'm going to do it. I'm going to call her. But stand here with me while I do. I need moral support."

The horse bobbed her head in what Trace thought of as an affirmation. He pulled his phone out of his pocket and dialed. She picked up right away. He told himself that was because she was waiting for his call. But her voice didn't sound quite right. It sounded strange. Maybe she was unhappy to hear from him. Maybe he was calling too soon.

Instead of getting defensive like he normally would, he asked, "Everything okay?"

She answered on a sigh, her words coming fast, too close together, like the cars on a train whose engine had stopped suddenly.

"Yes, everything is fine, thank you. How are you?"

She didn't sound fine.

In fact, Trace recognized in her voice the same sort of feelings he'd experienced a couple of times in his childhood. One of them: the day he'd come home from school and thrown his cowboy boots across the living room after the kids had teased him for being a country kid. On one hand, he wanted so badly to tell his parents what happened. And on the other, he didn't, because he was afraid it would hurt them knowing *he* was hurting.

"Everything doesn't sound fine," he said.

He heard her draw and release a breath, shaky. "It's fine. Really. I swear."

"Cross your heart?"

"Yeah. Cross my heart." At that, at least, her voice had calmed a bit, the edges smoothing out.

The plan Trace spent the morning developing didn't include seeing her that day, but something told him he needed to figure out what was behind her strange behavior. He was going to have to tread gently.

"What are you up to today?"

"Nothing, really."

She wasn't giving him much to work with. "Want to come over? Go for a ride?"

Louise's ears perked up at that. Even though they had just returned, she wouldn't mind going out again. He loved her for that.

From Abby, a long pause. And then, "Sure. That would be nice."

Normally, at that point in the conversation, Trace would say something suggestive, borderline raunchy.

How about visiting the swimming hole again?

Want to get wet together?

Let's go on down to the swimming hole and see what comes up.

But he could tell: there was something fragile hanging between them.

"I have a couple of things to do," she said. "Give me an hour?"

Trace thought an hour seemed reasonable. Some of the girls he'd dated in the past needed at least a two-hour warning.

"An hour sounds perfect. See you then."

Trace put his phone back in his pocket, and even though the call had ended, the worried feeling hadn't subsided. He took off his hat and scratched the back of his head, a nervous habit he developed as a kid. He'd probably copied it from Cody and Sawyer, his cowboy role models.

He hoped she hadn't agreed to come over just so she could tell him she never wanted to see him again. He hoped she really was okay. But, he would have to wait to find out. And because waiting was something he'd never been very good at, he walked back into the barn and saddled up his favorite team roping horse, Bravo.

Bravo was fast, fierce. And he loved to run. Trace couldn't run any other horse as hard as he could run Bravo. At that moment, a good, hard run was exactly what he needed.

———

Abby

ABBY WANTED to say no to Trace. She needed to be alone.

For one thing, she didn't want anyone, not even Trace (especially not Trace) to see how scared she was.

She didn't even know why she'd opened her front door earlier. Usually, when she was home, she spent Saturday mornings doing absolutely nothing. Well, besides drinking her coffee, scrolling through social media, maybe reading a little news. But that morning, she changed things up. She thought it would be nice to go for a walk. The weather was cooling, and the sun was still low in the sky, rather than blazing down on her. She threw on some leggings and a sweatshirt.

Then, she opened the front door and saw them. This time, there were two. Two little dead bunnies, lying on the concrete where her doormat used to be. They faced each other, their little front paws touching. The blood pooled between them.

Abby wasn't a screamer, but she found herself putting a hand over her mouth to stop the sound from escaping. Some insane urge to see if there was any chance of saving them took over. She knelt down, her eyes first on one rabbit and then the other, checking to see if they were breathing. But no. There was no chance of saving them. Abby's throat tightened. Her eyes began to sting.

She really wanted to retreat back into her apartment, but she knew she couldn't leave them there. The little boy who lived two doors down loved bunnies. He would be traumatized if he saw them. So she retrieved a plastic bag and carefully lifted their bodies into it. If she were home, at her dad's house, she would have buried them. But at the apartment, that wasn't really an option. She carried them to the trash bin, holding the bag down at her side so no one would see the blood.

When she returned to her apartment, she saw the stain of blood was still there. It shouldn't have shocked her, but it did, and she began to cry more openly. What kind of sick person would do this? she thought as she went back inside to get some paper towels. Why would anyone dislike her enough to leave dead animals at her door?

She knew why. To some of the people in Prescott, Abby represented change. And those people didn't like change. She tore off a few paper towels, and then a few more. She wet half of them, squeezing out the excess water. She got another grocery bag, and carried everything back to the front door. At that point, the blood was tacky. The dry paper towels removed most of it. No matter how hard she scrubbed with the wet ones, the stained didn't come clean. This made her cry even more. She felt the tears on her cheeks, cold thanks to the cool fall air. She scrubbed and scrubbed, the paper towels disintegrating, her fingertips becoming raw. Once she realized that no amount of scraping was going to remove the blood completely, she jammed the wet paper towels into the plastic bag along with the dry ones. These, too, she carried to the trash bin.

All the way up the stairs, down the hall, and into her apartment, she cried. Then, she shut the door and locked it behind her. That's when she got angry. How dare someone do that? Not just leave bloody animals at her doorstep, but kill three innocent rabbits? How awful. How terrible did a person have to be to do something like that?

Well, she thought as she washed her hands in the hottest water she could stand, she wouldn't let anyone intimidate her. She would carry on. She would keep doing exactly what she was doing. She didn't care how some evil guy felt about it. She would go for her run. She would come back. She would do Sunday morning spa day. And Monday, she would go back to work.

That's when her phone rang. Despite her resolve not to be scared, she jumped.

It was Trace. Typically, she didn't answer the phone when she was upset. But his voice was all she wanted to hear. And somehow, he used that voice to talk her into going for a ride.

She didn't even need an hour to get ready. But, she did need to run to the store and buy a new doormat. And bleach. She couldn't leave that bloodstain out there for her little neighbor to find.

Her parents had taught her to move about the world with confidence. And that's what she did. She locked up the apartment and looked right, then left, as she walked back to the stairs. She activated her sixth sense, hoping it would alert her if anyone was lurking around.

But she made sure that, if someone was, they would see she wasn't afraid.

———

TRACE WAS WAITING when Abby pulled up. He met her as she parked, and as soon as she stepped out of the truck, he wrapped his arms around her. She could have cried with relief. But she managed to hold it together. She wasn't quite ready to be that vulnerable.

She noticed he didn't ask how she was, or how her morning was. He led her to the horses and said, "Ready?"

They headed out in a different direction than they had the last time. As the horses walked toward the edge of the corral, Trace said, "I thought we would head east this time, so you could see the other side of the property."

"Sounds good," she said, and she was surprised to hear that her voice sounded calm.

Once they were out of the corral, Trace brought the horses up to a trot, and then a gentle run. Abby leaned forward, letting her body fall into rhythm with the horse's. She took in the rolling green hills, dotted with scrub oak and the occasional cottonwood tree. The clouds in the blue sky were so bright, they were almost blinding.

She could feel her stress melting away.

The rolling hills of Williamson Valley stretched out ahead of them, wide open.

The farther they got from the ranch, the more Abby felt like she could finally breathe. The horses ran side by side, the sound of their hooves so loud conversation was impossible. But Abby didn't mind. In fact, simply riding alongside Trace was as healing as alone time would be. Even though he hadn't asked her what was wrong, she could tell he sensed her stress … and she was beyond grateful he wasn't pressuring her to talk about it.

She glanced over at him as they rode, taking a couple of seconds to admire his strong jawline, the rippling muscles in his forearms. He turned his head, then, and flashed her an I-caught-you-looking smile. He returned his attention to the path before them, and they kept riding.

Being horseback — the rhythm of running, the focus required — had always been hypnotic for Abby. It forced her mind to clear. Nothing else in her life did that. It had been far too long since she rode regularly.

On the horizon, Abby could see another ranch property coming into view, which meant they would have to turn around soon. Disappointment crept in. She could keep riding for hours. But then logic took over. They'd been riding for so long, and they still had to go all the way back. Which meant she had time to enjoy the ride — to savor being completely in sync with the sexy cowboy next to her.

In sync.

A delicious shiver ran through her body as an image of the two of them, skin on skin between the sheets, came to mind. Trace pulled his horse to a trot, and then a walk. And, perhaps not surprisingly, he was giving her a look that said he knew what she was thinking. But that was impossible. Wasn't it?

"Guess we should head back," he said.

Again, that feeling of disappointment swept in. She wanted to ask whether they *had* to head back, or if she could stay longer. At least, on or around the Mint Creek Ranch with Trace, she felt safe. No one was leaving dead rabbits on Trace's doorstep.

As one, the two horses picked up speed as they headed back home.

Abby wanted to pull on the reins, to delay the end of this perfectly meditative moment. But all good things come to an end. Without warning, she felt the sting of tears in her eyes. The scene in front of her blurred. She knew it was ridiculous to cry over the end of a simple horseback ride. But she didn't want to say goodbye to such a beautiful moment.

CHAPTER FOURTEEN

TRACE

COMING to the end of their ride, Trace was proud of himself. When he called Abby, he could tell something was bothering her. At first, he'd thought it had something to do with him, or with *them*. But when she'd agreed to come to the ranch and looked so relieved to see him, he decided it must be something else. And he wanted so badly to know what.

If there was one thing he'd learned from working with horses, though, it was that when someone seemed uneasy, the best thing to do was give her a little space. Let her come to you. No matter how much you might want to solve the problem for her, you almost always couldn't. So, when Abby showed up at the Mint Creek Ranch and didn't immediately spill her guts, Trace knew a ride was exactly the right activity. There was nothing like being out in the sunshine, with the fall leaves changing, to get your mind off just about anything.

As they rode, he could feel the tension slipping away. Abby's face relaxed, and her shoulders, too. At one point, he caught her looking at him, and if he wasn't mistaken, she looked … dreamy. Yes, that's the word he'd use.

He thought she was enjoying herself, and the disappointment on her expression when it came time to turn around proved it. He felt it, too. He didn't want their time together to come to an end. But it was the weekend, and she probably had things to do.

The horses ran all the way to the barn. When they stopped, Abby said, "Apparently, that's what I needed."

"Feel better?" There. He'd let her know he could tell something was bothering her, without pushing.

"Lots. Thank you."

That answer surprised him. He'd expected her to deny anything was wrong.

"Want to help me put up the horses?"

They dismounted. Abby ran her hand down her horse's neck. "I would love to. I'm not quite ready to say goodbye to this beauty."

The horse nuzzled Abby's neck, and she laughed.

"She likes you, too," Trace said. "Come on in."

They led the horses inside, and the air shifted. Something felt off in there — Trace could feel it. And even if he couldn't, he could smell it.

"Something's wrong," he said to Abby, and she said, "I'm fine."

The misunderstanding would have been funny under other circumstances, and even though his heart was starting to pound harder and faster, he took a moment to turn to Abby and grab her hand. "You haven't been yourself this morning, but that's not what I'm talking about. Something's wrong, here. With the horses."

Abby surprised him by taking the lead, walking quickly toward the row of stalls. He caught up with her in a couple of strides, and they both looked over the half-door into Whistler's stall.

The horse trembled. When Trace said his name, he took a few dancing steps toward them, then away.

"Come here, boy," Trace said. As he looked over the horse, he was barely aware of Abby leaving his side. Whistler came close again, and when he put his hand on his neck, he noticed his fur felt damp. "Shit," Trace said.

Horses didn't get ordinary viruses like humans. There was no reason Whistler should be jumpy and sweaty. As he racked his brain to figure out what the issue could be, he heard Abby's voice. "Trace."

In that one word, he heard a warning: *Brace yourself.*

"Be right back," he said to Whistler. Abby stood outside the next stall, her hands on top of the half-door, her body canted forward. As if she wanted to go in, but —

"Something's wrong," she said. "It's not just Whistler."

Sure enough, the two horses in that stall, Cinnamon and Moonlight, were acting the way Whistler was. Jumpy. Nervous.

"Has this ever happened before?" Abby said.

Shaking his head, Trace said, "Only in dramatic movies. They've been poisoned."

"Call the vet."

Abby's voice sounded so sure, commanding. There he was, panicking, floundering, not quite sure what to do, and she was taking charge. She was right, too. He had to call the vet. He pulled out his phone and walked back over to Whistler's stall. He was among the steadiest horses on the ranch, and of all of them, he felt safe going into his stall with him. The vet, Mitchell Jameson, picked up right away.

"Trace."

Trace and Mitchell went to school together, from preschool through high school. Usually when Trace called, Mitchell had some kind of funny greeting. But it was Sunday, and Mitchell likely knew Trace wouldn't call on a Sunday unless it was an emergency. So Trace abandoned pleasantries and said, "Can you come on over to the ranch? Something's wrong with the horses. I think they've been poisoned."

"I'll be there in drive time."

On one hand, the conversation brought relief. Mitchell, and help, were on the way. On the other hand, Mitchell saying he'd be there in drive time scared Trace even more than he already was. It was definitely an emergency.

"It's all of them," Abby said, coming into the stall to stand next to him. "What's the likelihood they all got into something poison? Like a plant or something?"

"Slim to none," Trace said. He took off his hat and scrubbed a hand over his face. "Once, when I was a kid, one of my horses got into a poisonous plant. We were out on the trail, and she started eating it. I let her, because I thought horses were smarter than that. I figured they had some sort of built-in alert system that would stop them from eating something dangerous. But no. They're like dogs that way."

He gestured for Abby to follow him, and he headed for the barn's entrance. "By the time we got back to the barn, she was throwing up. We called the vet, and he took care of it. She ended up being fine."

The two of them were outside the barn by then, waiting for Mitchell. Trace didn't realize he was pacing until Abby joined him, walking back and forth with him, matching every stride. Feeling incredibly grateful for her presence, Trace took her hand.

"You'd better believe Cody, Sawyer, and I got a big lesson on plants that are toxic to horses. I don't think I've ever seen a poisoned horse since. But now. All of them. Someone did this."

The sound of tires on gravel ended the conversation there. Together, Trace and Abby approached Mitchell's truck. He got out and shook Trace's hand, and when Trace introduced Abby, he said, "I know who you are."

His tone was serious, which made Trace's hackles rise, but then he added, "I'm glad you're keeping Trace company."

Mitchell walked around to the bed of his truck and pulled out his bag. They began walking to the barn. "Tell me everything. What happened?"

"Everything was fine this morning. I went for a ride earlier, then came back and did some work around the barn. Then Abby came over, about eleven, and we took off for another ride." He glanced at his watch. "We were gone for maybe two hours. When we got back, we noticed Whistler didn't seem like himself. I called you right away. After we hung up, we checked on the other horses and saw that they're all sick."

Mitchell's mouth was set in a grim line, which made Trace nervous. He was a jokester, a witty comment or comeback always at the ready, even when he was at the ranch on business. At the entrance to Whistler's stall, he paused to watch him. As he had earlier, he stepped in place, seeming to have too much energy and no other way to displace it. When he saw Mitchell, he came over to bump his shoulder with his nose.

"Hey, boy," he said. "Is it all right if I come in there with you for a minute?"

The horse took a couple of steps back. Trace held his breath while Mitchell examined him. He checked his eyes, his mouth, his throat, his belly.

"This horse is Sawyer's, isn't it?"

Trace nodded, snakes writhing in his stomach. Again, Abby seemed to intuit his stress, and she put her hand on his lower back to calm him.

"You'd better call him down here," Mitchell said. "I'm going to have to run some tests. Might as well call Cody while you're at it, if they're all sick, like you said."

Trace swallowed against the lump in his throat and nodded again. "They're already on their way. I texted them as soon as we got back here."

———

ABBY

TESSA AND MONTANA came with Cody and Sawyer, and they seemed as baffled as Trace and Abby about the source of the poisoning. Abby stuck close to Trace for the next hour as the veterinarian, Mitchell, drew blood and started IVs on the horses, then ran the blood to the lab and returned to monitor them.

As calm, cool, and collected as he usually was, Trace was beside himself with worry. Abby understood. She'd been the same way when her dad was injured in the accident. When the thing you love most in the world is in danger, it's almost impossible to stay calm.

At one point, mid-afternoon, Trace took both of Abby's hands in his and said, "Now that the whole crew's here, you don't have to stay. Why don't you go home, get some rest?"

But Abby shook her head. "I'm staying."

She wanted to say more: *I wouldn't leave you. I couldn't. I know what this is like.*

But she didn't. It seemed Trace knew, though. He squeezed her hands and leaned forward to give her a kiss on the cheek. "Thank you. It means a lot."

A little while later, Mitchell's cell phone rang. "It's the lab," he said.

Everyone went silent as he answered.

"Dr. Jameson here." The caller said something, and Mitchell swore. "That's what I suspected. Thanks for letting me know."

He hung up and looked at each of the people standing before him, one at a time. Finally, he said, "Rat poison."

Trace, Cody, and Sawyer looked at each other, eyebrows raised, as if asking each other whether they'd accidentally left out poison. They all shook their heads.

"I'm pretty sure my dad banned rat poison that time Trace's horse got so sick. Remember? That's when we got the first set of barn cats."

"So if none of us left out the poison, how did they get it?"

"The answer to that question is obviously very important," said Mitchell. "But the more urgent matter is that we need to get all of these horses on vitamin K as soon as we can. I don't have enough here to treat all of them, so I'm going have to run back to the office."

"What can we do in the meantime?" Abby asked.

"Do your best to keep them calm. I'll be right back."

The group dispersed, and Abby followed Trace. He put fresh hay on the floor of one stall, so she did the same in another. He grabbed a brush and ran it over the side of one of the horses, so she did the same. Before long, Mitchell returned and went from horse to horse, hooking up vitamin K drips. Once all the horses were receiving the medicine, Mitchell called to the others. They gathered near the entrance to the barn.

"Fortunately, you found them quickly," Mitchell said. "I think you caught it in time. It may not be easy, but everyone should recover. If I know you all, you'll be here all night."

Trace nodded.

"I'm going to head home, get a little dinner, maybe play a board game with my kids," Mitchell said. "And then I'm going to come back. Check on everything."

Trace shook his hand. "Thank you so much for coming, man. I wouldn't trust anyone but you."

"Anytime. I'm glad we caught it when we did." Before he went out the door, he stopped and turned around. "Now that we know everyone is going to be okay, it's time to start thinking about the answer to that question you asked earlier. How did they all get into poison?"

A moment before, the mood had been lighter, buoyed by the relief that the horses were going to be okay. After Mitchell's comment, though, the atmosphere felt somber again.

He tipped his hat and left, and Abby broke the ensuing silence. "Well, no one ever figured out a problem on an empty stomach. Why don't I run into town to get dinner?"

"You don't have to —" Cody started, but Abby waved him off. "I know I don't. But it would make me feel useful. And you can't deny you're hungry. We can't have a bunch of hangry men staying up with the horses all night."

No one protested that.

"Want me to go with you?" Montana asked.

"No, but thank you," Abby said. "Stay with the horses. And Sawyer."

"I'll walk you to your car." Trace followed Abby out, and before she could climb into the driver seat, he wrapped her in a big hug. "Thank you so much for being here for me today," he said. "I don't know what I would've done if you weren't. I was about to lose my mind but somehow, you calmed me down."

Squeezing him around the waist, Abby said, "You're welcome. I'm glad I was here, too."

She watched Trace walk back into the barn and called in a pizza order before leaving. As she drove, Abby let her mind return to the thought she'd pushed away throughout the day.

The horses ingesting rat poison wasn't an accident, or coincidence. Just like the dead rabbits on her doorstep weren't an accident or coincidence. Someone had poisoned the Mint Creek Ranch horses just like someone had killed those rabbits and left them for Abby to find. It seemed impossible that it wasn't the same person.

Who would *do* that? What would motivate someone have to do such horrible things?

Abby didn't know for sure, but she had some ideas and she vowed to find out. In that moment, Abby thought, maybe she should tell Trace about the rabbits. If the two were related, they could figure it out together. But if she told him about the rabbits, he would be worried about her *and* his horses. And that wasn't fair to him. For the time being, anyway, she decided to keep it to herself.

———

Trace

AFTER ABBY RETURNED with the pizza, it was a waiting game. Trace hadn't wanted to admit how hungry he was. He didn't want Abby to feel obligated to get them food, and none of the Mint Creek Ranch boys would leave the horses. But after he ate — if scarfing down half a pizza in what felt like thirty seconds could qualify as an activity as classy as eating — he felt much better.

Less shaky, less jumpy.

Abby looked exhausted. Her hair in a messy bun, her eyes red, Trace wouldn't be surprised if she fell asleep standing up. All he wanted was to comfort her in the same way she'd comforted him.

"You don't have to stay," he told her for the twentieth time.

They sat on the floor in the entrance of the barn, backs against the wall, shoulders touching. Cody, Sawyer, Tessa, and Montana were at the far end of the building, outside the last stall.

"I know," Abby said. "But I want to. I know you have Cody and Sawyer, so our situations aren't *exactly* the same. But when my dad had his accident a few years ago, I felt really alone. The crew checked in on me. Some of their wives called me. They brought me food. They always asked what I needed, or what I wanted. Or how they could help. And I didn't realize until later that I couldn't put into words what I really needed, which was someone to be with me."

The emotion in her voice had Trace reaching for her hand, wishing he'd known her then so he could have done that. "I appreciate you being here for me."

She leaned her head on his shoulder. They sat there in silence for a while, and then Abby spoke again. "Any idea how the horses got poisoned?"

Trace sighed. "I've been thinking about it all day. And we talked about it when you went to get the pizza. It doesn't make sense. I've lived here most of my life, and I've never had any real beef with anyone. At least, not a beef big enough for something like this."

"Well, I hope you get to the bottom of this."

Trace nodded. "Me, too."

———

ABBY

ALL NIGHT, Abby remained by Trace's side. She insisted on taking rotations, hoping to let the others get as much rest as possible. The hours passed, and the horses seemed to improve, calming down and eventually sleeping. Abby was surprised they were able to rest with all the medical equipment in their stalls.

The vet said it could take a while for them to get back to normal. On one of her rounds at four in the morning, she crept into the stall where one of the horses, Lyla, lay on the floor. She knelt on the floor next to her and stroked her cheek, talking to her quietly. "I'm so sorry someone did this to you. You're such a good girl. I hope you get to feeling better."

Trace's voice startled her. "Oh, you're talking to the horses. You're officially a horse person."

She looked back at him then, and the way he was looking at her made her breath catch. No one had ever looked at her that way before. Something inside her unraveled, and she realized, then and there, that she would do anything for him.

———

TRACE

JUST AFTER DAWN, Mitchell came back, six hot coffees in a couple of cardboard carriers.

"I can't thank you enough," Trace told him, accepting the coffees with a deep sense of gratitude. "If you hadn't come, I hate to think what would've happened."

"So do I, to be honest," Mitchell said. "Have you given any more thought to who might be behind this?"

"We have. We'll get to the bottom of it, although, as much as I want to know, I also don't want to know."

"I get that," Mitchell said. "Somebody's got it out for you."

Acknowledging it hurt. "I need to think about it with a clear head, though."

Cody materialized behind him. "Thanks for the coffee, Mitchell," he said. He turned to Trace and said, "This coffee should get us through the next hour, right? My parents will come spell us then. They said they could hang out until noon or so, so we could get some sleep."

"That's great," Trace said, and his body practically melted at the idea of climbing into bed. He was literally weak in the knees with gratitude. Bed sounded like a slice of pure heaven.

He spent the next hour making the rounds with Mitchell, and

again, Abby was right there with him. By the time they had seen all the horses, Trace saw Cody's parents driving up on their Ranger. They all met outside the barn door, and Cody's mom, Elaine, hugged each of them. She gave Abby's shoulders an extra squeeze, and Trace knew she was issuing a silent thanks.

"We can hold down the fort here," Elaine said. "Why don't you all go on home, get in a good nap. We can stay until noon or so. That gives you a good five or six hours."

Abby started walking toward her car. Trace found the thought of her leaving unbearable. He called out a quick goodbye to Cody, Tessa, Sawyer, and Montana, and then he caught up with Abby. "Why don't you stay?"

"With the horses?"

"With me."

So much passed between them in that moment. Abby's answer, though, was simple: "Yes."

"We can take my truck," he said.

The moment both doors closed, Trace let out a huge sigh. Abby reached over and grabbed his hand. "Rough night."

"That's an understatement. I've never been so scared." He couldn't believe he was admitting that, but around Abby, he felt compelled to be one hundred percent honest.

"That *was* really scary," she said. "I'm so glad they're okay."

"Me, too. Thank you again for sticking around. I can't put into words how much it meant."

Their eyes met when she said, "Anytime. Really."

Trace was too tired to process all the feelings zapping back and forth between them. He put the truck in gear and drove back to his place. Inside, he shut and locked the front door. The house was as he'd left it the morning before. His coffee cup and breakfast plate sat in the sink. The newspaper lay on the kitchen counter. He took Abby's hand. "Come to bed with me."

She let him lead her to the bedroom, and, as tired as he was, when they both took off their shoes and stripped out of their jeans, he couldn't stop himself from feeling aroused. He pulled back the covers on what he suddenly thought of as her side of the bed, and gestured for her to get in.

She laid down and groaned. "This feels like heaven after the last twenty hours."

The rapture in her voice made him even more aroused. He went around to his side of the bed and slipped between the sheets. They turned toward each other. Trace tucked a lock of hair behind her ear and, his hand still wrapped around the back of her neck, he kissed her gently. "I can't believe I'm saying this, now that I finally have you in my bed, but I am *so* tired."

Her laughter in response unlocked something deep inside him.

"I can't believe it, either. And I can't believe that I'm about to say that I think we should get some sleep."

"The next time I get you in bed, we won't be sleeping."

Her eyes already closed, Abby said, "Is that a promise?"

"You bet it is."

———

ABBY

WHEN TRACE'S alarm went off at half past eleven, Abby was pleased to find herself in the same position she'd been in when they fell asleep: her head was on Trace's chest and his arms were wrapped around her. She would love to wake up like that every day.

He turned off his alarm and kissed the top of her head. "I don't think I've slept that hard since I was a little kid."

Abby snuggled in deeper. "That was really nice."

"I wouldn't mind doing it again."

"Me, neither. Only, next time, let's hope it doesn't follow a traumatic event."

"Let's," Trace said. He stretched. "I'd better go down and check on the horses. Relieve Elaine and Tom. I'll totally understand if you want to head home. I don't want to take up your whole weekend."

Wanting to prolong the moment for as long as possible, Abby stretched, too, letting her body press against his. With a familiarity that tugged at her heartstrings and made her want to straddle him then and there, he ran a hand along her side, knee to hip. "Keep doing that, and I'll never be able to leave this bed."

"That's the idea," she said, bringing her lips to his.

The kiss was long and deep, intense. It was sweet and desperate. His hand moved from her waist to her breasts, and back again, and she groaned, her body tingling. Slowly, he eased himself away, climbed out of bed.

"I'd love nothing more than to stay here in bed with you, all afternoon. But when I do take you to bed, like that, we're going to take our time."

With that — a statement that would have Abby thinking about sex with Trace for the rest of the weekend — he went into the bathroom.

The only thing to do from there was to get dressed herself.

CHAPTER FIFTEEN

"ABBY GO HOME?" Sawyer greeted Trace when he returned to the barn.

"Yeah. I kept telling her she didn't have to stay, but she insisted."

"That was pretty nice, man."

"I know it was," Trace said.

"She really likes you."

"I like her, too."

"Like, *like* like?"

Still smiling, Trace rolled his eyes. "This is like when we were in high school, man. Yeah, *like* like."

"Is it serious?" Sawyer wanted to know.

"Well, let's put it this way. I invited her into my bed and all we did was sleep. And cuddle."

Sawyer's eyes glinted with humor. "Like, *cuddle* cuddle? Or, actually cuddle?"

Trace gave Sawyer a friendly punch on the arm. "Where's Cody?"

"Inside already, with his parents."

"Why aren't we in there?"

"Because I had to give you shit about Abby."

"Well, now that we're done with that," Trace said, "let's go."

Inside the barn, Cody stood with his parents. They spoke quietly, and opened up their little circle to let Trace and Sawyer join them.

"Everything's still fine," Tom said, but the way his jaw worked implied otherwise.

"Then why do you look like you want to lambast someone?" Sawyer said.

"Because I do, darn it!" Tom said, causing the others to jump. "The horses are fine, for the moment. But who's to say something like this, or worse, doesn't happen again?"

———

FIRST THING MONDAY MORNING, Trace headed down to the barn to meet Cody and Sawyer and relieve Tom, who'd volunteered to stand guard overnight.

While the air was cool and smelled of smoke coming from nearby chimneys, the sun pooled against the east side of the barn, and the heat radiated off it, which meant the afternoon would turn warm.

Sawyer and Cody weren't there yet, so Trace let himself in. Tom, his gnarled hands wrapped around his rifle, leaned back in one chair with his feet propped on another. For the first time ever, Tom looked frail. Trace wondered if they should have left him alone all night.

"Morning," he said when Trace walked in. A couple of the horses nickered in greeting, too. A few of them came to their stall doors, ears pricked.

"Morning," Trace said, as much to the horses as to Tom. "I gather it was a quiet night?"

"It was," Tom said. "Everything's as it should be. I'd keep an eye on Old Red. He still seems a bit anxious to me."

Trace nodded. "Could be because you were here all night. That's unusual."

"True. Well, I'll leave you young 'uns to it. This old man's not cut out for all-nighters anymore. I've got to go home and get some sleep."

Trace shook Tom's hand and followed him outside, where he leaned against the warm side of the barn and closed his eyes to think. If they didn't get to the bottom of this mystery, he thought, more than the horses would be at risk. Despite the warmth, Trace shivered.

Cody's voice startled him, making him jump. "Saw my dad heading out. He barely managed a wave. I guess we need to hire an overnight security team. I woke up in a panic just now, thinking that we shouldn't have left my dad here alone."

"Great minds," Trace said, waving at Sawyer as he pulled into the driveway and got out of his truck. "I'll make some phone calls today, get someone over here tonight."

Cody nodded.

"Morning, fellas," Sawyer said, tipping his hat. "I heard you saying you'll make some calls to get us security. Sounds like a great idea. So, next step. We've got to figure out who did this."

"Any ideas?" Cody asked.

"Actually, yes." The thought struck Trace as if from out of nowhere. "I can't believe I haven't thought of this until now. I guess I was so worried about the horses. But I had a visit from Hector Inman last week. He wanted me to sign this petition."

"Ah, yes," Cody said. "The petition to get the City Council to reconsider Abby's zoning permit."

"Yes," Trace said. "How did you know?"

"Ronnie Sunshine," Cody said.

Trace pictured Ronnie's arrogant face, and sneered.

"I know," Cody said. "He came to me with it a few days ago. I told him to go to hell. Those two are thick as thieves."

"I suppose I shouldn't feel left out," Sawyer said. "But nobody asked me."

"Yeah, dummy," Cody said. "Because you already bought property. You're not going to sign the petition."

"You're right," Sawyer said. "But do you think Hector — I mean, we've known him since we were kids — would he go so far as to poison the horses?"

Trace shrugged. "Never know. He seemed pretty emotional when he was here. Hands shaking and everything."

"We all know how emotional the Williamson Valley men can get over a zoning change." Sawyer elbowed Trace, who elbowed him back. "Shut up, man."

"Maybe we should go over and have a little talk with Hector, though," Cody said. "Feel him out. See who else is gathering petitions. Get a few names."

"Play hardball with the guy," Sawyer said, cracking his knuckles.

"With all that knuckle cracking, you're going to scare the information right out of him," Trace said, rolling his eyes. "I do think that's a good place to start, though. Should we head over there, first thing after lunch?"

Cody and Sawyer nodded.

"That will give me time to make those calls, get us some security for the next week, at least."

"Sounds good," Sawyer said. "Why don't you go on home and work on that. Cody and I can take care of feeding the horses this morning."

"All right," Trace said. "Thanks."

"Oh, I almost forgot," Sawyer said. "I'm going to send you a picture I took."

Trace could see mischief in Sawyer's eyes.

He was walking through his front door by the time the picture came in, and it took his breath away. Sawyer had taken the picture the night before, in the barn.

In it, Trace and Abby sat side-by-side on the floor. They were in twin poses: legs stretched out in front of them, crossed at the ankles. They leaned up against each other, shoulder to shoulder, arm to arm. Abby's head rested on Trace's shoulder, and his cheek rested on top of her head. They were both asleep, their hands entwined.

Looking at the picture did something to Trace. It made him realize, then and there, that he would do anything to make Abby his. Forever.

———

"I'LL DRIVE," Trace said when the three men assembled after lunch to head over to the Bright Moon Ranch. "I don't want to listen to your music."

"You always listen to old-man music," Sawyer said.

"It's called the classics," Cody said, in a perfect imitation of Trace's drawl.

Still, though, Sawyer, and Cody headed toward Trace's truck.

"I've got shotgun," Cody said.

Sawyer punched him in the arm. The drive would take less than five minutes, but calling shotgun was an old habit. Once they were all in the truck, Trace pushed the preset button for the classic country station. Sawyer groaned, but it wasn't long before he was singing along.

"So, do you think we should have some sort of plan?" Cody said. "You know, a good cop, bad cop routine or something?"

"You've always been Hector's favorite," Sawyer said to Cody.

"True," Trace said. "I hear that whenever we're on tour, he's got the loudest voice in the bar, bragging that he knows you."

At one point in his life, Trace had been jealous of Cody's fame. But after everything that went down with Cody and his sister, Trace realized he preferred to be out of the spotlight.

Within a minute, they were pulling up at Bright Moon Ranch. Hector's old truck was parked in front of the house. In the distance, his Ranger made its way across one end of the field.

"I guess we'd better drive out to the field," Sawyer said. "That's Hector driving the Ranger. I can recognize his profile, even from this distance."

Cody made a sound, something between a snort and a laugh. "They say your nose never stops growing."

"Well, I'd say in Hector's case, that's true," Sawyer said.

Trace shook his head and drove down the long gravel driveway to the edge of the field.

The three of them got out and stood next to the fence, propping their elbows on the railing, waiting for Hector to spot them. It was clear when he did. He stopped the Ranger and raised a hand in greeting. He made a wide turn and came toward them, at a snail's pace.

"Walking might have been faster," Sawyer said out of the side of his mouth.

Trace smiled. "Might have been."

Eventually, the old rancher pulled the Ranger up alongside the fence. Trace could've sworn he heard Hector's bones creak as he got out of the driver's seat. Despite the fact that suspenders held his pants up, Hector hiked up his waistband as he made his way over. He wore an old straw hat, which frayed at the crown, and he tipped it at the Mint Creek Ranch boys. *Always the gentleman*, Trace thought. *Could he be capable of killing livestock?*

"Howdy, fellas. What can I do for you?"

Trace cleared his throat. "You came over to my house the other day. Asked me to sign a petition."

Hector's eyes glinted. "Something tells me you're not here to tell me you've changed your mind."

Trace shook his head. "No, sir, we're not."

"That's a damn shame," Hector said.

Cody took over. "Ronnie Sunshine was over at my place, too. Who else you got collecting signatures?"

"Well." With his gnarled fingers, Hector removed the cigar from his mouth. He licked his lips. "There's a few of us."

Out of the corner of his eye, Trace saw both Cody and Sawyer widen their stances and cross their arms.

"Who else?" Cody asked.

Hector shrugged. "Like I said, there's a few of us."

"So," Cody said, and Trace could feel the anger coming off his friend like heat waves, "you trying to be obstinate? Or do you not want to tell us?"

"Well, if we're being honest, I can't see as why it matters to you all."

Cody opened his mouth, inhaled, and leaned forward all at the same time. Trace breathed a relieved sigh when Sawyer put a hand on Cody's chest.

Seeing this, Hector rushed to give a more suitable answer. "Well, you got Ronnie Sunshine, you know that."

"Tell us something we don't know," Sawyer said, his voice deadly.

Hector held up both hands. "All right, all right. You got the Hernandezes, the Crenshaws, the Lees, the Tysons. To name a few."

Trace recognized all the names, which he'd expected. But he couldn't think of a single person on that list to would want to hurt his horses. They were old Prescott, all of them. And if there was something old Prescott loved as much as the town itself, it was horses. All animals, really.

"That'll do," Cody said.

"That's all you wanted?"

Trace looked at Cody and Sawyer, who each gave him a single nod.

"That's all we wanted."

"Thanks, Hector," Cody practically spit, obviously still seething.

The three of them turned to leave. They hadn't gone more than a couple of steps when Hector said, "Wait."

———

ABBY

MONDAY AFTERNOON, Abby's phone rang as she was heading back to her apartment. A feeling of excitement rose up inside her when she saw Trace's name on the screen. She couldn't remember the last time she'd had a physical reaction to a phone call from a man ... a little thrill. She liked it.

"Hey," she said.

"Hey, yourself," he said.

Again, her body responded. She felt all warm and tingly.

"What are you up to?" At a red light for the moment, Abby noticed the golden late-afternoon sun shining through the leaves on the big trees that lined the streets.

"I was just planning our evening," Trace said. She could hear something in his voice. Was it apprehension, maybe? Anticipation?

"Oh, yeah?" She definitely heard anticipation in *her* voice.

"Yeah." He cleared his throat. Was he nervous? "I want you to come for dinner. And stay."

"Stay? Like, for dessert?"

The sound of Trace's laugh, low and deep and rumbly, came through Abby's earpiece. The light turned green.

"I could arrange dessert," he said.

Abby practically melted on the spot. She wasn't sure whether they were talking about dessert or *dessert*, but she wouldn't turn down either one. "I'd like that." She stopped at another red light. The world outside her car looked so cheerful, picturesque. The sky was such a vibrant blue, the wispy fall clouds painted in broad strokes across it.

Trace said, "I'm asking you to spend the night."

Oh. A bolt of heat rushed through Abby's body and landed between her legs. *That* dessert.

"I'd like that."

She heard the smile in Trace's voice when he said, "Me too. What time would you like to eat?"

The light turned green, and before Abby put her foot on the gas pedal, she looked at her clock. A quarter after three. She might generally need an hour to get ready. But tonight, she was going to get *ready*.

"Eat around six? I'll be there at five-thirty for happy hour."

Again, Trace chuckled. Again, Abby found herself profoundly aroused.

"See you then," he said.
"See you then."

CHAPTER SIXTEEN

AT FIVE-THIRTY SHARP, Abby knocked on Trace's front door. The smell of something cooking greeted her when she stepped inside. Trace closed the door behind her and then leaned in for a long, deep kiss. Because Abby had spent the past two hours preparing her body for this eventuality, the contact immediately turned her on. She ran her fingers through his hair and let her hands rest at the back of his neck. She took the kiss even deeper, immersing herself in the delicious sensation of the man before her.

A fizzing sound came from the kitchen, and Trace groaned. "Soup's boiling over."

Abby followed him in and sat on a stool at the counter, admiring the way he filled out his jeans.

"How was your day?" he asked while he stirred.

"Pretty much business as usual," Abby said. "Which I consider a great day, by the way."

Trace gave her a sidelong glance. "Easy to please?"

She smiled. "You could say that. Also, William stopped by with baby Freddie. He had a pediatrician's appointment and said he figured the guys would skin his hide if they saw him drive by without stopping. He's probably right. And you should have seen them. The most sentimental group of honorary uncles you could ask for."

"How does he look?"

Trace had gotten a bottle of wine out of a cabinet next to the stove, and he held it up, eyebrows raised. Abby nodded, and he retrieved a couple of glasses and an opener.

"William? Tired, like any new dad."

"I meant the baby. Freddie."

"Oh." Abby laughed and accepted the glass Trace handed her. "He looks adorable. Obviously. Pretty much the same as he looked when we stopped by the other day, but a little less pink. She carried him in in his car seat, and he slept the whole time."

Abby took a sip of her wine. "How about you? How was your day? Wait! Before you answer, look at me, chatting away while you do all the cooking. Give me a job or something."

"I don't mind," he said. "I like cooking for you." The tone of his voice when he said it — husky — sent a shiver of anticipation up her spine. "If you insist on a job, there is a bunch of carrots in the fridge. And some radishes. You could slice those up for the salad."

"Cutting board?"

Trace pointed to a narrow cabinet next to the oven. From there, Abby pulled a big wooden board that looked like it had seen more than its fair share of meals. The idea that Trace was now sharing it with her made Abby smile. She set it on the counter and went to the fridge.

She wasn't surprised to find it clean and organized.

Suddenly, Trace was behind her, his hands on her waist, his mouth on her neck.

"I can't tell you what it does to me to see you standing there, looking through my fridge."

Chills made their way over every inch of Abby's skin. Trace's hand moved up her torso. She expected her voice to sound croaky when she said, "Yeah?" but it came out exactly the way she felt: sultry, sexy.

"Oh, yeah."

His breath in her ear, his hands sliding up her torso to cup her breasts, nearly took her breath away. "And I'm going to show you. Later. After we eat. Because I'm starving. Hand me the chicken broth, will you?"

Even that sounded unreasonably sexual, and by the time Abby

located it, grabbed it, and turned around to face him, her body was throbbing. She kissed him, hoping to convey how very much she wanted him. He responded like he felt it, with a guttural groan.

Abby smiled against his lips. "I'm hungry, too."

The refrigerator chimed, letting them know it had been open too long.

"Then I guess you'd better get to those carrots and radishes. And shut the refrigerator when you're done." He brought his lips to hers once more. She felt him wrapping her hair around his fist and giving it a gentle tug. His lips moved down to her throat, her collarbone.

Her need for him became more urgent. She could hardly resist the desire to unfasten his belt and put her hands on him. But she was hungry. For food. And besides, if they ate first, they could lay together all night. She slid her hands around to grasp his butt, which was solid muscle. His hands were on her breasts again, his thumbs lazily brushing over her nipples.

She groaned. "I'm afraid we're not going to make it to dinner."

Trace brought his hands to her waist and rested his forehead on hers. "You know what's better than the meal?"

Abby shook her head, licked her lips.

"The anticipation."

With that, Trace returned to the stove, where he gave her one more look over his shoulder before pouring the broth into the pot. Abby retrieved the carrots and radishes and returned to the cutting board. She washed the vegetables, and as she began to chop, she said, "So. Tell me about your day."

Trace told her about hiring security for the barn, at least for the time being. Again, she wondered if she should tell him about the rabbits. And again, she decided not to. She didn't want to worry him.

"Other than that, it was a normal day. Nothing too noteworthy."

Abby found that she enjoyed this rhythm: the talking, cutting, stirring, sipping, kissing. Why had she ever thought she disliked this man?

———

TRACE

THE NEXT MORNING, Trace woke before Abby did, his body attuned to the sun rising. He figured he could sneak out and feed the horses, then come back and make Abby breakfast.

Before he got up, though, he took some time to admire her in the brightening light of the sunrise. Her long, thick eyelashes cast shadows on her cheeks. Her lips, slightly open, looked perfectly kissable.

Looking at her lips made him picture them wrapped around him the night before, and that made him remember what he'd felt when he looked up at her as she straddled him. And, naturally, remembering those things made him want to do them again.

But if he gave in to the urge now, to wake her up and have his way with her, his hands on her skin, still warm from being under the sheets, he would feel rushed. The horses were waiting. The scent of coffee made its way into the bedroom, and the coffeemaker beeped to signal it was done brewing. So, with quite a bit of reluctance, Trace slipped out of bed and pulled on his underwear before going into the kitchen.

He poured the coffee into a mug, inhaling the steam. As much as he was anxious to get down to the horses and back, his mind wouldn't stop playing the film reel of the night before. He was still smiling when he heard footsteps behind him. Abby's bare feet whispered on the wood floor, but her voice sounded sure and sexy when she said, "Good morning."

He smiled at her over his shoulder — he didn't want to turn around and reveal that he'd been having anything but pure thoughts about her — and said, "Good morning, yourself. I was going to let you sleep."

She took a deep breath, and in the fraction of a second that took, Trace worried she was going to tell him she was going home.

"I'd like to come down to the barn with you," she said instead.

"You would?"

She nodded and walked across the kitchen to put her arms around his waist. Deciding he couldn't control his erection anyway, he turned to face her and kissed the top of her head.

"Are you sure you don't want to stay here and relax?" he said.

"Positive. The sooner we get done, the sooner we can come back."

She trailed a finger down his bare chest and hooked it into the waistband of his boxers. He groaned. "You're so right."

Although turning away from her was the absolute last thing he wanted to do, he got a coffee mug for her and filled it. When he turned around and finally *really* looked at her, her long hair tousled from sleep and sex, her cheeks rosy, her thin nightgown outlining every curve of her body, he had such a strong reaction, he almost dropped the coffee.

I love her.

"You okay?" she asked. "All of a sudden, you looked like you were going to keel over or something."

Trace swallowed. Cleared his throat.

"Fine."

As her hands wrapped around the mug, he brought his body close to hers, and kissed her mouth. It was a gentle kiss, a sweet kiss. But with everything that had gone through his mind in the past five minutes, and with her body touching his, he felt unreasonably turned on — again.

He wanted to drop to his knees then and there, and ask her to stay forever, with him. "How long can you stay today?"

She put her free hand on his lower back, and then cupped his butt. She kissed him again, deepening it slightly while his erection pressed against her. "All day."

"Good," he said. "Because I'm going to use every single minute."

———

ABBY

AS ABBY BRUSHED her teeth a few minutes later, she thought about how Trace seemed surprised when she said she would accompany him to the barn. Before she could stop it, a thought skittered through her mind about the other women he'd dated. From the whispers she'd heard around town, Trace had a type, and Abby wasn't it. He chose feminine, gentle, timid women. Well, she wasn't any of those things.

Actually, said a confident voice in the back of her mind, *you were pretty feminine last night.*

It was true. The night before, she felt confident, sexy, powerfully feminine. She thought back to how she took charge, taking him in her mouth, straddling him like some kind of sex goddess. A small groan — muscle memory pleasure — escaped, and she was glad she was alone in the bathroom. Done brushing, she went back into Trace's bedroom. He was already dressed in jeans and a flannel shirt.

"Looking damn good in those jeans," she said.

She meant it, too. Although she'd never taken much of an interest in cowboys, these days, she couldn't seem to stop checking him out every chance she got. Another surge of heat rushed through her body. And, along with it, another surge of lust.

She had to get dressed, and she was pretty confident she could make that routine as sexy as getting undressed. At first, Trace went about his own routine. He pulled a pair of socks out of a dresser drawer, and then sat on the bench at the foot of the bed to put them on. But when Abby started to remove her nightgown, as sinuously as she could, she sensed his movements stop. She turned her face away to hide her smile, and then bent down to pick up the jeans that were in her bag.

"Looking pretty damn good in those underwear, woman," he said then, and she could hear the barely restrained desire in his voice. She turned around as she stepped into her jeans and felt victorious when his eyes raked over her body. She'd never felt so reluctant to get dressed. She let him watch her as she put on her bra. Then, with what she knew was a wicked glint in her eyes, she said, "You'd better get your boots on, Mr. Walker."

Still seated, Trace rubbed his hands over his thighs. He shook his head and let out a breath. "I've got to tell you, I've never been so turned on watching a woman put clothes *on*."

"That's what I was going for." Abby walked over to stand in front of Trace. Her lace-covered breasts were at his eye level. She put her hands on his knees and kissed him. It was a promise. He ran his hands up her sides and cupped her breasts. Still, he kissed her back with a tenderness she wasn't expecting.

When she stood up, he wrapped his arms around her waist and laid his head on her chest.

"I don't know what you're doing to me."

Abby wasn't sure exactly how he meant it, but she sensed it was a good thing. Smiling again, she stepped back and took his hands in hers. "Let's get down to those horses, shall we? And back."

———

TRACE

ON NICE MORNINGS, Trace often walked down to the barn. And while the weather was definitely pleasant, he didn't want to waste any time getting down there and back.

Hand in hand, he and Abby walked to his truck. He opened the passenger door for her and didn't even bother resisting the urge to kiss her again once she got in. The kiss ignited some kind of fire, and her hands were in his hair and her tongue was in his mouth and his heart was beating hard.

After a few minutes, they were both breathless.

"We'd better get going," Trace said. "Even though there's nothing I'd rather do than this."

She kissed him one more time. Walking around the hood of the truck, he had to adjust his jeans, yet again.

As they worked together at the barn, Trace again marveled at how seamless it was. Abby learned quickly, asked good questions, and picked up on the nuances. At one point, they split up, each of them carrying a feed bucket, filling containers in each stall. He finished his row before she finished hers, and when he walked over to where she stood, he realized why.

She stood outside Louise's stall, talking quietly to her. "… and the weather's starting to get cold, isn't it? This is actually my favorite time of year."

For her part, the horse seemed very interested in what Abby had to say. She bobbed her head and made little chuffing noises while Abby spoke. Abby offered her a good scratch on the forehead and then said, "All right, my friend, I've got to finish up. Mr. Trace and I have some unfinished business back at the house."

Trace felt energy start to buzz through his body. "Did you say unfinished business?"

He'd stepped up right behind Abby, and she jumped. "You scared me!"

"Did I?" He took the bucket from her and set it on the ground. His imagination had him slowly unbuttoning her shirt to reveal her full breasts and that lacy marvel of engineering. But he didn't feel quite right about making love to her in the barn. That was teenager stuff. He put his hands on her waist and drew her closer, bringing their mouths together.

"I want you so badly," he said.

"Are we almost done with the chores?"

Hearing the desire in her voice made Trace laugh. It was nice to know he was getting to her in the same way she was getting to him.

"We're done."

"Oh, thank God!"

CHAPTER SEVENTEEN

TRACE ATTENDED his fair share of meetings, but this was potentially the most important one of his life. He'd mentioned to Cody and Sawyer that he was going out of town, but he'd been purposely vague, and left little room for questions.

An hour after landing at Cedar City Regional Airport in Utah, he knocked on Ernesto Flores's door.

It opened almost immediately, and Trace wondered if Ernesto was as anxious about this as he was. Abby's father beamed at him from his wheelchair, and Trace's first thought was that he embodied the phrase, "larger than life."

"I've really looked forward to meeting you," Ernesto said.

"Likewise."

They shook hands. Trace breathed a little easier. Ernesto seemed friendly, unguarded.

"Come on in," Ernesto said. "I'll get the door. Want a drink?"

Trace felt at ease, like Ernesto was a friend. "Sure, what are my choices?"

"Beer, seltzer water — Abby makes me keep that around, so I won't drink too much soda. Soda — I keep that around, too, but Abby doesn't know."

"I'll take a beer," Trace said. Beer was the perfect accompaniment to man-to-man discussions.

"Coming right up. Living room's on your left. I'll meet you in there."

The living room was stunning. High ceilings with exposed beams, a gorgeous rock fireplace, and one wall made up entirely of windows took Trace's breath away. Outside, a generous deck featured the same view as the windows: the striking red rocks of Utah, silhouetted against a bright-blue sky.

"Nice, huh?" Ernesto came up beside him and handed him a beer.

"Actually, I was admiring the house more than the view. You build it?"

"Sure did. Well, my daughter and I did."

"I love what you did with the view."

"The wall of windows," Ernesto said, nodding. "Abby's idea."

"I'm impressed," Trace said.

Ernesto looked up at him, then, one eyebrow arched. "Better than you expected, right?"

Trace had to give it to the guy. He wanted to be friendly. But he'd also made his point. He knew how Trace had treated his daughter. And although he'd invited Trace into his home for a beer and conversation, he wouldn't soon forget it. The thought should have scared Trace, but it made him admire Ernesto even more.

"Can we go out on the deck?"

"Of course." Outside, Ernest said, "Have a seat." He gestured at one of the cushy chairs that overlooked the view. Trace did, and Ernesto positioned his wheelchair next to him.

"Although it would be nice to enjoy a beer and a chat with you," he said to Trace, "I suspect you might have something on your mind. You didn't fly all the way out from Arizona for small talk, did you?"

Trace thought he was nervous before, but his nerves revved up at that. He cleared his throat and gripped the arm of his chair with his free hand, so Ernesto wouldn't see it shaking. "You're right. We might as well cut to the chase." He took a deep breath and looked over at Ernesto. This part of their talk was worthy of eye contact. "I'm in love with your daughter."

Ernesto didn't look surprised. He gave a little nod, and Trace continued. "I'm sure you've heard how things were between us. When we first met."

Ernesto smiled. "When you came to Abby's rescue, helping her change the tire on that confounded car? Or when you shared with the entire City of Prescott why you thought her dream project was a terrible idea?"

"I deserve that," Trace said as his face burned. "Both, I guess. The very first time I saw Abby, I knew she was different. Special. I shouldn't tell her father this, but I thought she was drop-dead gorgeous, too. And when I saw her at the City Council meeting and heard about the Sunset Valley subdivision, I saw red. Not just because no self-respecting snake would agree to being turned into those impractical excuses for shoes. But also because I'm an old-fashioned jerk."

Ernesto chuckled. "I admit, I may have heard that about you."

Feeling a little more confident at that point, Trace nodded. "I deserve that, too. Really, though, I was worried about having a subdivision out there. Once I cooled off and really listened to Abby's vision, I realized I was overreacting. For that, I'm sorry. I'm sure it was stressful for you to have Abby so stressed."

"Thank you. And it was. But I accept your apology."

"Thank you," Trace said. His knuckles were bright white where he gripped the arm of his chair. "That's not why I'm here, though." His vision started to go black around the edges. He took a deep breath, so sudden and deep, he felt like a fish out of water. His vision cleared, as Ernesto said, "I suspected it wasn't."

Well, he wasn't making it easy on Trace.

"Like I said, I'm in love with your daughter. I'd like nothing more than to ask her to marry me. But I would really like your blessing before I do."

The silence stretched between them. Interminable. Trace took another gulp of air. And another. Finally, Ernesto spoke. "We don't know each other well."

Trace stopped gulping and held his breath.

"What I do know is that my daughter is in love with you, too. Since the two of you started 'talking,' as she calls it, she's a different person. Happier. I've never seen her like this over a man."

Trace exhaled.

Ernesto went on, "I also know that it means a lot that you've come to me. It gives me a great deal of respect for you. As does your apology for hurting my daughter."

More silence.

"I'm going to tell you what I told Abby when I first observed how much you meant to her: I told her, 'Don't guard yourself so carefully that you miss out on one of life's greatest blessings.' It's true love, Trace. That *is* life's greatest blessing. I'm sure you know by now that my daughter guards her heart. But the fact that you're here shows me that she let you in. Don't underestimate the weight of that, son. She loves you, and that didn't come easily for her. All I ask is that you guard her heart, the same as I would."

"I will, sir," Trace said, his throat tight with emotion. "I wouldn't do anything else."

"Then you have my blessing."

In the next span of silence, Trace felt himself relax. His breathing came easier, and he released his death grip on the arm of his chair.

Ernesto, his own voice sounding tight, said, "Should we eat?"

———

THE NEXT DAY, Trace woke up with a plan. He'd been thinking about it for a while — well, a short while, but long enough to know. Before getting out of bed, he texted Cody and Sawyer and invited them for lunch and beers.

Cody wrote back, *Lunch and beers? Must be a special occasion.* Sawyer wrote, *You had me at beers.*

Abby stretched and rolled toward him as she woke up, wrapping her arm around his waist and nuzzling his neck. Over the course of the past few days, he'd grown accustomed to waking up next to her. The sound of her breathing, deep and even, gave him a sense of calm, readying him for the day.

"Good morning," he said. He kissed her on the top of the head.

She ran a hand down his stomach and giggled. "Good morning to *you*." She stroked him, slow, lazy, to which his body responded with anything but laziness.

"What do you have on the agenda for today?" she asked, her breath warm on his ear.

"I can't remember just now," he said. "But I know what I'm doing first."

He could hear the smile in her voice when she said, "Oh yeah? What's that?"

"You."

Afterward, they went through what had become their morning routine: they fed and watered the horses. He made breakfast while she showered, they ate together, and she cleaned up while he showered. Dressed and ready, they met at the front door to say goodbye. Trace couldn't believe he'd ever thought this type of domestic partnership could feel mundane. Every moment somehow felt special.

After Abby left, Trace spent most of the morning doing paperwork … and thinking (which he couldn't seem to do when they shared the same space). He paid bills, sent invoices, and researched new water troughs for the corral and north pasture. And he thought about what Hector Inman told them: "Ronnie Sunshine is real fired up about this new development. To tell you the truth, I think he might be off his rocker."

Sawyer and Ronnie had been something of rivals in high school, but Ronnie loved his position as mayor. Trace had some serious doubts about whether Ronnie would poison an entire herd of horses over the Sunset Valley issue. But why would Hector say that? Trace didn't know, but he decided to let his subconscious work on it while he tied up loose ends.

As noon approached, he started to feel jittery. He hadn't yet told Cody and Sawyer his plan, because he wasn't sure how they would take it.

On one hand, he thought they would be surprised. He'd sworn off marriage when he was seven, and although he dated, he never changed his stance on becoming a husband. But, on the other hand, he figured Cody and Sawyer could tell Abby was different.

He made his way to the Horseshoe, arriving a few minutes early so he could get a booth — and the upper hand on the situation by having his friends' beers ready when they got there. They came in the door and grinned at the frosty bottles waiting on the table.

"So, what's the occasion?" Cody held up his beer for a toast, an eyebrow raised, waiting for Trace to say what they were toasting to.

Enjoying the performance, Trace leaned back in his side of the booth, stretching both arms across the top of the seat. "Well, fellas, I'm sure you never thought this day would come. But, after I treat you to lunch and a couple of beers, we're going ring shopping."

Their reaction was exactly as he'd hoped. Surprised, they looked at each other, and then back at him, grinning. Then they were laughing, shaking their heads, and holding up their beers for that toast.

"I can't say I was expecting it so soon," Sawyer said, "but we had a feeling, didn't we, Cody?"

Cody nodded. "We knew you had eyes for Abby. The first day you saw those snakeskin high heels. Cheers to snakeskin high heels and a wedding dress."

"And ring shopping," Sawyer added. The three of them clinked their beer bottles together over center of the table, and then took long drinks.

"So, tell us the story," Sawyer said. "What led to this ring shopping?"

"One thing and another," Trace said, "I guess you could say."

"One thing I have noticed is that I haven't seen Abby's truck in its parking spot over at the apartment complex," Cody said.

Trace raised an eyebrow at him. "You keeping tabs on her?"

"Nah," Cody said. "I guess you could say I'm an observant guy."

Trace nodded. That was true. Then he said, "Why didn't you guys tell me?"

This time, the look his friends exchanged was quizzical.

"Tell you what?" Sawyer said.

"That when you find the right woman, all that mundane, day-to-day stuff is actually not boring. It's actually … kind of magical."

Dead silence.

After a couple of beats, his friends were laughing again. Cracking up. Trace felt his neck getting hot, then his face, and even his ears. He shrugged off the embarrassment, though. It was true. His time with Abby felt magical.

Hooting with laughter, Sawyer said, "Hence, the ring shopping."

"Why didn't we tell him?" Cody said, his voice gently teasing. His face grew serious, and he said, "Dude, even if we *had* told you, you wouldn't have believed us."

That was probably true. "Live and learn, I guess you could say."

Sawyer and Cody laughed some more. Simultaneously, they managed to squeak out, "I guess you could say."

The jewelry store was a couple doors down from the restaurant, and as Trace walked with his friends down the sidewalk, he experienced a heady feeling of anticipation. It was as if he had reached the peak of the tallest mountain in the world and was about to turn around and see the most beautiful view of his entire life. He felt almost breathless at the thought of choosing a ring for Abby.

"Come to think of it," he said to his friends as much as himself, "I'm going to have to buy her two rings. Something sparkly for sure. And something more practical that she can wear to work."

"Well," said Cody, drawing the word out into three syllables. "Who knew our boy could be so thoughtful?"

Trace elbowed him and was rewarded with a grunt of pain.

"I was going to say something similar," Sawyer said, "but instead I'll say, that's really good thinking."

Trace elbowed him, too, for good measure. They were all still laughing when they walked through the door of the jewelry store. Trace had been inside only a handful of times. He'd bought a piece of jewelry for a girlfriend or two. But never something like this. He knew where the wedding rings were. He'd studiously ignored them in the past. He headed straight for the display case centered against the back wall. His friends followed him, and they each let out a long whistle as they looked down at the contents.

"That's a lot of hardware right there," Sawyer said.

"Sure is," Cody said.

As the three of them stood there, peering down at the sparkly hardware, a salesman came out of the back room. He looked vaguely familiar to Trace, but Prescott was a small town, so that didn't mean much.

"Can I help you gentlemen?"

"The first thing you can do is stop referring to us as gentlemen," Sawyer said. "That's the farthest thing from the truth."

"That can't be all true," the salesman said. "I suspect you wouldn't be looking at engagement rings if at least one of you didn't have some gentlemanly qualities."

"Yeah," Trace said to Sawyer. "Speak for yourself, man."

The salesman made eye contact with Trace. "You must be the gentleman, then. I'm Ryan."

"Trace."

"Nice to meet you, man. Who's the lucky lady?"

"Her name is Abby," Trace said.

Cody reached around behind Trace and punched Sawyer on the arm. "Did you hear that? He's all twitterpated."

Trace shook his head. "I'm beginning to regret bringing you guys with me. I thought I was going to get moral support."

"What do you think this is?" Cody asked.

"Tell me more about this Abby," Ryan interjected.

Trace considered. What would a jewelry salesman need to know about Abby? He didn't need to know that her laugh was contagious, or that she had the prettiest smile he'd ever seen. He didn't need to know that she was tough as nails, but her gentle touch drove him wild.

"See those hearts coming out of his eyes?" Sawyer said.

Cody cleared his throat. "First of all, she's in construction."

Sawyer added, "But she also likes to dress up. We were thinking of getting her two rings."

As much as he pretended his friends' witty banter annoyed him, Trace was so grateful they were there. Sawyer's use of "we" made him feel all warm and fuzzy inside. Not that he would ever say that out loud. Trace nodded. "Yeah. We were thinking something simple that she could wear to work, and then maybe something a little more flashy for, you know, wearing around town."

Ryan nodded. "Smart. Thoughtful. See? Definitely gentlemen. Let me show you some sets. If you get a slightly simpler wedding band, with a more sparkly engagement ring, she can always remove the engagement ring when she goes to work."

Trace thought that seemed reasonable. Ryan took out a piece of black velvet and unrolled it on top of the case. He took several pairs of rings from inside the case and set them on the black velvet. All three of the men looked down at the rings for a full minute without speaking. Both Cody and Sawyer pointed at the set on the far left and said, "Not that one."

"Too dainty," Cody said.

Trace nodded in agreement. "I agree. And that one, on the far right, is too flashy."

Within a few minutes, they'd narrowed down the selection to two sets. Trace knew which one he liked. He'd spotted it immediately. The rings were made of white gold, with a matte finish. The wedding band had a single round diamond set into the top. The engagement ring was a little more showy, featuring a setting that incorporated four diamonds of a shape and size similar to the one on the band, with a fifth, larger diamond in the middle. The rings were elegant and practical, sparkling and radiant. Like Abby. He didn't say anything at first. He wanted to see what Cody and Sawyer said.

Without speaking, as if they'd planned it, they both pointed at the very set Trace had his eye on.

Trace grinned. "That was my first pick, too."

"Nice choice," Ryan said. "Want me to box them up?"

———

ABBY

SPENDING ALMOST an entire week at Trace's house — away from her apartment and whichever creep was leaving nasty messages on her doorstep — was beyond amazing. Not that she wouldn't have enjoyed it anyway, but knowing she wasn't alone made her feel so much safer. Unfortunately, she couldn't stay away from her apartment forever. When she finally made it back that afternoon, Abby felt like she was walking on clouds, wrapped in a protective layer of bliss.

Things like the cold, staring eyes of dead bunnies weren't even part of her reality at that moment. So when she approached her apartment door and saw what had to be yet another dead animal on her doormat, it was as if someone had dumped a bucket of ice-cold water over her head. She heard a horrible moaning sound, and slapped a hand over her mouth when she realized it came from her.

She'd long since stopped wondering why someone would do this. Sure, she'd been nothing but a model citizen since coming to Prescott. But she represented change, and some people *hated* change. Her sense of dread grew as she forced herself to put one foot in front of the other and move toward the apartment. It was like what people said about car accidents. It would be horrible to see, but grotesque curiosity drove her forward as she tried to figure out what exactly made up the lump on her doormat.

A tiny voice in the back of her head whispered that she should tell Trace. He would know what to do. He would be able to find out who was behind this. But she didn't want to worry him.

Even up close, the lump was unidentifiable. It was an animal of some sort. Spiky, dark fur matted with dried blood stuck up from the body. Abby stopped trying to figure out what it was when she saw the piece of paper taped to her door. It was folded in half, the outside left blank. With a shaking hand, she pulled it off.

Not for the first time, she wondered if someone might be watching her. As quickly as she could, she unlocked the door and went inside. After turning the deadbolt, she unfolded the paper. It read: *You don't belong here. If you don't pack up and leave, your loved ones will be next.*

Abby crumpled the note in one hand as she leaned against the door. "Stupid," she said. "Juvenile."

She didn't know who was killing the animals. But what she did know was that she had to get out of there.

Yes, she'd absolutely loved being at Trace's place for the past few days. But there was only one place where she could trust completely. And that was at home. With her dad.

She didn't waste another minute. She packed a bag. She put the little dead body in a grocery sack, which she set into the trash bin before driving away. She didn't even text Trace until she was on the interstate, and there was no chance of her turning back. And even then, all she wrote was, *I'll be out of town for a couple of days.*

She hesitated before sending it, wondering if she should add something like, *I'll miss you,* or, *I wish you could come with me,* or, *I love you.* But she didn't.

She thought she could trust Trace. She had slowly but surely become part of the Mint Creek Ranch gang. But what if — it was almost too horrible a thought to finish — what if Trace still considered her an enemy, and was spending all this time with her only to keep her close, so he could keep an eye on her?

Hadn't everyone heard the phrase, "Keep your friends close and your enemies closer"?

Common sense spoke up and told Abby it was impossible. Trace's feelings for her seemed genuine. He cared about her. He hadn't said as much, but he loved her. She sensed that. But still, there was always that chance. She shut off her phone and focused on the road ahead. She needed a few days to think.

CHAPTER EIGHTEEN

FOR THE NEXT SEVERAL HOURS, Trace felt like he was walking on clouds. Everything seemed so beautiful, so wonderful. So magical. The leaves around town were changing color. He admired the way the sun shone through them, casting a glowing light on every scene. He put the rings in his nightstand drawer, at the back. He had to come up with a plan for the proposal. He wasn't one of those fools who thought it had to be perfect. No, he wanted it to be right. The right moment. The right place. For the right woman.

Trace was running errands in town. He'd parked at the grocery store, and he planned to buy something special for dinner. Maybe that night would be the night. Maybe he could propose over a glass of wine. No, a shared bottle of wine. That seemed more romantic. He got out of the truck thinking of what to pair with it. Walking in, he ran through the list: bread, cheese, olives. Maybe some of those fancy meats. Grapes. His mouth watered. He'd filled his day with lots of activity, and now he craved a quiet evening at home with Abby. He chuckled to himself as he walked through the door. Craving quiet time with a woman — especially Abby — would never have occurred to him a month before.

"Hey, Walker."

Trace froze, both hands on the handle of a shopping cart.

Ronnie Sunshine's voice didn't usually strike fear into Trace's heart. But today, it did. There was something about his tone. Trace pulled his cart away from the others, and Ronnie fell into step beside him as they walked into the produce section.

"I hear you were ring shopping earlier."

There it was again. Trace's sixth sense was on high alert. He resisted the urge to look around. Surely, Ronnie wouldn't have hired an assassin to take him out at the grocery store.

"I was. News travels fast."

"I heard the lucky lady is a woman named Abby."

"Did you?"

Not that there was any point in denying it. But something told Trace not to confirm it.

The less Ronnie knew, the better.

"Don't bother trying to hide it. The two of you have been seen together around town."

The phrase grated on Trace's nerves. His senior year English teacher, Mr. Moore, had drilled active voice into their heads. He wanted to ask Ronnie, *who* saw us? He knew engaging would only add fuel to the fire, though, so he bit his tongue.

"You know she can't stay here, right?"

The hairs on the back of Trace's neck prickled. "Of course she can."

"Not if I have anything to say about it."

Anger rushed through Trace's body, like lava through a volcano.

"I'm sorry to tell you, not everyone in this town agrees with you. Retailers and businesses haven't been shy about signing leases in her buildings. And she's sold almost all the lots in her new subdivision. If you don't like it, you're in the minority."

Ronnie shrugged, his thin lips forming a sneer. "Maybe so. But I'm sure you've heard about the squeaky wheel."

Although Trace had made a mental list while walking into the store, he'd forgotten all the items on it. He and Ronnie had meandered through the produce section without Trace so much as thinking about grapes. He shook his head, irritated with himself for letting Ronnie get to him.

"Well," Trace said, doing his best to keep his tone neutral, like he wasn't milliseconds from punching Ronnie in the face. "I doubt your squeaky wheel will be able to gain much traction. The more people who get to know Abby, the better they like her. She won't be run out of this town."

"Not if you sign the petition, she won't."

"You can forget about that. I'm not going to sign it."

"Yes, you are. If you, Cody, and Sawyer — the golden boys of Prescott — sign the petition, it'll really get its teeth in. That's how we're going to get our traction."

So that was the crux of the issue, then, Trace thought. Ronnie and his gang needed the Mint Creek Ranch boys' signatures. He wasn't going to get them. Remembering the grapes, Trace turned around his basket, carelessly enough to run over one of Ronnie's feet. Ronnie winced, which gave Trace no small level of satisfaction.

"We're not going to sign. None of us."

"Oh, I imagine you'll think differently, the more time passes."

"What's that supposed to mean?" Trace all but threw a bag of grapes into his cart. "Are you threatening us?"

"No," Ronnie said, his voice going perfectly neutral. "Not making threats. Just letting you know that if you don't sign, Mint Creek Ranch will no longer be on the map. We'll eliminate you, so we never have to rely on you again."

Trace's head spun. Although Ronnie's words sounded overdramatic, designed to get a response, Trace couldn't help but feel uneasy. He wanted to push for more information, but he didn't. He didn't want Ronnie to know he was getting to him.

"Message received. Now I'd like to do my shopping in peace."

Trace shook his head as Ronnie walked away. He grabbed a loaf of bread, a few packages of cheese and meats, and a bottle of wine. He didn't even check the label, just looked for something in the right price range. He couldn't believe how flustered he was over everything Ronnie said. "Ridiculous."

———

CODY AND SAWYER were waiting for him when he got home. His heart sank. Their presence could mean only one thing. They approached his truck as he parked. Sawyer opened his passenger door and grabbed a couple of bags of groceries. Always ready with a joke, he held up the bottle of wine and said, "Planning for romance tonight? Is this, like, a *fancy* bottle of wine?"

Trace's phone dinged. The text message was from Abby: *I'll be out of town for a couple of days.*

Alarm bells went off. Why now?

"Just a minute." He responded: *Everything okay?*

His mind was going a million miles an hour, trying to figure out if he'd said or done something to spook her.

"What's up?" Cody said.

Trace shook his head. "It *is* a good bottle of wine, and yes, I was planning on romance. Until I got a text saying Abby's going out of town."

"Why?" Sawyer wanted to know. "Everything okay with her dad?"

Trace felt a rush of gratitude. "I don't know, she didn't say. Anyway, I ran into Ronnie Sunshine at the grocery store ... and since I came home and found the two of you here, that could only mean —"

"You're right," Cody said, cutting to the chase. "We had chats with Ronnie today, too."

"Crazy son of a gun," Sawyer said.

Trace didn't even have to ask what Ronnie said to them.

"He wants us to sign the petition," Cody said as the three of them made their way to the front door. "Basically threatened us."

"Basically proved that he's the one who poisoned the horses," Sawyer said.

Trace's thought process had brought him to a similar conclusion. "Can we go to the cops?" he asked, even though he already knew the answer. He unlocked the door and used the toe of his boot to push it open.

"I don't think so," Cody said. "We go running to the cops, they make it even worse for us. Anything that happens, they can make it look like an accident."

"Yeah," Sawyer said. "Remember that year Ronnie lit the trash in the boys' bathroom on fire? The entire bathroom had to be gutted. Everyone knew it was him, but they could never pin it on him."

The three of them went to work putting away the groceries.

"Right," Cody said. "He beat up the only witness before that kid even had a chance to go to the principal."

"And we all know that's how it is with the Council."

Trace sighed. They were right.

"We've got to sign it, man," Cody said. "Remember, signing it doesn't mean —"

"I know what it means," Trace said, his words clipped. "It puts it on the agenda. People vote. But if Abby were to find out —"

"You think *I* want to sign the petition?" Sawyer said. "The property Montana and I bought is part of this. If the vote goes the wrong way, that dream is down the toilet."

Trace's mind flashed to the ring he'd bought. To the images he'd conjured of his marriage to Abby. Her in a dress, smiling up at him. He removed three beers from the fridge and opened them. "Yeah, mine, too."

"You think she'd break up with you over it?" Cody asked, taking his beer with a nod of thanks.

Trace shook his head. He didn't want to think so, but he knew she'd feel betrayed. Cody and Sawyer signing it was one thing, but if she saw his signature on that petition …

He hated to think how she'd react.

"Well, couldn't you explain it to her?" Sawyer said. "Tell her none of us felt like we had a choice? I'm sure she would understand."

When both Trace and Cody said, "No," and Trace added, "Absolutely not," Sawyer shrugged. "I thought it was a pretty good idea."

"It is," Trace said. "But I don't want her to know how strongly people feel about getting rid of her. Think of how hard it would be for her to live here after that. She'd probably pack up and move out."

"Actually, that makes sense," Sawyer said. "It just stinks."

A few seconds of silence passed while the guys sipped and thought.

"I hate to let these guys bully us into submission," Trace said.

"Me too," Cody said. "What if we didn't sign the petition?"

"I don't know," Trace said. "I'd like to believe they're making empty threats. But look what they did to the horses. Who knows what else they'd do?"

"I do know that even if they didn't literally wipe Mint Creek Ranch off the map, they could make our lives miserable for the foreseeable future," Cody said. "It's not like they're bullying us into canceling Abby's project. It's just signing a petition. Putting it to a vote. Actually —"

Trace cut him off. "Even if we sign the petition, we could go on a sort of marketing campaign afterward," Trace said.

"You took the words out of my mouth," Cody said.

"So we sign it?" Sawyer asked.

Cody nodded. With a growing sense of dread and the knowledge that that wasn't going to be the night after all, Trace said, "I guess we sign it. We don't really have a choice."

CHAPTER NINETEEN

ABBY

THE FIRST AFTERNOON after returning from her dad's, Abby stopped by her apartment to get some clothes. Fortunately, her doormat was free of dead animals, and she breathed deeply to get herself to relax as she unlocked the door. She glanced around her apartment, which was bare of decorations and photos, except for the framed picture of her and her dad that sat on the single bookcase in the living room. Although Trace's house was sparsely furnished, it felt a lot more like home than the apartment, Abby thought. Chiefly because Trace lived there.

After packing her bag, she filled a mug with water and put it in the microwave. Once she'd dropped in a teabag, she sat down at the kitchen table and opened her laptop. While it booted up, she did some more deep breathing. She didn't know why she still felt so anxious. She'd needed time away. But she knew she couldn't avoid the situation forever. After taking a mental break, Abby was ready to research — to do her best to figure out who was leaving dead animals in front of her apartment. She wasn't sure if she wanted to know. Even if she did figure it out, what would she *do*? It wasn't like she'd confront anyone. At least she could steer clear of that person and potential danger, though.

As a reporter, Tessa might have some good ideas for research methods. But Abby wasn't quite ready to let Tessa, or anyone for that matter, in on what was going on.

During the past couple of days, Abby had decided that the City Council meeting transcripts might serve as a good starting place. She could go back to the meetings where she'd first presented and find out who expressed opposition to the Sunset Valley subdivision. Back then, she was new to town, and with no frame of reference, she wasn't able to remember everyone's name.

But time had passed, and she knew the main players.

She navigated to the City of Prescott's City Council page and clicked on the *Agendas and Transcripts* link. She scrolled down to the first meeting she attended when she was going for the rezoning and took a deep breath. The meeting had been borderline traumatic for her. All those nerves.

"Thanks to the man himself," she said into the empty space.

Yes, Trace was one of the people originally most opposed to her project.

She sat up with a start. In a horror movie, Trace would be the prime suspect. With a shiver, she reminded herself, "But this isn't a horror movie. Yet."

While she waited for the transcript to load, she pulled her notebook out of her purse. If she remembered correctly, she was going to have a lot of notes to take. It was going to be a long process. If it were any later in the day, she would have poured herself a glass of wine. But she still had so much to do. She sipped her tea and started scrolling.

A few hours later, Abby had a long list of names and an excuse to pour that wine. She scrounged up a bottle from the back of a cabinet. Immediately upon taking her first sip, she wondered how she'd be able to drive to Trace's house that evening — she was going to need more than one glass of wine, and she didn't see herself waiting until she left — but then she realized she could probably have him come get her. Although, she'd have to explain why she was two (or three) glasses in, alone at her own place, when they were both expecting her to be at his place. She groaned.

"Just the one glass, then," she told herself.

Sipping slowly, Abby worked her way through the list. She had formed tenuous bonds with some of the people on it, and she figured she could cross off a few names. One or two had moved away, from what she knew. And while they could return to Prescott to leave her nasty surprises, she doubted they would. She crossed those off, as well. Her trimmed-down list included about ten people. Absently, she tapped her pen on her paper.

"So, now what?" With her free hand, she rubbed her forehead. "I have no idea."

She could run a quick Internet search on each person, see what they were involved in, what they did around town. She could spend a day following them around … maybe catch someone in the act of capturing a poor, defenseless rabbit. She shivered again. The truth was, she didn't have time for either of those things. Internet research could take hours, and she'd rather spend that time with Trace.

A sensible voice in the back of her mind piped up, reminding her that she could always make a police report. Surely, leaving dead, bloody animals at someone's door was against the law. Harassment, maybe? The note was an overt threat.

But — and she hated to think it, because she'd always thought of the police as protectors — she didn't know if she could trust anyone. Maybe the best course of action was to let it go, just a little longer. Maybe it would run its course. She groaned. Five minutes before, she felt like she was doing something productive. At the moment, she was at a standstill. Sure, a few paths forward existed, but none of them seemed viable.

Feeling defeated, Abby packed up her computer. She grabbed a few changes of clothes, corked the wine bottle, and carted out the rest of her things. She got into her truck and drove over to Trace's.

———

AS WAS HER ROUTINE, Abby stopped at the convenience store the next afternoon to buy a sports drink. And, as usual, a few people waited in line before her. The night before, with Trace, had felt different. He felt different. Undoubtedly, he thought it was odd that she didn't explain her two-day absence, but he didn't push for details. That aside, he seemed subdued, himself. They made small talk, watched a TV show, and went to bed early. When they lay together, they clung to one another like they were holding onto lifelines. They slept like that, which brought her comfort.

That morning, they went through the motions: chores, breakfast, showers. She sighed. Maybe everything *was* okay. They were both stressed, after all.

Directly in front of her, two men dressed in paint-spattered clothes chatted. At first, they talked about the Arizona Cardinals, who had won their game the day before.

"I think they're going all the way this year," one of the men said.

The other guy scoffed. "It's early in the season. My money's on the 49ers."

"Time will tell."

The line moved forward, and there was a brief lull in the conversation. Then the 49ers fan, said, "Hey, did you sign that petition?"

"Haven't heard of it, so, no."

"You know that subdivision? The one in Williamson Valley?"

The Cardinals fan nodded. "Yeah. I saw it in the paper. I thought I heard the boss saying he was going to put in a bid on it, if it passes."

"Don't count on that, either. The petition is to see if they can't get subdivision canceled."

Abby felt the floor drop out from under her. A petition? But —

"The Council already approved the zoning for it, though. They can't change it back, can they?" asked the Cardinals fan, his thought process obviously mimicking Abby's.

The 49ers fan shrugged. "I guess they can. But anyway, you know, it's just a petition at this point. All that means is that it goes to a vote."

The line moved forward again, and the two men stepped up to the register. Abby sucked in oxygen, her vision going black around the edges. She couldn't believe her ears. How was this possible? After everything she'd done —

Her hands shook as she paid for her drink. She rushed out to the parking lot and thanked her good fortune when she saw the painters sitting in their truck, eating the burritos they'd purchased. She walked up to the driver's side window and offered what she hoped was a friendly smile (it felt more like a grimace). The driver — the Cardinals fan — smiled back, rolling down the window. It seemed unlikely he had any idea who Abby was.

"I overheard the two of you talking about a petition. Any idea where I can go to sign it?"

The Cardinals fan had his mouth full, so the 49ers fan answered.

"Last time I saw someone out with a clipboard, it was at the grocery store."

"I saw someone walking around the Prescott Public School parking lot," the Cardinals fan said. "You know, after school?"

Abby checked her watch. She didn't know exactly what time school got out, but she did know that she often noticed a full parking lot while she was making her end-of-the-day rounds. So, sometime around three. Thirty minutes. "Well, thank you, gentlemen."

"No problem," they said.

Back in the car, Abby used her phone and did an Internet search for Prescott Public School's bell schedule. The last bell rang at quarter 'til. "Perfect."

As always at that time of day, the school was abuzz with activity. Kids poured out of open classroom doors, laughing and shouting as they made their way to the buses or their parents' cars, or started their walks home. While some parents waited in a long pickup line, others stood outside their cars in the lot, talking as they waited for their kids. Abby parked and then wandered over to where the parents were standing. She knew that in that tight-knit community, she'd stick out like a thumb someone hit with a framing hammer, but she wasn't too worried about it.

She did her best to act casual, strolling along behind the waiting parents, searching for someone holding a clipboard. A couple of people gave her odd looks — and why shouldn't they? None of them recognized her as a parent. But mostly they ignored her, preferring to talk to the people they knew as long as she wasn't snatching up any kids.

People held water bottles and school projects, books and snacks, but not a clipboard among them. If only it had been that easy to find the petition.

Biting back a curse, she trudged to her truck, navigated carefully out of the crowded parking lot, and drove over to the grocery store. There, her luck didn't seem much better at first. Typically, the people from various organizations who used the store to raise money for charity — Girl Scouts, the Lions Club, firefighters — stood outside the double doors near the produce section.

Abby drove across the front of the store, and not seeing anyone outside either set of doors, she almost headed back to work. But something caught her eye then: the flag at the bank next door waved wildly in the wind, sticking straight out from the flagpole in an almost perfect rectangle. Before that, she hadn't noticed how windy it was. But if she were trying to get people to sign a petition, she would wait inside the store, not out.

After parking, Abby made her way to the first set of doors, thinking she'd never been filled with hope and dread at the same time. On one hand, she hoped she could find someone with the petition. On the other, she dreaded reading it.

Even more, she dreaded the potential outcome of the petition. It didn't seem fair that, after a City Council approved a certain rezoning measure, they could rescind their approval. She wondered briefly if it was even legal, but before she had a chance to think it through, she spotted her: inside the doors, next to the shopping carts, a middle-aged woman stood, clipboard in hand. Abby made eye contact right away, then strode up with as much purpose as she could. Without waiting for any sort of introduction, she said, "I take it that's the petition to have the Sunset Valley subdivision rezoned?"

The woman's expression would have been funny if it weren't such a personal matter. First, surprise. Then, uncertainty. Then a bolstering of courage and a squaring of the shoulders. "It is. Would you like to sign it?"

Abby snatched the clipboard from the woman's hand. She closed her eyes, briefly, inhaled, and then opened her eyes and read the petition.

We, the undersigned residents of Prescott, Arizona, request that the Prescott City Council hold a special election regarding the rezoning of parcel 10 – 04 753. We believe the proposed subdivision will decrease the quality of life for Prescott residents, and we believe the matter deserves further consideration.

Abby took another deep breath. On the surface, the petition didn't include any new information. Which was good for Abby. Yet that didn't mean that whoever created the petition didn't *have* any new information. What information they could possibly have up their sleeves to change the minds of people who already voted to approve her initial rezoning request, Abby didn't know.

The woman cleared her throat, startling Abby. She said, "Aren't you going to sign it?"

"Oh!" Abby forced a tittering laugh, which she hoped would

convince the woman that she was so engrossed in the petition that she lost track of how long it took her to read it. "Do you have a pen?"

Now the woman's expression showed disbelief. She pointed at the clipboard. "It's attached."

Another tittering laugh. "I guess I'm not on my A game today, am I?"

The woman didn't respond. Abby ran one finger down the list of names on the first page. She flipped up that page and was alarmed to see a second page, entirely filled out. She ran her finger down that page, as well, committing as many names as possible to memory. Taking a picture might be a red flag. Only half the lines were filled out on the third page. Abby's finger made its way down the row, stopping at the very last one.

Until that moment, she felt like she was reading a roster of her enemies.

Then she saw their names: Cody Davis, Sawyer Nelson, and finally, Trace Walker.

All the noise around her — the beeping self-checkout machines, the clanging of the shopping carts, the people talking as they came and went — faded away.

That didn't make sense. Even if the Mint Creek Ranch boys believed the City Council should take another look at the zoning, and even if they believed that doing so would simply solidify the decision they'd already made, seeing their signatures felt like a betrayal.

Abby realized then that she had made a huge mistake. She'd let herself believe that she was one of them. In that moment, she knew just how wrong she'd been.

PART 3

CHAPTER TWENTY

ABBY BURST into tears the moment she saw her father. He couldn't hold her like he used to, but when she fell to her knees next to his wheelchair, he wrapped his arms around her shoulders and kissed the top of her head.

"My goodness, Abby," he said. "I sensed from your messages that something was amiss, but I guess I didn't quite grasp the magnitude of it."

That made her sob harder. Ernesto stroked her hair. "Fifteen years ago, I would have offered you hot chocolate. In fact, I'm sure I did, on more than one occasion."

This earned a watery half-chuckle. It was true. Ernesto's antidote to crying was almost always hot chocolate. When Abby got her driver's license and cried because her mom wasn't there. When Abby's second — and most serious — high school boyfriend, Benny, broke things off with her because the star soccer player, Vanessa, batted her eyelashes at him. When she received her first college rejection letter.

"Hot chocolate always helps," she said through the tears.

"I know it does, my girl. But I think we should try a little something extra in our hot chocolate this evening."

A cold front had moved across Utah, and the icy air followed Abby into the house. She closed the front door, but could still feel the cold coming through the windows. Hot chocolate with Peppermint Schnapps would warm them both right up, she thought. She offered to go into the kitchen and make the drinks, but her dad waved her off.

"Go get a warm washcloth and wash your face. I'll make the drinks. And then we can talk."

Five minutes later, they were in the living room, Abby curled up on the sofa and Ernesto sitting comfortably in his recliner.

"So," he said. He paused, took a sip of his drink, and said, "Oh, this isn't going to work. I didn't make it quite strong enough. Would you mind?"

Abby smiled and went into the kitchen. She brought back the bottle of Peppermint Schnapps and added a generous pour to each of their mugs. Ernesto held up a finger, sampled his again. "Perfect. Now. Where were we?"

Abby curled up on the couch and wrapped her hands around her mug.

"I don't even know where to begin."

And it was true. He already knew how Trace had been one of Abby's most outspoken opponents, and how she slowly brought him around to her way of thinking. He knew she and Trace had been an item. And he'd said the last time they saw each other that he could tell how much Trace meant to her. What he didn't know — what he *couldn't* know — was how hard she had worked to become part of Prescott ... part of the Mint Creek Ranch crew.

Befriending Montana, and then Tessa, had been relatively easy. Being social was out of her comfort zone, but the two women had accepted her and brought her into the fold. The men, though, they'd been a little trickier. Though her natural inclination would have been to do absolutely everything she could to prove her value, she hadn't. She quietly went about her business. In her resolve, she had finally shown them that she didn't mean to damage their way of life. At least, she *thought* she had. Because Ernesto didn't know any of this, he didn't know how badly it hurt to realize she was still an outsider. She wasn't part of the Mint Creek Ranch crew after all. Sighing, she sipped her drink.

Ernesto's smile was kind and gentle, when he said, "Why don't you start at the beginning?"

Abby nodded and took another deep breath.

"As you know, when you and I first went to Prescott, we knew it was the place. We wanted to make it our new home, together."

Ernesto nodded. "It was the first place that felt like home since your mother left us."

"Right. And, as you know, when the locals saw that I wanted to bring in some new retail spaces, new commercial spaces, they were thrilled. They love all the community service I've done. All that changed when they learned about our plans for Sunset Valley."

"Yes. I remember."

"But eventually, we got the approval. And the locals started to come around. Once they got to know my charming personality."

Ernesto's eyes crinkled at the corners. "Naturally. Like I knew they would."

Abby shook her head. "I had my doubts."

"I didn't. I knew that once they got to know you, saw the quality of your work, they'd love you."

"Which I thought was happening."

The liquor started to hit Abby's bloodstream, making her limbs heavy and pliable. She stretched out her legs, let her body relax.

"I thought they were coming around. But then, a few weeks ago, someone started leaving ... *messages* at my door."

Ernesto stilled. "What kind of messages?"

"Let's just say, someone made it very clear they didn't want me around."

Ernesto's expression changed from one of curiosity to one of suspicion, his eyebrows drawing closer together. "What did they do?"

Abby took a deep breath. "They started leaving dead rabbits."

Ernesto swore. "You have no idea who would do such a thing?"

Abby saw the fire in her father's eyes. "No, no idea. And, the way you look right now, I'm not sure I would tell you, even if I did. Because I think you might end up in jail."

Ernesto laughed. "I'm sure you are right about that. But I wouldn't regret it. You'd better believe that."

"Oh, I do."

"If I know you, you've already tried to figure out who it could've been."

"I have." Silence stretched between them.

Finally, Ernesto said, "And?"

"And, there's a long list of people. That list is in the form of a petition."

Ernesto perked up again like an animal, scenting its prey. *Or maybe its predator,* Abby thought. "What is this petition?"

Abby took a deep breath. "Basically, it's a call for a special election where people will vote whether to rezone the property that we already rezoned."

"Wait. So you're telling me that some buffoons got it in their heads that they could undo something that was already done?"

Abby nodded. "Basically, yes. The petition says something about how these concerned citizens want to uphold the integrity of Prescott. Blah blah."

"Blah blah, indeed."

Although years had passed since Abby had seen her dad walk, she pictured him standing up and pacing the room, much as she had done earlier.

"Those —" he slammed one fist into the other palm.

Abby held up her hand. "Wait. That's not even the worst of it. I haven't even gotten to the climax yet."

"It gets worse?"

Ernesto didn't need to stand. His voice stood for him.

"I heard about this petition while I was standing in line at the convenience store. Some guys were talking about it, as casual as they were talking about a football game. So after I paid, I went outside and asked them where they'd signed it. I'm sure they thought I wanted to sign it, too. They told me they'd seen people collecting signatures at the grocery store and at the school."

"At the school? I can't believe these people."

"I know. You're telling me. I went to the school straightaway. There was no one there with a clipboard. So I went to the grocery store, and there she was."

"Who?"

"I don't know. A lady. Anyway. I asked her if I could read the petition. She handed it over. There were so many signatures, Dad. So many. And I know, I know. That doesn't mean they don't want the development. It means they want it put to a vote. Again. It was bad enough to have to turn to the second page. But then there was a third page. And I got to the last three signatures on it. And there they were, in black-and-white. Cody Davis, Sawyer Nelson, and Trace Walker."

This time, Ernesto was silent. Which seemed even scarier than when he raised his voice. Abby took another drink.

"My hot chocolate is warm now. I'm going to reheat it. Want me to put yours in?"

"Mine's gone. Make me another."

"But the sugar —"

"Fine. Pour me a shot of bourbon, then."

Abby didn't argue. She went to the kitchen and put her drink in the microwave. While it heated, she poured a double shot of bourbon into a fresh glass. When she carried the drinks back into the living room, a calm seemed to have settled over her dad. She handed him the glass, and she expected him to toss the contents back in one go. But he didn't. He sniffed the bourbon, then took a small sip.

"Abby," he said. "Did you tell Trace about someone leaving those rabbits at your door?"

"No," she said slowly.

"And why not?"

"I didn't want to worry him. Same reason I didn't tell you," she rushed to add.

"I thought so."

"What do you mean?"

"Did it occur to you that perhaps someone was threatening Trace, as well? That if you saw all three of those guys' names on the petition, all right next to each other, that they might have felt forced somehow?"

Oh.

"It didn't, no."

"Did it occur to you that perhaps Trace and his friends signed the petition only to protect themselves, and possibly, you?"

Abby set her drink on the table. She rubbed her eyes. "No. But why wouldn't he tell me?"

"For the same reason you didn't tell him — or me — about those rabbits."

It was possible. Possible, but unlikely. Nobody ever forced the Mint Creek Ranch boys to do anything they didn't want to do. They weren't afraid of anybody.

Abby shrugged, feigning nonchalance, even as the emotions swirled around in her body. "It's possible, but unlikely."

"Abby," her dad said, "from everything you've told me about

Trace, signing the petition doesn't seem like something he would do, unless he felt like he had to. I know I don't know him very well, but I do think he deserves a chance to explain."

———

THE NEXT TWO weeks in Utah felt at once comforting and agonizing. On one hand, spending so much time with her dad was amazing. For old time's sake, they ate frozen dinners and watched reruns of old cartoons. They went out for pizza and beers at their favorite pizza parlor, Slice of Pie. They worked on puzzles.

Abby didn't completely ignore her life in Prescott. She knew that the City Council would consider the petition at the next meeting, which meant members would decide whether to hold a special election where people would vote on whether to kill Abby's dream. She didn't text or call her friends, other than to let them know she was safe at her dad's.

Every time Ernesto started to bring up the petition, the upcoming City Council meeting, or the Sunset Valley subdivision, Abby held up a hand. It became a bit of a joke, with him starting to talk, her shushing him, him starting again, her shushing him again.

At one point, though, after they'd shared each of their favorite pizza pies, watched every episode of *Tom and Jerry*, and gone through a full twelve-pack of microwave popcorn, Ernesto had his say.

They sat across from each other at the kitchen table, working on a puzzle picturing an amusement park.

"You're going to have to face this, Abby. I know it's hard, and I know it hurts. But Prescott is where we belong. I know you're going to be upset with yourself if you don't go back and fight for this."

Suddenly, all those feelings Abby held at arm's length came rushing in. "But what if it's not? What if we *thought* it was? What if the friends I thought I made were not actually my friends? What if those people who smiled and waved at me in the grocery store don't actually want me there? And what if Trace —"

She couldn't even finish the sentence.

Ernesto reached across the table and wrapped one of his hands around one of hers. "Trace loves you. I know he does. I wish you would give him — and yourself — a chance."

"But I did give him a chance, dad! I gave *us* a chance! Maybe it's not meant to be."

Ernesto squeezed her hand.

"In all my fatherly wisdom, I suspect it *is* meant to be. And I suspect he wants, more than anything, for you to go back. I know you do, too. As I've always told you, never turn down a chance at real love."

That sent Abby into yet another crying jag. Ernesto passed her the box of tissues, again. With kindness in his eyes, he said, "You need to go back to Prescott. You'll regret it if you don't."

Abby knew he was right. But she was scared. She put her head down on the table and cried.

"That's it," her dad said. "Have yourself a good cry now. Tomorrow morning, fix yourself up, put on some lipstick, and head back to Arizona."

Unable to speak, Abby nodded. Her dad's hand settled on the back of her head, his thumb gently stroking her hair. At least if she lost everything else, she thought, she would always have her dad.

CHAPTER TWENTY-ONE

ABBY

THE FLIGHT WAS ON TIME, but almost nothing else went right after that. In a series of events that mirrored those of that fateful trip to Prescott when she first met Trace, Abby started to wonder if the universe was trying to send her a message that maybe Prescott *wasn't* the place for her.

Another harried-looking woman stood at the rental car counter, talking with the employee there.

"What do you mean you don't have my reservation? How is that possible? I got an email receipt."

"Do you have the confirmation number, ma'am?" The agent looked like he was holding on to the very last thread of his patience.

"I have it here somewhere. These darn smart phones. They're not actually very smart, are they?"

After an eternity, the woman found the confirmation email. When she showed it to the agent, a smug look on her face, he smiled. With what Abby imagined was the very last of his kindness, he said, "Ma'am, you're at the wrong counter. You want Frugal Rentals, over there."

The woman turned her head to look in the direction the man was pointing, and her mouth dropped open. Her face turned a shade of red that rivaled Trace's summer tomatoes (and when Abby would stop thinking of Trace as a reference point for every single thing, she didn't know). The woman *harrumphed* and gathered her things before stomping off to the Frugal counter.

"I hope processing my rental is easier than that," Abby said to the man behind the counter, who smiled back at her.

"I'm almost certain it will be. What's your last name?"

She gave it to him and waited as he typed it into his computer. *This isn't good*, Abby thought as she watched the man's smile transform into a frown.

"I found your reservation, but it doesn't look like we have the car you selected."

Oh, wonderful. Not that it mattered. Abby didn't really care what she drove, as long as it wasn't —

"We have a really nice Ford Mustang. Bright blue. It's a big upgrade, actually. You'll still pay the same rate."

Abby could scream. Surely, the rental car employee wondered why she didn't look more pleased. Who wouldn't want to drive a car like that up the mountain to Prescott? She offered him a tight-lipped smile and said, "That'll be fine."

With an expression that read, *They sure make them crazy around here*, the employee handed her the paperwork and pointed to the door. "Out those doors. Jaime will get you to your car."

It was the same car. Its shiny blue blared at her from its spot in the lot. She didn't need Jaime or anyone else to show her where it was. But she followed the tall man over there anyway. Once he left and she stowed her bag in the back seat, she slid into the driver's seat.

"We meet again."

The car didn't respond.

She got out of Phoenix okay, and through the outskirts of the city. But as the interstate turned windy, the check engine light came on. Abby growled. She still had about 85 miles to go. Her dad had always cautioned her about going too far if something was wrong with the car. But — she checked the clock — she was going to be cutting it close to get to the City Council meeting on time.

"I'll go straight to the meeting," she told the car. "And then I'll take you to a mechanic right after. Can you just get me to Prescott?"

The car gave her an answer a few miles later. Smoke billowed from the engine. There was no way she would get to the meeting on time if she didn't keep going. But she couldn't. If she did, the engine could catch on fire. Explode, even.

She looked at the clock again. The meetings usually started one or two minutes late. And then the City Council had to go through all the obligatory housekeeping stuff. They said the Pledge of Allegiance, and someone usually gave some kind of opening speech. That would buy her five minutes, six, tops. Maybe the fix was something as simple as putting water in the radiator reservoir. She had filled her water bottle at the airport. It wasn't enough to fill the whole reservoir, but maybe it would hold until she made it to Prescott.

Abby wasn't ready to give up hope. She had been through so much, worked so hard. Gritting her teeth, she found a wide spot in the shoulder and pulled over. Even though it was early fall, the temperatures on the pavement were borderline blazing. Fortunately, because she'd had to locate the trunk-opening button the last time she drove the cursed Mustang, she knew the lever to pop the hood was down by her left leg.

When she opened the hood, a giant cloud of smoke — or maybe steam? — billowed out into her face. The smell of it, acrid burnt rubber, stung her throat and nose and she coughed. Her eyes watered. Once the cloud cleared, she looked around for the radiator. The reservoir looked almost full, which she knew was how it should look. No greenish liquid leaked from anywhere. The problem likely wasn't the radiator, then. Hope started to slip away.

The tears came before Abby even realized she was crying. She wasn't a mechanic. She didn't know what to check next. There was no way she would make it to the meeting on time. Yes, the discussion on whether to hold the special election could be the last item on the agenda. But a tow truck would take time. Maybe even hours.

She wouldn't have a chance to speak, to fight for herself. How could she have come this close, only to lose everything? All the anger and angst and sadness and disappointment of the past few weeks boiled up inside her, and she let a loud, guttural scream erupt from her mouth. Her throat was really raw. She cried some more. A semi-truck drove past, sending out a big gust of hot air that nearly knocked her over.

The best thing to do was to pull the car further off the road. "If it will even start."

It did start, and Abby offered up a silent prayer as she inched it into the dirt beyond the shoulder. She rolled down the windows and picked up her phone. Her dad answered right away.

"Calling for a pep talk? You must be in Prescott now."

"I'm not," Abby wailed. "I'm on the side of I-17 with smoke coming out of my engine."

A long silence passed.

"Have you called for a tow?"

Abby closed her eyes and shook her head. A couple of tears ran down her cheeks. "No. Not yet." She said, "I checked the radiator," as he said, "Did you check the radiator?"

"That's all I knew to do. It's not the radiator. Smells like burning rubber."

"It's probably a belt, then."

"Want to hear the kicker?"

Abby heard her father sigh. "Do I?"

"I'm driving the exact same car I was driving that day I met Trace."

Another beat of silence. And then, the last thing she expected: laughter. Ernesto laughed, the loud, high-pitched laugh that meant he was in hysterics. She could picture him, sitting up straight in his wheelchair, his head thrown back, his eyes squinting, tears on his cheeks. And, despite everything, she found herself smiling.

"I'm glad you think it's so funny."

"Call a tow, Abby. Have them take it to Prescott. If you hurry, you can have him drop you at the meeting."

The tow company's estimated time of arrival was one to two hours, which meant there was almost no way she would make it into Prescott before the meeting was over. She didn't even bother calling her dad back. Experiencing her own disappointment was enough. She couldn't bear to hear his, too.

Instead, she texted him and told him a tow truck was on the way, and that she would let him know when it got there. She put her phone down and had a good, long, hard cry. She cried because she wasn't going to make the meeting. She cried because she hated the stupid blue car. Because Trace signed the petition. And because she wasn't going to get to build Sunset Valley. She cried for herself — the loss of her dream home — and she cried for Montana and Sawyer, who planned to start their married life there. She cried for her dad, too, because it would take that much longer for the two of them to start their next chapter.

Although her subconscious recognized the sound of a diesel engine approaching, Abby didn't fully realize someone had pulled up behind her until a shadow blocked the sun coming through the window.

"Abby Flores, is that you?"

Suddenly aware that she probably had tears and snot all over her face, Abby sat up straight and looked around for a tissue or a napkin. The Mustang being a rental car, it contained neither of those things. She made an attempt at wiping off her cheeks. A woman's hand thrust a handkerchief through the open window. "Here you go."

Abby still didn't know who it was, but she appreciated the handkerchief, nonetheless.

"Thank you." She wiped her eyes and nose. "I don't think you're going to want this back right now." Once she balled up the handkerchief in her hands, she finally took a good look at the at its owner. "Elaine."

Cody's mom looked down at her, nothing but kindness in her expression. "Hi, honey. Looks like you're not having the best day. Smells like this hot rod is going to need a new belt."

Abby nodded. "You're right about the former. The latter? I'm no mechanic, but I do know there was a lot of smoke involved."

"I take it you're on your way to the meeting?"

Stifling the sob that threatened, Abby nodded. "I was." She cleared her throat, then, because she thought she might cry again. "But now I've got to wait for a tow truck. And I'll never make it before the meeting ends."

"Actually," Elaine said, reaching in and squeezing Abby's shoulder. "Tom and I are headed there now. We're running a little behind schedule ourselves, but if we hurry, I think we can make it. Come on, why don't you catch a ride with us?"

"Don't I have to wait for the tow truck?"

Elaine looked south, as if she would be able to see how far away the tow truck was. "We'll leave a note. Have them tow it back to the rental company, and good riddance."

The idea seemed reasonable. The rental company would be responsible for paying for the tow, anyway.

"I guess I'll leave the keys in the ignition," Abby said. "If someone tries to steal this piece of junk, it's not like they're going to get very far."

"My thinking, exactly. Let me get you a pen and paper."

A couple of minutes later, Abby buckled into the back of the Davises' truck, and Tom pulled onto the interstate. "We may miss opening remarks, but in case Elaine hasn't told you, I am an excellent driver."

He winked at Abby in the rearview mirror, and Elaine swatted him on the arm. "Be careful. Drive fast, but be careful."

"Yes, ma'am."

"We saw the petition," Elaine said. "To point out the elephant in the room."

"I figured you had. I saw it, too, and based on the number of signatures on it, I think everyone in town did, as well."

Elaine looked over her shoulder at Abby. "I don't understand some people. You're doing great things in Prescott, honey. You almost single-handedly brought back a major retail area everyone else left for dead. Those of us with any sort of vision can tell it's going to be vibrant, and profitable, for the town."

"Thank you," Abby said, her voice thick as tears threatened again. "It's so hard not to take all of this personally."

"It *is* personal, though, isn't it?" Tom asked, his voice gruff but gentle.

Abby nodded. "It is."

"Believe it or not, it's personal to us, too." Tom turned up the music, then, and Abby leaned back against the seat and closed her eyes.

———

"WE'RE HERE, and we made good time," Tom said.

Abby blinked awake. "How good?"

"We're only seven minutes late."

"And only that late because we hit a little snag coming into town. Someone drove straight through the roundabout," Elaine said.

A rush of gratitude swept through Abby's body, giving her goosebumps. "I didn't say it before because I was so overwhelmed," she said. "But thank you guys so much for stopping. And for offering me a ride. I didn't know what to do."

Elaine turned around in the front seat. "You're welcome, honey. No matter what's going on between you and Trace right now — and whatever it is, I'm sure it has nothing whatsoever to do with his ego — you're part of the family now."

Elaine couldn't possibly know how much those words meant to Abby, and when Abby couldn't form a response, Elaine gave her knee a quick squeeze. "Let's go."

The three of them rushed across the parking lot, which was packed. A sense of dread started to creep in. Most of the people surely were there to support whoever had started that petition. Although Abby felt like she could cry, yet again, she straightened her shoulders. She was the daughter of Ernesto Flores. He was a brave and determined man. If she was going to go down, she would go down fighting.

Still walking, she pinched her cheeks to give them some color and then ran her fingertips under her eyes one more time to get rid of any smeared mascara. Tom reached the door first and held it open for Elaine and Abby. She thanked him as she walked in, and he winked at her, producing in her another rush of gratitude.

Sure enough, it was standing room only in the Council chambers. The air held the energy of anticipation. A few people shifted in their seats and cleared their throats, and Abby heard the sounds of someone adjusting the microphone. He began to speak just as her gaze landed on his face. Trace.

"Hello," he said. "I'm Trace Walker, part owner of the Mint Creek Ranch, and therefore, the future neighbor of the Sunset Valley project." His eyes met Abby's, and her heart beat so hard and fast, she could hear it in her ears and feel in her fingertips. "I'm here to ask you — implore you, actually," he said with a smile, "to deny the request for a special election, leave the zoning as is, and allow the Sunset Valley project to move forward."

Abby felt her mouth drop open. She shut it.

"As many of you know, I was one of the project's most outspoken opponents."

A low murmur came from the audience.

"I thought the project would threaten the character of Prescott. More specifically, the character of Williamson Valley. The area hasn't changed much in the past few decades, am I right? And that's because we all love it so much. We love the open space, the fresh air, the pastures, the barns. We love the dark sky at night, the open sky during the day. And, we love each other."

Hector Inman snorted. Abby saw the movement, and immediately recognized him, thanks to his worn denim overalls.

Trace spotted him, too. "Go ahead and snort, Hector," he said. "But I love you, man." This earned a few laughs. "I'm serious, though. Think about all the ways we've supported each other over the years. The weekend almost everyone spent baling hay for the Lochsteins when Henry Lochstein had a heart attack … the week neighbors filled Marcy Brown's freezer with casseroles after her kid was in a car accident … the Friday night we all came over and stood by when two of Luis Garcia's horses foaled at the same time."

People in the audience nodded, chuckled quietly.

"As you probably know," Trace went on, "my friend — well, Montana Hart is practically my sister — befriended Abby the moment she moved into town, and to my grave disappointment, I was forced to spend time with her."

More laughs. Trace's eyes met Abby's again.

"Then, I fell in love with her."

Abby could have sworn her heart stopped beating.

"Just like we are all in love with this town. I think I fell in love with her because she represents the same qualities we love about Prescott. She wants to be part of this community. Every project she's taken on represents a better quality of life for all of us. Better shopping for those of you who like to shop. Quality housing the regular folks can afford. Every project she's taken on has really embodied the spirit of Prescott. *Abby* embodies the spirit of Prescott. Most of you probably haven't seen her at her job sites, or with her construction crew." Trace let his gaze roam over the audience. "A few of you probably saw her at Cody and Tessa's wedding, and you probably saw that she fit right in. Abby treats everyone she meets with the utmost respect. She genuinely cares about them. Her crew is like a family, and that's because of her."

Abby could feel the mood in the room shifting. Her own mood shifted, too. She hadn't realized Trace noticed all of those things. And to hear him put it in words, in front of almost the entire City of Prescott … *Maybe he does love me.*

"My guess is that most of you don't even know about the community service projects she's done. She built a little shed at the elementary school, so the gardening club would have somewhere to store their supplies. She donated money, tens of thousands, to help launch the community college's new construction program. The new barn at the high school? The one that saved the ag program? She built that. After taking care of all the permits. And she paid for it out of her own pocket."

At that point, people started looking at one another, surprised. They had no idea. If she wasn't so scared, Abby would be completely giddy.

"Whether you know it or not, she's already contributing to the community she loves, and its people. She has made Prescott even better. She's brought in more of the things we love about it. She's a valuable member of this place, and because of that, I know Sunset Valley will do nothing but enrich it. I sincerely hope that you leave the zoning as it is and allow Abby — Ms. Flores — to build the Sunset Valley subdivision."

Abby was completely stunned. Trace had made her speech *for* her. He didn't know what she'd planned to say, but he said it all. And he'd announced that he *loved* her. In front of *everyone*. She didn't know whether to laugh or cry. Or both. She didn't have time to decide, because as Trace made his way back to his front-row seat, Tessa was making her way to the podium.

CHAPTER TWENTY-TWO

TRACE SENSED Abby the moment she walked in. She looked breathless. Beautiful. Silly in those ridiculous snakeskin high heels. And she looked shocked.

Shocked to see him standing there, and to hear the words he said. And when he said he loved her, in front of everyone, she looked downright stunned. His speech over, he wanted to run up to Abby and pull her through the doors and out to the parking lot, where he would explain everything. But first, he thought as he watched Tessa adjust the microphone at the podium, he wanted to see how she reacted to what everyone else had to say. The front row was packed, but Trace did his best to sit slightly sideways, so he could see Abby out of the corner of his eye.

"Well," Tessa said. "I'm not used to being on this side of the microphone."

Trace smiled. The newest reporter on the *Daily Dispatch* staff, Tessa usually sat in the audience, taking notes.

"Most reporters prefer to stay out of the spotlight," she said. "That's true for me. I'm an observer by nature. And I'd like to share what I've observed in this town over the past several months. The first night I came to Prescott, I felt welcome. *Really* welcome."

A few people chuckled. Some people shifted in their seats, and next to Trace, Cody winked at Tessa. They'd met at the rodeo dance her first night in town and hit it off, until he realized she was the reporter covering his championship bull-riding tour. Having been burned by a reporter before, Cody made Tessa work to earn his trust.

"As for my first few weeks," she continued, "I was given a bit of a cold shoulder. You all didn't trust me right away. I understood it. After hearing about what happened with Cody and his sister, I could see why I had to prove myself to you. From my point of view, that was tough. So tough. I thought about quitting the assignment and going back to Phoenix. But I decided to stick it out. And I'm glad I did. Because what I observed after that initial trial period was the loyalty people in this town have to each other. A different reporter almost brought harm to a member of this community. And you, every single one of you, were ready to protect Cody and Annie. That is really special. You won't find that just anywhere. I don't know if you all realize how special that is. I see that same loyalty in Abby. Did you know that she took over her father's business after he had an accident that left him paralyzed? She designed and led the building of the beautiful gazebo we used for our wedding. Even though our own Trace Walker was constantly throwing her shade."

Trace laughed, felt his ears turning red. He glanced at Abby, trying to look at her without her noticing. He couldn't quite see her reaction.

"You probably don't know that some big developers have contacted Abby, to see if she'd be the local contact for huge developments. Developments I know for a fact none of you would like. Remember, I attend almost every City Council meeting. She turned down every single developer, even though she stood to make a pretty penny. The real reason she wants to build the Sunset Valley project is because she'll be able to move her dad out here and into a house with better wheelchair accessibility. If that's not loyalty, I don't know what is. She's got a pretty face, but she is so much more than that."

Tessa's eyes glistened with tears, and Trace actually felt his own eyes start to prickle. Before Tessa made it to her seat, Sawyer was at the microphone. Then Montana, and then Cody. Cody's parents walked to the front of the room next, hand in hand.

Each person spoke about Abby with exactly what she deserved: admiration and love.

The Mint Creek Ranch crew had planned this speech-making

parade as soon as it became clear that the petitioners gathered enough signatures to make an official request that the rezoning be put to a vote. But they hadn't planned what happened next. Other Prescott residents came to the microphone, and every one of them had a story about Abby — about her loyalty, her dedication, her kindness. Trace wasn't surprised. He had seen and fallen in love with all of those qualities.

Finally, one of the City Council members announced they wouldn't be able to hear any more speakers. It was time to put the special election matter to a vote. No matter what happened, Trace knew he had done everything in his power to help the woman he loved. And, he thought, so had his friends.

If only he could convince Abby he deserved another chance.

ABBY

AS PERSON AFTER PERSON SPOKE, emotion overwhelmed Abby. Gratitude, joy, and that sense of belonging she so craved mingled together, filling her to the point of bursting.

Abby didn't need to know how the vote turned out. Whether the Council voted to hold a special election to reconsider the rezoning, or to deny it and leave the zoning alone so she could build Sunset Valley, Abby knew she had something even more important than a one-hundred-acre parcel. She had the love of the people in the community; the people she'd been living with, working with, and building for over the past year.

Hugging every single person who stood up to speak was impossible, at least in that moment. And thanking them adequately would be forever impossible. How could she possibly convey how much she appreciated each one of them standing with her?

Again, the space in the room filled with anticipation.

The Council chairman gathered his papers into a pile, which he tapped on the table in front of him.

"Well, folks," he said. "I guess it's time for us to vote."

Abby knew she should stick around. Her dad was waiting for her call. But she couldn't. She couldn't bear to hear the outcome, even though she had told herself it didn't matter. So, while the chairman read the wording of the vote, Abby slipped out the chambers door.

————

AN HOUR LATER, alone in her apartment, Abby paced the floor. After leaving the meeting, she'd turned off her phone and power-walked home, where she'd continued power-walking in circles.

The air inside was just cool enough to be uncomfortable, even with the power-walking. "I really should get a sweatshirt," she muttered, pacing her way into her bedroom. "Probably better to change my path anyway. I'm bound to wear a track in the floor."

Sweatshirt on, she resumed. She needed to see Trace. To talk to him. Wrap her arms around him.

But she'd fled that meeting immediately after he publicly declared his love for her. Would he even want to see her? And there was that matter of his signature on that petition. Even if he loved her, he had some explaining to do.

Letting Trace Nelson get under her skin was the stupidest thing she could have done. Yes, he had the most amazing blue-gray eyes. And yes, he turned out to be way more thoughtful than she'd expected. He liked shopping for *babies*. He was talented. Animals liked him.

He loved her.

I love him. Maybe being stupid — for once — was a good thing.

Abby stopped walking. She had to think. She had to be *sure* before she drove over to his house. If she were going to dissect every second of her relationship with Trace, including the possibility that she *loved* him, she preferred to do it with a clear mind. She had to calm down. She paced into the kitchen, where she filled a mug with water and put it in the microwave. While it heated, she paced some more. Over to the pantry to get a tea bag, once more around the loop in her apartment. "Where was I?"

Oh, yes. There were plenty of good things about Trace. But. He was also stubborn. Hardheaded. Old-fashioned. And, okay. If she were being honest with herself, the polite part of old-fashioned — the way he opened doors, carried things, took the side closest to the street when they were walking down the sidewalk — those were endearing.

But the rest of it — the way he seemed to believe nothing should ever change — "Well, forget that."

By that time, the microwave had finished heating her water. She dropped in the teabag, then lifted the mug in both hands and inhaled, letting the steam kiss her skin and the scent of the tea soothe her. She breathed deeply, in and out, in and out. There. She was already feeling calmer.

Regret and relief mixed, in equal parts. She regretted that she'd let herself drift apart from Trace when things got tough.

For a few weeks there, she thought their relationship was pretty much perfect. If only … but no. Things weren't perfect. He'd signed the petition and hadn't even told her about it. Was there any way the two of them could ever work?

Without warning, she remembered the way he looked at her when she was holding William's baby, Freddie. He never said as much, but she knew he was thinking he wanted to see her holding *their* baby. His expression said so, plain as day. One of her hands dropped from its place on her mug to rest on her lower abdomen. The regret and relief stepped offstage, and a deep yearning, a heavy desire, replaced them. She groaned, briefly wondering if she had anything to spike the tea with. Started pacing again. She wanted to have Trace's baby. More than one.

"What if it wasn't meant to be?" she asked herself again.

Even though she'd already convinced herself it might not ever work with Trace, and even though she knew the relationship might be over because she'd run out on him after he declared his love, and even though, just the day before, she'd sworn she never wanted to see him again, in that moment, she felt like she *had* to see him.

She knew she'd see him around town. But if this was goodbye, it would be more about closure. Saying goodbye to their romance. And if it wasn't … she couldn't hope for that. Not yet.

"Great," she said, as another tear made its way down her cheek. "Now I'm crying again."

Tea still in hand, Abby went back into her bedroom, took off the pajamas she'd put on only a few moments before, and pulled on her sexiest jeans and a light sweater that showed off her cleavage and complemented her skin. She finished the look with her snakeskin heels. Impractical, yes. Sexy, yes. They were her power shoes, after all.

"Perfect."

———

A FEW MINUTES LATER, Abby was about to turn onto the Mint Creek Ranch driveway when she smelled smoke. At first, she didn't think much of it. Fall had fallen, and people were building fires in their fireplaces. But the weather that day was warm. Too warm for a fire.

Looking around for the source of the smoke was an automatic response. It was already near dark, and Abby didn't see anything at first.

She made the turn into Mint Creek Ranch and gasped. There, in front of her, was the source of the smoke.

Bright-orange flames ran around one end of Trace's house. And, worse, at one end of the barn. Abby slammed on her brakes. She heard the sound of her tires crunching on the gravel. She slapped a hand over her mouth. She had to do something, but what? She reached across the console to get her phone out of her purse, but her hands were shaking so badly, all she could do was fumble it, dropping her wallet and her lip balm and her spare keys on the seat.

"Where is my phone?" she growled.

Then, it clicked: all she had to do was get to Trace.

Goodbyes could wait. But Trace — and the horses — couldn't. She gripped the steering wheel with both hands, hard enough to steady them, and put her foot on the gas pedal. Within seconds, the car was lurching to a stop in front of Trace's house. She started to get out, and quickly remembered her shoes.

Pulling them off and tossing them onto the passenger seat, she muttered, "Damn inappropriate shoes."

CHAPTER TWENTY-THREE

ABBY

SHE WAS OUT AND RUNNING, pounding on the door.

"Abby," Trace said. He looked surprised to see her, but his expression turned to shock as he smelled the smoke.

"The barn," Abby said. "Your house." She shook her head. She couldn't quite get the words out.

"Is that fire?"

Abby nodded.

"The barn?"

"It's the back corner. I was coming over to talk to you — and then I saw the flames. We've got to get the horses."

Leaving the door open, Trace stepped inside and grabbed his boots. He pulled them on while he started to run.

"How bad is it?" he was asking.

She shook her head. "I don't know. It looks like it's just at the far end right now."

Trace swore. He didn't even close the door. They ran, side by side. Phone in hand, he dialed Cody.

"Barn's on fire," he said when Cody picked up. "You and Sawyer, get here quick."

Abby could hear the fear — and anger — in his voice.

As soon as he saw the flames and the smoke, Trace swore again. "Someone did this. On purpose."

He broke into a full-on sprint, and Abby matched his stride. When they reached the barn, Trace threw open the doors, and they both ran toward the burning end. So far, Abby noticed, only the wall was on fire. The stalls were untouched at this point. But it wouldn't take long before they, too, went up in flames. Still in sync, she and Trace ran to the stalls closest to the fire. He took the one on the left, and she went right.

Abby grabbed a lead rope off the hook on the wall, slipped it over the horse's head — was it Lucky Charm? It didn't matter — and coaxed him out of the stall and through the barn.

"Should we let them loose?" Abby asked. "If the fire spreads, they'll be trapped in the corral."

Trace, who'd led Louise to the door, considered. "Good thinking, but I'm worried about traffic on Williamson Valley Road. Let's put them in the corral for now, and when Sawyer and Cody get here, hopefully soon, they can run them out to the north pasture."

Abby nodded. "I'll take Louise. You go on back and get the next ones."

Without a word, Trace handed Abby Louise's rope. She jogged out to the corral, the horses plodding along agreeably. Although she could feel the buzzing energy of adrenaline surging in her veins, a strange sense of calm made her movements sure and smooth. She let the horses into the corral and swung the gate closed. By the time she ran back to the barn, Trace was emerging with two more. He handed her their lead ropes and went back in.

The rhythm continued, horse by horse. Abby felt like hours had passed, but in reality, it had probably been only a few minutes.

Cody and Sawyer came down, the headlights of their trucks shining on the barn.

Within seconds, they'd grabbed saddles out of the barn and were on their horses, leading the whole group toward the north pasture, where they'd be safe from the fire as long as the wind didn't change.

Abby ran back to the barn door, only to find Trace carrying a saddle himself.

"All the horses out?" Abby asked.

"Yeah," Trace said, "but I'm hoping to save some of the gear."

Again, Abby nodded, and ran into the barn. Because she'd been meeting him at the door, she hadn't seen the progression of the fire. It had now eaten up at least half the stalls as it marched forward. For a moment, Abby felt herself freeze. Panic set in. Not simply because of the fire, but because of whoever had started the fire. What would they do next?

"Abby! Move!" Trace's voice startled her out of her daze. She felt his hand wrapping around her upper arm, pulling her back. And then she looked up. The roof of the barn above her had caught fire, the flames eating away at the boards, and the boards were coming loose. As Trace's arms came around her waist, one of the rafters fell.

"Come on, let's get out of here."

Holding hands, they ran together toward the barn door. At the same time, Cody and Sawyer returned from the pasture. They were on foot, out of breath.

"How much do you think we can save?" Cody said.

Trace shook his head. "We got what we could. It's not safe to go back in. Roof's coming down. We got most of the saddles. Some of the tack. The fire department should be here soon. Once they come, we'll see what's left."

TRACE

AS TRACE WAS CATCHING his breath, Abby said, "Your house."

Cody and Sawyer looked at Trace, then at Abby.

"Your *house*?" they both said. "Shit."

"All I could think about was the horses," Trace said. "The barn. But I guess we'd better go up and see what's what."

As the group approached Trace's house, he was surprised to see that Montana and Tessa were already there, carting out what they considered valuable: his cowboy boots, his best jackets, the buckles he'd won at rodeos.

"I got your computer," Tessa said. "I stuck it in my car for now."

Montana said, "We've got your boots, your jackets, that old cowboy statue your parents left behind. What else? I think we still have time. We've got your closet cleared out."

What else?

On reflex, Trace looked at the only other valuable thing in his life — Abby.

In the rush of activity, and the panic, he hadn't had a chance to really dial in on what he was feeling. But she was there. She had come to him in a time of need and helped him. Once again, they'd worked as a team. Seamlessly. Without her, the horses — he couldn't even finish the thought.

The ring.

Neither Montana nor Tessa knew about it. Without saying another word, he ran back into the burning house.

CHAPTER TWENTY-FOUR

Abby

ABBY WATCHED Trace run back into his house. Without conscious thought, her body made to follow him. But Montana grabbed her hand to stop her. "I don't think it's safe to go in there. I'm sure he'll be right back."

She didn't sound sure. The sound of sirens came through the air. Abby turned around to see the firetruck trundling down the driveway, lights flashing.

"Thank goodness," Montana said. "It felt like they'd never get here."

"We're lucky," Tessa said.

As the five of them watched, the truck stopped and the doors opened. Firefighters, already in their full gear, jumped out. One of them — Abby assumed he was the captain — shouted orders at the others. They unrolled hoses and turned spigots and started dousing the fire.

"Looks like they'll be able to save some of it," Cody said.

Sawyer, who had come to stand behind Montana, his arms around her waist, said, "Guess that's something. It won't be a total loss."

As the steam rose, illuminated by the hungry flames, a loud crash came from Trace's house.

Abby, Montana, Tessa, Cody, and Sawyer ran toward the front door.

Cody got there first. As if he knew Abby was right behind him, he stuck out one arm to stop her. "You're not going in there."

Abby bristled. Anger flared, as hot as the fire that now lit up the night sky. "If you're saying that just because I'm a woman —"

Cody gave her a look that stopped her in her tracks. "You know me better than that. But if Trace knew that we got here at the same time, and I let you go in before me, and something happened to you, he would never forgive me. This is as much for me as it is for you. Stay put. I'll find him."

Sawyer was next. Before going into the house, he paused long enough to say, "What he said. Hang tight."

The three women stood outside, listening to the snapping and crackling of the fire, which consumed the house little by little.

Watching any structure burn was hard enough, Abby thought. The hours of hard work, all the sweat, the labor, the care. Up in flames, literally. But watching a building burn when the man you loved — and she *did* love him — was inside? It was the worst kind of waiting.

Tessa and Montana came up on either side of her. Montana held her hand, leaning up against her left side. Tessa had her arms around Abby's shoulders from the right. They didn't move.

"They'll get him," Montana said. "They'll bring him out."

Abby nodded, as a tear rolled down her cheek. She thought, *But in what shape?* Despite the heat radiating off the house, Abby shivered. Tessa took off her own sweatshirt and draped it over Abby's shoulders before wrapping her arms around her again. They waited.

Abby was aware of the firefighters wrapping things up at the barn. She heard the captain calling for a mop-up. The engine roared back to life, and the flashing lights came closer, casting the women's shadows in flickering relief. A few seconds later, the captain was barking orders for the firefighters to work on Trace's house.

"The guys are in there," Tessa said to the captain.

His reaction sent Abby's nerves into overdrive. She felt nauseated. His eyebrows shot up, and he looked at the house like he couldn't believe someone would be stupid enough to go in there.

Well, Abby thought, they were.

"Damned Mint Creek Ranch boys," he muttered before holding up a hand, signaling that the firefighters should wait. They paused, but

Abby recognized their impatience. They looked like a team-roping horse waiting for the go ahead.

Finally, *finally*, there was movement at the front door. When Abby saw all three men, her body sagged with relief. If Montana and Tessa hadn't been holding her up, her knees would've buckled. Trace was in the middle, one arm draped over Cody's shoulders and the other draped over Sawyer's. The two of them moved as quickly as they could, but it was obvious Trace wasn't much help. The phrase *dead weight* came to Abby's mind, but she dismissed it.

Hustling, Cody and Sawyer dragged him away from the house, while the three women watched, helpless.

"He's unconscious," Sawyer said, and the fire captain hollered, "Paramedic!"

One of the firefighters grabbed a medical bag out of the truck and ran over, and the three men helped Trace onto the ground. Although he was mostly in one piece, a huge, bloodied wound slashed across his neck and shoulder.

Abby could hardly resist the urge to go to him, but she knew, from experience, that the paramedic needed space to work.

She couldn't help but picture her father's body, oddly bent after he fell on the job site all those years before.

"Anybody else in there?" the captain barked, bringing Abby back to the present moment.

Tessa shook her head. "No, sir. It's all clear."

The captain pointed at Trace's house and shouted, "Hit it!"

The hoses were on full blast, and the scene was a spectacle of sparks and steam and flames and water. But Abby couldn't take her eyes off Trace. Despite all the activity, he was still unconscious.

———

AFTER LOTS of rushed words passed between Cody, Sawyer, Montana, and Tessa, almost none of which Abby could comprehend, they shuffled her to the back of the ambulance and helped her climb in. She squeezed into a tiny seat alongside the gurney. Before Abby even realized what was happening, a paramedic climbed in next to her, pulling the doors shut.

"You his girlfriend?" The woman spoke fast, no nonsense. Abby licked her lips, and nodded. It was the simplest response.

"Obviously, he's unconscious," the paramedic said. "But he can probably hear you. You can hold his hand, if you want. Talk to him. Try to get him to wake up, if you can."

The wild urge to grab his hand seized Abby, as if she were starving, and it was the biggest, juiciest cheeseburger. She managed to restrain herself, though, and slid her palm under his, curling her fingers around his hand. She couldn't say any of the words she wanted to, not with the paramedic sharing that tiny space.

"Trace." Her voice sounded hoarse. She cleared her throat and tried again. "Trace."

The back of the ambulance was anything but silent. The sirens wailed, the equipment creaked, the engine roared. When she didn't say anything for a minute, the paramedic said, in a voice much softer and gentler than she'd used before, "Keep talking to him. Talk about anything. It doesn't matter what you say, only that he can hear your voice."

Abby nodded. "Okay," she whispered. "The first time I saw you, you know what I thought? I thought you were the handsomest man I've ever seen, riding in on your horse — literally — to save the day. I actually thought I was imagining you. I mean, who is that good-looking?" She laughed a little. The paramedic handed her a tissue. "I thought I imagined the whole interaction. If it weren't for the fact that you actually helped me change that tire, I probably would've kept right on thinking I'd conjured you out of thin air. When I went back to Utah, I couldn't stop thinking about you. I made up all these scenarios where we would meet again. And then we did. When I saw you at the City Council meeting, I thought — can you believe this? — I thought, well thank my lucky stars."

Abby knew that if Trace was conscious, he'd be giving her that wry smile. Because when they met at the City Council meeting, Abby was anything but lucky.

"I know what you're thinking. You're thinking I was deluding myself. I was your absolute worst nightmare. A developer. In faux snakeskin high heels." She sniffled. "You probably wished you'd never come to my rescue. Left me out there in the desert to dry up and blow away."

In the movies, the unconscious person always started waking up at some point, squeezing their loved one's hand, or blinking. But Trace lay on the gurney, unmoving.

"To be fair, *I* kind of wished you hadn't come to my rescue. If we never met, I wouldn't have lived through those fantasies of meeting again — only to have you turn up at that meeting, arrogant and old-fashioned. And as handsome as ever."

She leaned closer and kissed his fingers. "Boy, am I glad there was time for the ice to thaw out. I don't know if it was those snakeskin high heels or how good I look in a pair of carpenter jeans, but I'm glad you came around. You've surprised in more ways than one."

At that thought, Abby's throat tightened, and because she didn't want to full-on cry in front of the paramedic, she took a slow, deep breath.

The ambulance slowed down. Looking out the back window, Abby saw that it was pulling into the bay at the hospital's emergency department. She looked up at the paramedic for guidance.

The woman smiled at her. "You can stay with him. I wish I could, too. I'd really like to hear how this story ends."

Abby offered her a watery smile in return. "So would I."

Everything moved quickly after that. The paramedics and emergency room nurses traded information as they moved the gurney out of the ambulance and wheeled Trace inside.

Although almost two decades had passed, Abby couldn't help but picture the chaotic scene after her father's accident. She leaned against Trace's gurney to steady herself. Suddenly, she heard someone saying, "You okay, girlfriend?"

She blinked, bringing into focus the face of the paramedic from the ambulance.

"I'm all right," Abby said. "Just got a little discombobulated."

Within minutes, after lots of frantic activity — measuring, monitoring, listening, checking — the doctors and nurses finally left Abby and Trace alone in a room.

One of them, a young woman with piercing blue eyes and wild, curly blonde hair pulled into a giant ponytail, had paused long enough to tell Abby to sit tight … that Trace likely wouldn't wake up for a while yet. Even with the beeping and whirring of machines, the room felt still and quiet. And although Abby had spent the past forty minutes (which felt like an eternity) thinking about what she really wanted to say to Trace, the words she would speak when they were finally alone, she found she couldn't quite string any together.

So, she pulled her chair up close to his bed, folded her hands around one of his, and rested her head on the bed rail. She'd once read that every idea forms twice: once in the mind and once in reality. She took some time to formulate the idea — the apology she owed him — in her mind.

I'm so sorry I didn't trust you. I'm so sorry I left without talking to you. Sorry doesn't even cover it. I hope you can forgive me. All those things I said earlier, in the ambulance? Those were all true. I've always said I'm great at first impressions. And my first impression of you was that you had come to save me. I still think maybe that's true. Before this, I never counted on finding love. I figured I would spend my life as a single woman — and, happily, too. I told myself I didn't need a man. But now I know I was wrong. I need you. I don't think I can do this without you. You have to be okay. I want to say you have to forgive me. But you don't. I just hope you will.

Then, she spent a little while listening to his breathing. It was shallow, but steady.

A few minutes later, Abby said the words out loud. She spoke quietly, but with a calm certainty. Part of her feared Trace waking up and telling her to get lost, to go back to where she'd come from. But another part of her knew Trace needed to hear what he meant to her. If she had to say it a hundred times, she would.

CHAPTER TWENTY-FIVE

FINALLY. Trace felt himself moving into clear consciousness from a deep, dreamless sleep. There was none of the confusion he'd noticed the last several times he pushed through the heavy drowsiness. As he woke fully, he knew exactly where he was: the hospital. Snatches of memories came back to him, grabbed from those times he'd surfaced. He'd run back into the house to get the rings — the rings! Where were they now? A loud, fast series of beeps came from the machine next to him.

He'd been in his bedroom when he stuffed the ring box in his pocket before running back toward his front door. That's when he passed out. The first time he woke up, he heard Cody and Sawyer talking. When he heard the serious tone of the conversation, he let himself fall back into that comfortable sleep. He came to again while the firefighters strapped him onto a gurney. In the dark, the flashing lights from the firetruck and ambulance hurt his head and he closed his eyes again. He woke up once more in the ambulance, and listened to the cadence of Abby's voice. At that point, he wanted to remain conscious for as long as possible. But the swaying of the ambulance made him sick, and as soon as he closed his eyes, he was out.

He figured the fact that he could remember all of that was a good sign. The horrible burning in his chest and his lungs, and across his shoulder, was probably a bad sign. The way his skin felt — he wished he could look down and make sure it wasn't still on fire! They wouldn't leave him in the hospital room if he was still on fire, would they? That was probably a bad sign. He heard Abby's voice again.

The way she was talking, and the words she was using? Definitely a good sign. He tried to squeeze her hand, but his fingers didn't seem to want to work. She had stopped talking — likely because the machine was beeping so loudly. He heard Abby say, "This doesn't seem good," and then, after what felt like less than a second, he heard several pairs of feet running into the room.

———

HE WOKE UP — again — because he felt someone looking at him. His chest still burned, and he groaned as he blinked his eyes open. Once he was able to focus, he realized someone was, in fact, watching him. And he was overjoyed that it was Abby. He did his best to twist his features into something resembling a smile. She gasped. He must look pretty ghastly.

He felt her hand tighten around his. "You're awake."

"Seems like it."

"I would ask how you're feeling, but..."

Her voice trailed off.

"I feel pretty rotten," he said. He cleared his throat, which felt raw. "I'm alive, though. And that's good. I think."

Even in his half-alive state, he could tell her eyes softened. "It's good."

The rings, Trace thought. Hopefully the box was still tucked into his jeans pocket. He tried not to panic.

"Could you get my jeans for me?"

"Your jeans?" Her eyes narrowed. "You can't leave here, yet. The doctors haven't released you."

"Not leaving," he rasped. "Just need my jeans."

Abby stood up and went to the cabinet in the corner. He heard her going through a plastic bag. She came back, his folded jeans in her hands.

"Thank you so much," he croaked. "You can set them right here, next to me."

He had to figure out how to get her out of there for a minute. He took a couple of deep breaths, as torturous as they were with the fire in his chest. The fire. Those two words brought on a true panic. "The horses — are they —"

"They're fine," Abby said. She practically collapsed into the chair next to the bed and grasped his hand again. "They're fine. Everything's fine. We might have to rebuild the barn, and we definitely have to reconstruct the back end of your house. But the horses are completely unharmed. Everything else is fixable."

Abby might think Trace was too out of it to notice her use of the word, *we*. But he did. Offering up a prayer of gratitude, Trace said, "Thank you. I'm so glad to hear that."

"It all would've been the same without you running back into a burning building," Abby said.

Trace thought he detected a hint of disapproval in her voice. He wondered how many times he would hear that in the coming years. Didn't wives often disapprove of their husbands' shenanigans?

"I had to," he said.

"You had to?"

Trace wanted to laugh. She had no idea. She probably still thought he'd signed the petition because he wanted her to leave town. Which couldn't be farther from the truth.

"What's so funny?"

She watched him carefully, obviously uncertain about his thoughts.

"Could you get me a drink?"

Eyes still narrowed, Abby said, "Sure. Here's your water." Her efficient movements as she held the straw to his lips reminded him of how much she'd been through. For half a second, he considered proposing then and there, without even knowing whether the ring was in his jeans pocket. He stopped himself. He wanted to do it right.

"Thank you," he said after taking a drink of the cool water. "I could really kill for a soda. Anything bubbly. Do you think you could hit up the vending machine?"

Abby shook her head. There was that disapproval again. "Sugar is probably not the best thing for you right now. But I guess after everything you've been through, it's not the worst, either. Something that makes you happy is probably just as well."

"I have that, right here." He looked into her eyes as he said it.

She simply gave him a questioning look, and paused in the doorway on her way out. "I'll see what they have."

He waited a couple of seconds, in case she came back to ask him something. When she didn't, he pressed the button to move his bed into a more upright position and then rushed to unfold his jeans. He saw it right away. The lump in his right front pocket sent a wave of relief through his veins. It was there. He removed the box, tucked it under his right leg, and refolded the jeans. Abby came back in, carrying a lemon-lime soda.

"Perfect timing."

———

ABBY

SOMETHING WEIRD WAS GOING ON. Trace's eyes sparkled. His energy bordered on giddy.

"What do you mean, 'Perfect timing'?"

"I was really thirsty."

Abby twisted the lid off the soda and handed the bottle to Trace. He took a drink and held his hand out for the lid. "Thanks. That hit the spot."

"You're welcome." She sank back into the chair. "You seem a little perkier. How are you feeling?"

A megawatt smile came her way. She blushed.

"A lot better, thanks to you."

"If I'd known all it was going to take was a soda, I would've gone to the vending machine hours ago."

"Abby, do you know why I signed that petition?"

So many thoughts went through Abby's mind.

You regret saying you understood my vision. You regret saying you understood me. You regret supporting me. You regret me.

"I regret it so much," he said. "I felt like I had to do it. After someone poisoned the horses, Ronnie Sunshine told us things would only get worse if we didn't sign. It was the last thing any of us wanted to do."

"But why didn't you tell me?" Abby asked. It wasn't lost on her that the question was hypocritical, considering she hadn't told him about the rabbits.

Trace shrugged. "We wanted to. But also, we wanted to protect you. We didn't want you to know how badly someone wanted to get you out of here."

Abby nodded. "I already knew."

As she told him about the rabbits, she saw him becoming angry. She finished the story with, "And, for the record, I didn't tell *you* because I wanted to protect you. I didn't want you to worry, when you already had so much going on."

"I understand. I wouldn't have, before. But now I do."

"I'm sorry," she said. "Maybe if I'd told you about the rabbits, we could have figured it out together. Before someone set the barn on fire."

"They would have done worse. Whether I signed the petition or not."

"If I'd had any sense," he went on, "I would've talked to you before I signed. The truth is, I was afraid that if you knew, you might leave."

Abby shook her head. "It takes more than that to scare me off."

"Still. I wish I'd handled things differently."

Abby nodded. "I hold as much blame as you do."

Trace reached for Abby's hand, and when his fingers curled around hers, she nearly cried at the familiarity of it, the perfect fit. "I'm sorry," she whispered. "So sorry."

"I'm sorry, too," he said. "And I have something to ask you."

Abby held her breath.

"Will you forgive me?"

Caught by surprise, Abby laughed. "Yes. Do you forgive me?"

Trace's eyes shone with tears, and Abby felt tears on her cheeks, too.

"Of course I do."

"Thank goodness. Because I have another question."

From under his leg, Trace withdrew a velvet box. He opened it, revealing a ring, five diamonds set into its center, sparkling up at her.

"I'm sure you've guessed what the question is. But before I ask it, officially, I want you to know something. I said some of this at the meeting, but I want to say it to you. Abby, I know we didn't get off on the right foot. But after I grudgingly accepted you into the Mint Creek Ranch crew, I started to see what everyone else saw in you. Your smile is contagious, and your laugh literally creates endorphins. You are one of the hardest working people I know, and hands down, the most beautiful. I admire you. I admire your dedication to your work, your loyalty to your dad, your creativity. When I thought I'd lost you because I was too stubborn to communicate with you, I couldn't envision a happy future for myself. And that's because for me, a happy future doesn't exist without you. I want to spend the rest of my life with you. Starting right now. Would you do me the honor of marrying me?"

———

SAWYER, Cody, Montana, and Tessa came through the door, talking in hushed voices. As soon as Sawyer saw that Trace was awake, sitting up, and alert, he shouted, "You're alive!"

Everyone laughed, which broke the worried tension.

"I'm alive," Trace said. "And we have news."

Abby saw everyone's gazes shift to her left hand.

"You did it?" Cody said, moving in for a high-five. "Way to go, man."

"I assume she said 'Yes' since she's wearing the bling," Sawyer said.

After the group broke out in cheers, the three men formed an awkward group hug, and before she knew it, Abby was in the middle of her own embrace with Tessa and Montana.

"You knew?" Abby asked them after they offered their congratulations.

"Of course we did," Montana said. Tessa added, "You think these guys can keep a secret? They had to explain what would make Trace so crazy as to run back into his burning house."

"Hey, we can keep a secret," Cody said. He winked at Abby, and again, she felt that rush of belonging. "We didn't tell her before this, did we?"

"Let's celebrate!" Sawyer said.

"I don't think we're going to be doing any real celebrating until Trace gets some rest," Tessa said.

Trace held up a finger. "Doctor says I can go home tonight. But Abby and I have some private celebrating to do."

Abby felt her face glowing bright red. She also felt herself smiling.

Tessa wrapped an arm around her shoulders. "No privacy. You'll get used to it."

Abby looked at each of her friends in turn.

Trace, a complicated, loyal, stubborn man who wanted nothing but happiness for the people he cared about. Cody, his serious, hard-working best friend, who would do anything for him. Sawyer, who loved fun, but his friends even more. Montana, who'd brought Abby into this circle with the friendliest smile. Tessa, who knew the struggle of being an outsider, and worked all that much harder to make Abby feel a part of things.

Abby loved them, and after she and Trace had a more intimate celebration — which she very much looked forward to — she couldn't wait to celebrate with all of them, as well.

CHAPTER TWENTY-SIX

TRACE

SINCE TRACE MOVED to the Mint Creek Ranch when he was eight years old, it had been his favorite place. Its laughing creek, the whispering leaves of the cottonwood trees, the peaceful emerald-green rolling hills … those formed the perfect backdrop for a magical childhood. One filled with joy, a little heartbreak, and growth.

On a cold winter day, Trace slipped out of bed and went into the kitchen. Cup of coffee in hand, he looked out the window at the scene he'd loved for the past two decades.

Three months had passed since someone attempted to destroy the Mint Creek Ranch, he thought. Police detectives had arrested a small group of men in connection with the crime.

Three months had passed since the moment when Trace thought he might lose his home and the woman he loved — and he experienced a surprising realization: *Abby* was his home. They could be anywhere, and as long as they were together, nothing else mattered.

She came up behind him and wrapped her arms around his waist.

"Excited for the big day?" she asked, laying her head on his back.

He set down his coffee and turned to face her. "I'd be more excited to take you back to bed. But we don't want to miss the ground-breaking, do we?"

"No, we don't."

She tilted her face up, and kissed him good morning before going to the coffeemaker for her own cup.

While they got ready for the day, Trace thought about their plans. The two of them had decided they would live in Sunset Valley, as neighbors with Sawyer and Montana.

Trace wouldn't be much farther from Cody and Tessa than he was in this house … a hop, skip, and jump.

Trace and Abby's home would include a father-in-law suite, and the whole property would be wheelchair accessible. They had the best builder in town, and she could make it work. Despite everything that had changed, Trace thought as he and Abby headed down to the barn hand in hand, he felt more content than ever.

In Abby, he'd found his favorite place.

The End

ABOUT THE AUTHOR

Hilary Dartt loves great adventures, whether she's writing, reading, or living them. The author of twelve novels, Hilary lives in Arizona's high desert with her husband, their three children, her Weimaraner and running partner, Leia, a failed barn cat, and a flock of chickens. She loves camping, exploring in the Jeep, and dance parties with her kids. Learn more at www.hilarydartt.com